Ka-thunk! Irene was first. Her skull cracked as the claws connected with her scalp. Her body jumped and twitched, but she didn't cry out. The impact snapped her neck and she died instantaneously.

But the noise and movement made John sit up in bed. He wasn't fully awake yet, his breath heady with the aroma of alcohol, and he couldn't see much at all in the darkened bedroom. His hand felt the bed, made contact with his wife's body, and he tried to wake her with gentle nudges to her midsection.

"Irene?" he whispered when she didn't respond. And then the hammer hit his head with a force that sent his toupee flying clear across the room. Blood gushed from the wound in his temple and he screamed in pain.

The second blow hit him in the mouth. His teeth broke into tiny fragments and blood flooded his throat, stopping the scream so abruptly that none of the neighbors knew the night had been invaded by violence. The scream died in his throat before John Koster could die in his bed.

The third blow took off the skin of his nose before the deadly claws buried themselves in his left eye. Hard steel penetrated the brain behind his eye socket and John Koster's misery ended as quickly as it had begun.

He never felt the blows that followed.

Special thanks to Elizabeth Aisling Flygare for doing a line edit while I was at World Fantasy Con, and for Lizza who urged me to kill again...

Copyright © 2016 by Paul Dale Anderson
Cover design by David Dodd
All rights reserved. No part of this book may be used or reproduced in any manner whatsoever without written permission except in the case of brief quotations embodied in critical articles and reviews.
Gordian Knot Books is an imprint of Crossroad Press Publishing
For information address Crossroad Press at 141 Brayden Dr., Hertford, NC 27944
www.crossroadpress.com

Crossroad Press Trade Edition

CLAW HAMMER

BOOK 1 OF THE INSTRUMENTS OF DEATH

BY PAUL DALE ANDERSON

ROCKFORD PUBLIC LIBRARY

DEDICATION

For Gretta

When you are an anvil, hold you still; when you are a hammer, strike your fill.

—George Herbert, Jacula Prudentum

Cruelty has a human heart, And Jealousy a human face; Terror the human form divine, And Secrecy the human dress.

—William Blake, Songs of Experience, "A Divine Image"

PROLOGUE

Awakened from a sound sleep by Robin's blood-curdling screams, Joyce ran instinctively to her mother's bedroom. But the big bed her parents slept in was empty, the covers still tucked neatly at the corners. The bed hadn't been used. Mommie wasn't home. Mommie was never home when Joyce needed her. Never ever.

Robin's screams had stopped. The house was silent as a tomb. Joyce began to wonder if she'd been awakened by a nightmare, her own terrified screams and not Robin's still echoing through the house. Bad dreams were nothing new to the six-year-old.

Often, in the past, she'd come back from the depths of a dream to find herself screaming at the top of her lungs; and just as often she'd run to Mommie and not be able to find her. Then she'd run to Robin's room. Robin was eleven and Joyce's older sister. "Go back to bed," Robin would tell Joyce. "You had a bad dream. That's all it was. A bad dream."

"I'm scared," Joyce would say.

"Act your age," Robin would chide. "Six-year-olds shouldn't be scared of the dark. If you're too old to believe in Santa Claus, you're too old to believe in the boogeyman."

"Trevor's nine," she'd argue. "He gets to sleep with a night light to keep the boogeyman away. Why can't I?"

"Boys are dumb. Especially Trevor. Haven't you noticed that yet? Geeze, Joyce! You wanna act dumb as a boy?"

"I'm scared," was all Joyce could say.

"What's to be scared about?"

Joyce didn't know.

"Look. Go back to sleep. Nothing's gonna hurt you."

Joyce didn't want to bother Robin at all, didn't want to rush into

Robin's room. But Mommie wasn't home. Mommie was never home. And Joyce was scared.

And Robin's door was open a crack. Almost like an invitation. Joyce hesitated outside the door. What if Robin was in one of her foul moods? What if Robin didn't want to wake up? What if she wasn't willing to listen to a scared little girl's nonsensical babblings about the boogeyman? What if…?

Joyce pushed open the door. There was no tiny night-light glowing in the corner of this room as there was in Trevor's room, but some light streamed in from the hallway as Joyce opened the door even more. Joyce stood silhouetted in the open doorway feeling vulnerable, a little silly, and very, very scared.

She could barely see her father leaning over Robin's bed. He held something in his hand. His back was to the door. Joyce didn't dare intrude. She thought of her father as someone sacred, almost a god. Though seldom seen, his presence was always felt.

Gordon Roberts was an entrepreneur, someone who devoted all his time to a thing called "business." He never had time for his children. Less time, certainly, than Mommie. And Mommie was never, ever around.

What was Daddy doing in Robin's room in the middle of the night?

Joyce didn't dare disturb Daddy. When Daddy was home, he had more important things on his mind than a six-year-old could possibly understand. So Joyce stood in the doorway and said nothing.

Daddy's hand went over his head. He held something in his hand.

Joyce glanced at the bed. It looked like the bed was covered with blood.

And then Joyce saw Robin's face. And it wasn't a face anymore.

And Joyce screamed.

BOOK ONE

If you strike a child, take care that you strike it in anger, even at the risk of maiming it for life. A blow in cold blood neither can nor should be forgiven.

—George Bernard Shaw, *Man and Superman, Maxims for Revolutionists.*

CHAPTER ONE

"He's here, Joyce!"

"I'll be ready in a minute, Grandma."

"Need my help, dear?"

"No, don't bother. I'm almost finished. Tell Tony I'll be right down."

Joyce checked her makeup again. Although ready and impatiently waiting for more than an hour, she was absolutely certain she must have overlooked something. Leaning over the bathroom sink, her face almost touching its twin in the mirror, Joyce pushed back long bangs that completely covered her forehead. She, very carefully, inspected every inch of skin. She could barely see the scars.

Satisfied, she let the hair drop back into place. In ordinary light, with her thick auburn hair covering most of the heavily powdered flesh above her eyebrows, Joyce looked perfectly normal. No one need ever know.

Joyce stepped back and tried to see herself in the mirror as others would see her at a distance. She wore a pink, long-sleeved prom dress with a high lace collar that covered her neck to the chin. Beneath the dress she wore a pink slip that added depth to the dress. The slip felt silky next to her body, not rough and scratchy like the lace. The bodice of the dress was layered with more of the pink lace. Her breasts looked full and round, sensuous. She smiled at herself with approval.

Her face—angular, adolescent, and pale in comparison to the dress—was simply highlighted with dabs of blush on both cheeks. Her lips were coated bright red with Revlon.

Her eyes looked naked.

The eyes that met hers in the mirror were light blue, dotted with tiny specks of hazel not unlike the shiny mica chips that intermittently dotted the Formica countertop downstairs in the kitchen. Her lashes were long and naturally curled. Deep-set on both sides of a narrow nose, those eyes gave her face a hollow, haunted look. She had to do something else with the eyes, she decided. But what?

Very carefully, Joyce unscrewed the lid on a jar of foundation. Using a cotton pad, she applied base to both eyelids and the area under the eyes. She added mascara and eyeliner. By the time she finished, her eyes were the new focal point of her face.

She smiled. Her brightly painted lips and dazzling eyes lit up her face like a neon sign. No one would ever notice the scars.

She screwed the cap back on, and dropped the jar, two clean cotton pads, brushes, pencils, mascara, and liner into a small handbag. She was ready to go.

And then, on impulse, she raised her skirt and slip and dabbed a touch of perfume to each thigh. Now I'm really ready, she told herself.

But when she began to descend the stairs, a moment of pure panic gripped her heart in icy fingers. Joyce wanted desperately to turn around, run back to the bathroom, barricade herself inside, and never ever come out.

You're acting like a scared child again, she chided herself. You've got to do it, Joyce. You've got to. If you botch this chance, you'll never be able to go out on your own. You'll end up hiding in this house, living with Grandpa Fred and Grandma Grace for the rest of your life. You'll probably become exactly like them. You wouldn't want that, would you?

Joyce walked the rest of the way down the stairs telling herself that the past didn't matter tonight, nothing mattered but the prom and Tony and having a good time; and that, finally, after eleven years of pain and doubt, she could begin to believe a normal life might be possible after all. Possible!

Even for her.

Tony was waiting on the living room sofa with Grandma Grace. When Joyce made her entrance, Tony rose from the couch and looked Joyce up and down with ravenous eyes that threatened to devour all of her in a single bite. He smiled his approval. His smile was instantly infectious and Joyce smiled back.

At six-foot-six and two hundred and twenty pounds, Tony Virusso was the star athlete of West High. Besides football and basketball, Tony had varsity letters in baseball and track. Was it any wonder that the senior class had voted Tony Virusso the most popular man at West, officially bestowing on him the title of "Big Man on Campus"?

Dressed in a dark brown tuxedo, a cream-colored pleated shirt, and milk chocolate bow tie, Tony looked a lot like a young but tall John Travolta. His dark brown, almost black hair was naturally wavy. Neatly trimmed and sprayed so every strand stayed smartly in place, he was manicured to perfection. Tony Virusso was easily the handsomest man Joyce had ever seen.

Tony turned back to the couch, opened a small white box, and produced a gorgeous corsage composed of miniature pink and red roses. "Can I pin it on?" he asked.

Before Joyce could voice consent, Tony's left hand reached the bodice of her dress and tugged gently at the fabric. His fingers quickly separated dress from undergarments with a practiced familiarity that left Joyce speechless.

Holding the corsage to her dress, Tony tried to slip an ordinary straight pin through the fabric without scratching her skin or catching her slip. He almost succeeded. But the point of the pin looked like something else to Joyce—something that had hurt her badly not once but a thousand painful times—and she recoiled in total terror.

Her mind saw a hypodermic needle instead of a pin. A hypodermic needle aimed to pierce her naked flesh. A hypodermic filled with pain.

Not the needle itself, she knew, but what always followed. The real pain came later, after the effects of the needle wore off. And when she awoke, parts of her would be missing. Big patches of skin—long strips of pink flesh peeled from the most sensitive parts of her body—would inevitably be missing.

Joyce screamed. She flailed wildly with both arms, knocking the man with the needle off-balance.

And he accidentally pierced her skin with the straight pin.

"No, please!" she shrieked. "Don't hurt me again. Oh, God!" Her voice keened at the edge of hysteria. "Please! Not again!"

"It's all right, dear," Grandma Grace soothed, pushing Tony aside. "Nobody's going to hurt you. I'm here to protect you."

"What the hell did I do?" a bewildered Tony asked. "I didn't mean to hurt her. Honest. What'd I do wrong?"

"It's not your fault," Grace said, slipping both arms around her granddaughter. "You didn't do anything wrong."

"Jesus," Tony whispered. "I didn't mean..."

"It's okay," Grace said. "Isn't it, Joyce?"

An almost painful silence seemed to settle over the room. Tears ran like rivers from the girl's eyes, streaking both cheeks with long lines of ruined mascara.

"But what'd I *do?*" Tony demanded. "Whatever it was, I don't wanna do it again."

"You didn't do anything, Tony," Joyce whispered, startling Tony with the sound of incredible pain in her voice. "It's me. I'm the one who's messed up. I'm sorry, Tony. Can... can you ever forgive me?"

"Sure. I mean, there's nothing to forgive."

"I've ruined our evening, haven't I?"

"Nothing's ruined but your makeup, dear," Grace said. "Let's go upstairs and I'll help you freshen up. Then you and Tony can go on to the prom just like you planned."

"Go ahead," Tony said. "I'll wait."

"Why don't you sit on the couch and watch TV," Grace suggested. "The remote control is on the coffee table. We won't be long."

"And I'll make it up to you," Joyce promised as she and Grace disappeared up the stairs. "Just don't leave, Tony... oh, please... don't leave..."

Tony had no intention of leaving. He found the TV control and settled comfortably into soft sofa cushions, flipping channels until he found a baseball game. No, he wouldn't leave for a million dollars.

Joyce Roberts was an incredibly beautiful young woman, well worth whatever wait. Tony had already waited months for this single date. What would a few minutes more matter?

He'd been irresistibly attracted to Joyce that very first moment sixteen months ago when she'd walked into his algebra class as a new student. Unlike other girls at West High, Joyce Roberts always managed to look beautiful, even after an entire day of classes.

Red-brown shoulder-length hair covered most of her forehead and framed her gorgeous face, and bright-colored makeup tastefully highlighted her eyes and mouth, making her look sophisticated and somehow older than sixteen or seventeen. And she was always—always!—impeccably dressed in long skirts and turtle-necked sweaters, even on warm days when other girls wore T-shirts and shorts. There was something curiously sensuous, delightfully mysterious about Joyce Roberts that attracted Tony Virusso like a magnet.

More than once Tony had thought Joyce looked too good to be true. Her facial features were almost perfect, sculptured, like the faces decorating the covers of *Vogue* or *Cosmopolitan* at the news stands. Like every man's dream of how a girl *should* look. She made other girls seem unattractive by comparison.

And her body! What a body Joyce had! Large breasts, obviously always encased in a bra (Joyce was one of the few girls Tony knew who looked as if she needed a bra for support rather than vanity), and even though her oversized sweaters hid most of her figure, he was sure she had a flat stomach and gently curving hips.

But what really made Joyce Roberts special was her unattainability. She'd made it quite clear to everyone at school that she didn't go out on dates. Every guy who asked her out was politely rebuffed. And Joyce never went to varsity games or parties nor participated in any of the after-school activities where guys and girls put moves on each other.

At first Tony suspected Joyce might be a lesbian like Sheila Gilbert and Rhonda Lewis. But Joyce didn't seem interested in girls any more than guys. She was a loner, a private person, too aloof to be bothered by the banalities of high school. And that made Joyce a challenge.

Tony loved challenges.

He bided his time. There was more than enough to keep him busy anyway. Every available girl in school was constantly putting moves on *him*, for Christ's sake! When he wasn't sweating his balls off at practice or breaking his balls on the field during a game, Tony could pick and choose from dozens of good-looking young women who wanted to suck his balls *dry*. He didn't need to bruise the old ego by hitting on a girl who'd certainly turn him down.

But Tony couldn't get Joyce Roberts out of his mind. All through his junior and senior years he watched and waited. Three months before the senior prom, knowing no one else had dared to ask her for a date, Tony took a desperate chance. Cornering her in chemistry class, he blurted out, "I want you to go to the prom with me. Will you?"

Without lifting her beautiful eyes from a beakered precipitate she was carefully measuring on a gram scale, Joyce said, "I'm sorry. I can't go."

"Got another date?"

"No."

"Why can't you go with me then?"

"I simply can't." She recorded the measurements neatly in a spiral notebook. "I'm sorry," she said, still not looking at him. "Really I am. But I can't go. Please ask someone else."

That night Tony got drunk with a few friends and told them he wasn't going to sit still while some hotshot bitch cut off his balls. He'd work on her until she changed her mind. And then he'd stick it to her good.

And work on her he did. For more than a month he lavished her with compliments, followed her around like a lovesick puppy, sent flowers to her home, offered to carry her books between classes, and told her his life wasn't worth living if she wouldn't go with him to the senior prom.

That, finally, did the trick. "Why me?" she asked. "Why not one of the other girls I've seen you hanging around with?"

"Because you're special," he answered honestly, sensing an opening at last. "You're not like any of the other girls. You're you. And no one else will do."

"Oh. God. Tony. It's impossible. Can't you see that? It's impossible. I'm not right for you. I'm not right for anybody."

"If you won't go, I'll slit my wrists."

"No!" Her eyes pleaded with him. "Don't say that!"

"I mean it."

"You're acting like a spoiled child."

"Maybe. But I can't help myself." He knew now was the time to push her into a corner. "I swear, Joyce. If you don't go to the prom with me, I'll slit my wrists."

The horror in her eyes was nearly enough to make Tony laugh. He even thought of relenting, admitting he was putting her on. Tony Virusso had too much going to ever seriously contemplate suicide. He'd never slit his wrists over a girl, not even a girl as pretty as Joyce Roberts.

He waited and said nothing. The next move was hers. He'd gone as far as he could go, pushed her to the brink.

"All right," she gave in, looking as if her iron will had been shattered by a sledgehammer. "I'll go to the prom if it means that much to you."

Tony saw tears in her eyes, big glistening tears that should have told him something of the terrific battle that raged inside her and the significance of the monumental victory just won. But Tony was too elated to notice; he was too self-centered to be concerned, too rapturous to do anything but kiss her lips as hard as he could.

After her acceptance, Tony backed off and gave her room to breathe again. Though he continued his compliments, he stopped sending flowers. He carried her books only between classes they had in common. And he never again mentioned suicide.

As the days and weeks went by and the prom date grew closer and closer, Joyce became more and more enthusiastic. She told Tony about the dress she was making, the shoes and handbag she'd bought at Sears.

Tony knew she was hooked.

He began making plans for the big seduction scene. He paid his older brother, Steve, for the use of Steve's apartment after the prom. He got Steve to buy bottles of booze and cases of beer. And he invited a half-dozen close friends and their dates to attend "a wild fucking party that'll knock your socks off."

And every night, whether alone in bed playing with himself or in the back seat of his car playing with one of the many girls he still dated, he would fantasize about Joyce and what he'd do to her after the prom.

And his erection would get rock-hard and he couldn't contain his ecstasy.

Looking down at his lap he realized he had another erection that wanted to split the seams of his tuxedo trousers. What if Joyce and her grandmother came back now and found him sitting on their living room couch with a raging hard-on bulging in his pants?

He tried to concentrate on the TV baseball game, but it was too early in the season to hold his interest. Even the Cubs were tied for first place and a single game didn't make a whole hell of a lot of difference one way or the other.

When Joyce and her grandmother started down the stairs, Tony stood up. He quickly checked his fly, smoothed the back of his jacket down over his butt, and smiled pleasantly as they entered the room.

Joyce knew she owed Tony some sort of explanation. But she didn't know how or where to begin. It seemed so silly to be scared of a simple, ordinary straight pin. She didn't think he would believe it if she told him the truth.

Dr. Joshi had warned her this might someday happen. This or something similar. It was only a matter of time, Joshi had said.

"The body cannot be scarred without the brain being also scarred," her shrink had told her. "The body and mind are intertwined, inseparable. What affects one affects the other."

Gephardt Joshi was the psychiatrist Joyce had seen twice monthly since she was eight. A hulking, obese man with a white neatly-trimmed goatee, he sometimes reminded her of an aging Orson Welles trying to fake a German accent.

"What will you do, *Liebschen*, if your mind plays these tricks on you while you are out in public?"

"I've got to take that chance, doctor. I can't stay cooped up with Grandma and Grandpa in that old house forever. Now can I?"

Joyce loved to answer the doctor's questions with other questions. If he insisted on using Zen-Socratic techniques and make her find her own answers to her own problems, then Joyce would use it right back on him.

"Do you think you're ready to break out of your shell and fly away like a sparrow? Or are you an ostrich about to hide your head in the sand?"

"What do you think, doctor?"

"I can't answer that, Joyce. Only you know the answer."

"I'm ready to fly," she conceded.

"And what will you do, *Liebschen*, if your mind plays tricks while you are out in public?"

"You already asked me *that* question, doctor. Why are you repeating yourself?"

"Because you didn't answer *that* question, *Liebschen.* Did you?"

"Didn't I?"

"What will you do, *Liebschen? Have you* thought about it?"

"No."

"Will you think about it?"

"Do I have to?"

Maybe Joshi was right after all. This time when Tony pinned the corsage to her dress, she wasn't afraid of the pin because she'd thought about what it was and knew it wouldn't hurt her. Even the accidental jab she had received when Tony was knocked off-balance was nothing more than a minor pinprick. There would be no lasting scars, no excruciating pain.

With the corsage firmly in place, Grandma Grace kissed Joyce good-bye and wished them both a good time at the prom. Tony gave her his arm and escorted her out to the car, his father's Buick Regal borrowed for the night. He opened the door and held it while she climbed in. She slid to the middle of the front seat, trying to keep her skirt modestly tucked around her thighs. Tony smiled, slammed the door, walked around to the driver's side, and climbed in behind the wheel while trying to fish the car keys out of his pants pocket.

"Thanks for being patient with me," she said shyly.

He put his arms around her and kissed her quickly on the lips. "No big deal," he said. "I'd wait for you forever, if I had to."

She pulled him back to her lips. Her hands held the back of his head while her tongue probed his mouth. He was gasping for breath when she finally let go.

"Thanks, Tony. You're sweet."

Flustered, Tony started the car and pulled away from the curb with a squeal of rubber. The sun was beginning to set and shadows stretched from the trees to cover the streets and sidewalks. He switched on the Buick's beams, turned left onto North Main, and headed for the high school.

"Will we be really late?" Joyce asked. She wasn't wearing her watch.

"Don't sweat it," Tony answered with a smile. "This way we can make a grand entrance. Everyone'll already be there to watch us come in."

Joyce settled back in the seat, laid her head softly against Tony's shoulder, and tried to think of ways to tell him.

"I've got a secret," she might say. "It's a deep, dark secret you don't really want to know. It's ugly and sickening."

Or how about, "I'm not normal, Tony. I just thought I'd tell you so you'd know what you were getting into." Or, "I told you to find someone else to take to the prom. Don't say I didn't warn you."

Or maybe even, "A long time ago I was hurt really bad, Tony. My mind and my body will always have scars."

Tony swung the Buick into the high school parking lot, found a space at the end of a long row of cars, and edged in quickly before some other latecomer could ace him out.

"Hope you don't mind a little walk," he said. "Otherwise I could drop you off at the door and come back for this spot."

"It's a beautiful evening," she said. "I don't mind walking if you don't."

As he opened his door and got out of the car, Joyce knew she'd missed her chance to tell him. They'd arrived at the prom and whatever she would eventually tell Tony would have to wait until later.

Much later.

And maybe, if she was lucky, she wouldn't have to tell him anything at all.

CHAPTER TWO

Decorated with flowers and streamers and special lights, the high school gymnasium was bathed in a soft, warm glow and the heady odor of fresh carnations and roses from hundreds of corsages and table decorations. Over the stage, where a ten-piece band played, there hung a huge silver circle wreathed with flowers. Since "June Moon" was this year's prom theme, Joyce supposed the cardboard circle covered with aluminum foil was someone's silly idea of the full moon.

Though certainly not the last to arrive, they were late enough to be noticed. Heads turned and people stared. No one expected Joyce to be there. Her presence at the prom was oddity enough. That she had entered on the arm of Tony Virusso, Mister Popularity of the senior class, was shocking.

A delayed murmur began at one end of the gymnasium and spread to the other. Couples stopped dancing and congregated in small groups. Everyone was whispering.

A hundred pairs of eyes riveted on Joyce. They scanned her body from the tips of her toes sheathed in high-heeled pink pumps to the long strands of layered hair hiding her ears and forehead.

Some of the men mentally undressed her with their eyes. Envy, and often outright dislike, radiated from the eyes of many of the women.

Gary Brandt, president of the senior class and star linebacker for the varsity football team, came up to Tony and shook hands. Gary shot Joyce a sly wink, implying that he had badly misinterpreted their reason for late arrival.

"You know Elaine Flanders, don't you?" Brandt asked, introducing his date to Joyce. Joyce nodded. Everyone knew Ellie.

Elaine Flanders was captain of the cheerleaders, a bottle blonde rumored to have slept with half the football team. Looking at Ellie now, Joyce could easily believe the gossip.

Dressed in an expensive evening gown with cleavage that didn't allow for a bra, Ellie was a very close Britney Spears lookalike. Everything about her seemed to suggest an unbridled sexuality that someday would get her into big trouble.

Unlike Britney, however, Ellie Flanders seldom acted like just another "dumb blonde." She was one of the smartest girls in her senior class, maintaining a straight A average without opening a textbook. Ellie had earned an academic scholarship to Northwestern next fall, something no other student in their class had managed. If she didn't get pregnant, she'd surely graduate college *cum laude* and become an instant success when she entered the business world.

Joyce, on the other hand, had to study constantly merely to make the honor roll. She hadn't received a single scholarship, not even one from a state university. Of course, Joyce hadn't applied until just recently. College had always seemed out of the question for her. Going away to college, living away from home, seemed simply impossible.

But Tony's constant flattery during the past few months had built her ego to the point where she now knew it *was* possible. Three weeks ago she'd sent her application, copies of transcripts, and a financial aid form to the University of Illinois at Chicago. Although she hadn't heard a word from the university, didn't expect to be accepted, and didn't think she'd applied in time to be eligible for a scholarship, at least she felt better for trying. And maybe next year, she would try again.

Ellie smiled, giving Joyce the impression she was secretly laughing. She looked as if she were right on the edge of revealing the punch line to some ridiculous joke without first telling the rest of the joke.

"I like your dress," Ellie said, her smile growing into a grin. "Did you make it yourself?"

"Is it that obvious?" Joyce asked, uncertain of Ellie's compliment. Was it meant to be sincere? Or was it meant as a put-down?

"Not at all. You did an excellent job. Almost professional even."

Though Ellie's smile hadn't wavered beyond a grin, Joyce was certain that Ellie was indeed laughing. Laughing at Joyce as if Joyce were the joke.

"She's jealous because she wouldn't know how to make a dress if her life depended on it," Tony said. "Take away her mother's credit cards, and Ellie'd have to go naked."

Ellie's grin faded. "Bet you'd like me to go naked, wouldn't you?" she taunted.

"Hell," Tony replied with a grin of his own. "Everyone here's already seen everything *you've* got. You could take off your clothes and nobody'd even bother to notice."

"Hey!" Gary interrupted. "If you can't be nice to each other, at least be civil."

"C'mon." Tony grabbed Joyce's hand in an iron grip. "Let's dance."

On the dance floor Tony pulled Joyce close and whispered in her ear. "Don't let that bitch get under your skin," he said. "She gets her kicks by being a pain in the ass."

Joyce forced her feet back and forth in a shuffle, trying to follow Tony's practiced lead. Though she'd never danced before, she had read several books with fancy diagrams that outlined most of the steps. Her mind raced desperately, trying to recall the simple difference between a foxtrot and a waltz.

Slowly she got the hang of it, and soon she was able to relax and simply enjoy the closeness of a male body pressed tightly to her own. Tony's after-shave filled her nostrils with the sweet scent of musk.

"It isn't the dress," she said with a sense of sudden insight.

"What?"

"It isn't the dress that made Ellie jealous."

"Not the dress?"

"No, not the dress. Ellie isn't jealous over the dress. She's jealous over *you*."

"Over me?"

"Didn't you used to go out with her?"

"Once or twice."

"See? I bet she thought you'd ask *her* to the prom and she's disappointed you didn't."

"She's here with Gary."

"Is she Gary's steady'?"

"She's nobody's steady."

"Then I was right. She probably waited for you to ask her, and when you didn't and Gary did, she came with him instead."

When Tony didn't try to argue, Joyce knew it was true. She had seen it in Ellie's eyes and hadn't recognized it at first. But now she knew. Ellie wanted Tony, wanted his body pressed close to hers, wanted to smell his sweet musk.

Wanted it so badly that she hated anyone who got in her way.

The band finished their set and announced a ten-minute break. Tony took Joyce's hand and led her to the punch bowl.

They had to stand in line to be served. Three large crystal bowls, filled with fruit cocktail, orange juice, grapefruit juice, pieces of frozen fruit, and dry ice, were being constantly replenished by caterers. But by the time Joyce and Tony reached the head of the line, all three bowls were empty.

Tony grabbed two of the plastic glasses from the table and motioned Joyce to follow. He headed to the far end of the gym and entered the varsity locker room.

"C'mon," he said, holding the door.

"I can't go in *there*," Joyce rebelled. "That's the boys' locker room."

"So what?" He laughed. "C'mon. No one's in the showers. You don't think I'd try to embarrass you, do you?"

She entered cautiously, feeling very nervous and out of place. This was obviously male domain that both looked and smelled ruggedly-masculine. There were long rows of metal lockers with wooden benches where she knew men dressed and undressed, where they hung dirty jock straps and smelly sweat socks up to dry, where they swapped dirty jokes and ribald tales, where they talked about their sexual prowess and their fantasies of future conquests. Tony belonged here, but she didn't.

"Hold these." Tony shoved a plastic glass into each of her hands. He dug around in the inside pocket of his dinner jacket and brought out a pint bottle of Jack Daniel's.

He emptied the bottle equally into each of the glasses.

"Tony, no! We'll be expelled for drinking on school grounds. We won't get to graduate next Friday or even next year!"

"Only if were caught," he said. He threw the empty bottle into an unlocked locker. "And who's gonna catch us?"

"A chaperone, maybe? One of the kids?"

"Naw. No one's allowed in the varsity locker room except team members. And the coach, of course, but he ain't here tonight." Tony took one of the glasses from her trembling hand. "Don't worry, love. Nobody'll see us."

Tony sat down on the bench and pulled Joyce to sit beside him. Then he took a long swallow of the amber liquid, sighed a long sigh, and said, "I needed that."

Joyce didn't know what to do. She'd never before in her entire life tasted even a drop of liquor. Fred and Grace, diametrically opposed to alcohol, didn't drink. And they condemned anyone and everyone who did.

"Demon rum is the downfall of any man or woman who touches but a single drop," Grandpa Fred had hammered into her head. "It's the Devil's brew. Its only purpose is to corrupt and degrade decent folk who should know better but don't. Look what it did to your mother."

Joyce had been told repeatedly of her mother's alcoholism. Too young to remember much about her mother at all, Joyce had been led to believe Leona Roberts was a real souse. According to Grandpa, Leona had been a drunk even before she'd married Gordon Roberts. Drink, Grandpa claimed, was responsible for ruining not only Leona's life, but also the lives of those around her.

"Go ahead," Tony said. "Drink up."

Joyce put the glass to her lips. The strong alcoholic fumes made her head swim and her stomach churn. Why would anyone want to drink such foul-smelling, unappealing stuff?

Grandpa Fred had been quite a drinker himself in his early days, before he'd seen the light and got religion. To hear him tell it, he could outdrink everyone at a bar and still be standing after everybody else had passed out. But something had happened to make him see the light. And whatever it was, it wasn't something he liked to talk about.

"It's too awful to tell," he'd said, avoiding her eyes when Joyce had tried to probe. "Much too awful to tell."

"Can we go back and dance some more?" Joyce asked Tony. "The band's playing again. Don't you hear them?"

"Give me a minute," he said. He tilted his head and downed half the glass in one gulp.

"Want mine too?" she offered.

"Aren't you drinking?"

"I guess I don't like gin."

"It isn't gin. It's bourbon. The best bourbon you can buy."

"Bourbon, then. I don't like bourbon."

Tony looked at her funny, as if he was really disappointed in her. "Don't drink much, do you?" he said. It was more a statement than a question.

"Not much," she admitted.

"That's okay. I don't wanna get shitfaced yet either. Give me your glass and I'll pour it down the drain in the shower room."

Tony was gone for ten minutes. When he came back, without the glasses, he was smiling. He didn't seem in the least upset.

"Let's go cut a rug," he said.

He led her out of the locker room and back onto the dance floor. When he pulled her close, she was disappointed to learn that she could no longer smell the musk in his after-shave. All she could smell was the strong odor of liquor on his breath.

Henry Mancini's "Moon River" was the last dance of the evening. Many of the couples had already left, and those who remained rocked back and forth without really moving much. The other kids looked as if they were asleep on their feet. Joyce was tired and ready to sit down, but she didn't want the evening to end. After a brief rest, she was sure she'd be back on her feet and able to dance until dawn.

When the song ended, bright overhead fluorescent lights came on and the spell was broken. For nearly an hour Joyce had lost herself in the strong, masculine arms of Tony Virusso. Never in her life had she felt so secure, so protected. She didn't want to think about going home.

So when Tony told her about the party at Steve's, told her they could dance all night long to music from Steve's stereo, she didn't hesitate to say yes.

And when they got to the car and Tony took her in his arms and kissed her long and hard on the lips, she kissed him back. Tony's tongue danced in her mouth and her tongue followed his lead. She didn't stop him when she felt his hand on the bodice of her dress. She didn't even stop him when his fingers searched for an opening, found none, and settled finally on fondling her nipple through three layers of lace.

This was the first time that any man had touched her in anything other than an antiseptic, clinical fashion. Joyce was surprised at the warm feelings that flooded her body. She'd read about such reactions in countless books, but never knew until now how pleasurable a mere touch could be. She didn't want him to stop, ever. She wanted him to keep touching her. He broke away, panting for breath.

Then he quickly started the car. "Let's go to the party," he whispered. "We can take up where we left off when we get to Steve's apartment."

Steve's apartment was the entire second-floor of an old wood-framed house. An enclosed back stairway led directly into the kitchen. The party was already in progress when they arrived. Tony had passed a key to Gary Brandt at the prom, and Gary had opened the house a half-hour before anyone else had left the dance.

Besides Brandt and Flanders, Joyce recognized three other couples. Tom Torino and Linda Michaels were sprawled on the living room couch, seeming more interested in a TV movie than in each other. John Grabowski and Sharon Davidson were sitting on the floor rolling cigarettes on a huge mirror that had obviously been lifted from a bare space on the wall over the fireplace. Claire Kelly and Jeff Schilling stood behind Grabowski and Davidson to supervise the making of cigarettes.

It suddenly dawned on Joyce that they were rolling joints, not cigarettes.

Joyce didn't know any more about drugs than she knew about alcohol. She'd heard about drugs, of course. She had read about them and studied about them in high school health classes. Drugs were supposed to be dangerous. And Joyce was afraid of being around them because she knew drugs were even more dangerous than alcohol.

Before Joyce could say anything to Tony, Ellie Flanders came between them and handed Tony a large glass of Jack Daniel's on ice. "I'm playing cocktail waitress tonight," she told Tony in an imitation sexy Southern drawl. "I'm working for tips, y'all surely understand. Will you give me a big tip?"

Tony laughed. "Think y'all deserve a tip?" he mimicked.

"I deserve all you got to offer, mister, not just the tip." She licked her lips suggestively. "But I'm not greedy. I'll settle for what I can get."

Tony laughed again. "Look," he said. "Do me a favor, Ellie. Fix a drink for Joyce. I gotta go use the bathroom." He turned to Joyce and pecked her cheek. "I'll be right back, honey. Why don't you go into the kitchen and get a drink?"

Tony quickly ran off and Joyce was left alone with the blonde. "What's your pleasure, honey?" Ellie asked sweetly.

"Coke," Joyce answered.

"Mine, too," Ellie admitted with genuine surprise. "But we've got to wait until Keith gets here. There's lots of booze, though. And Jeff'll pass a joint as soon as he gets three or four rolled. Meanwhile, let's go to the kitchen and get ourselves a drink. Gary's making kamikazes."

Dumbfounded, Joyce followed Ellie to the kitchen, where Gary Brandt stood at a counter pouring lime juice into a blender.

"Second batch is almost ready," he announced, flipping the switch on the blender. "Get your glasses from the pantry."

"What are kamikazes?" Joyce asked.

"You don't know?"

"No," said Joyce, feeling stupid.

Ellie and Gary exchanged glances. Both seemed to smile sympathetically.

"They taste real sweet," Gary said.

"A lot like lemonade," Ellie added. "They're good and they're good for you, too. There's lots of vitamin C in the lime juice."

"Go ahead," urged Gary. "Try one. If you don't like it, you don't have to finish it."

Ellie brought three eight-ounce water glasses from the pantry. "Are kamikazes alcoholic?" Joyce asked nervously.

"A little triple sec to take the tartness off the lime," Gary admitted. "But you won't notice an alcoholic taste."

"No more than you notice the alcoholic taste of vanilla extract when you put vanilla in cookie batter," Ellie said.

"Go ahead," Gary said. "Try one, just one, and see for yourself." He switched off the blender and filled all three glasses. He handed one to Joyce, one to Ellie, and kept one for himself.

"Cheers," Ellie said, raising her glass.

Clinking his glass against Ellie's, Gary said, "Down the hatch."

Joyce held her drink so tight she was sure the glass would shatter in her hand. Though she didn't want to try the kamikaze, she didn't want to appear juvenile in front of Tony's sophisticated friends, either. For eleven years, Joyce had been overly protected by her grandparents. She hadn't been allowed to mature normally, to experiment with life, to make decisions on her own. Her entire life, she realized, had been controlled as tightly as the glass she held in her hand.

She watched Gary and Ellie sip their drinks. Gary was a star athlete and Ellie was valedictorian of their high school class. Neither had ruined his or her life by drinking. One little drink couldn't hurt, could it?

She licked the edge of the glass. A sticky-sweet taste titillated her tongue.

She took a small sip. One little sip wouldn't hurt. It did taste a lot like lemonade, she discovered. Or maybe a little like iced tea with lots of sugar and honey spooned in. She took a larger swallow. Despite the crushed ice that cooled her lips, the liquid warmed her throat.

"What do you think?" asked Gary.

Joyce smiled. "I like it," she said. She gulped down the rest of her drink and asked for more.

Gary refilled her glass and topped off the other two. "I'll make another batch and put it in the refrigerator," he said. "When you want more, just open the fridge and help yourself."

Ellie and Joyce returned to the living room and sat on the floor next to Sharon and John. It seemed silly to be sitting on the floor in formal attire, and Joyce giggled. The other girls had already removed their shoes, and Joyce slipped the high-heeled pumps off her own feet with a sigh of relief. After hours of dancing and standing, it felt good just to sit down and take off both shoes. She wiggled her toes and giggled again.

John and Jeff lit two of those funny cigarettes—joints, Joyce corrected herself—and passed them to their dates. Sharon and Claire inhaled, coughed, inhaled again. Then they passed the cigarettes to Ellie and Joyce.

Joyce had never smoked a cigarette before, didn't know how to inhale or even hold it in her mouth. She watched as Ellie put the paper to her pursed lips and sucked. Ellie's cheeks grew hollow and the fire at the tip of the cigarette flared a bright orange.

Joyce was about to take a puff of her own cigarette before she remembered that these weren't just ordinary cigarettes. These were marijuana cigarettes. *Drugs!* She quickly peeled the paper from her lips and passed the joint on to a grateful Linda Michaels. The next time one came her way, Joyce passed the joint on without delay.

"Don't you want any?" Linda asked. "I can wait till you take a hit."

"I don't like drugs," Joyce said.

"Different strokes for different folks," Linda quipped. "That just leaves more for us who do."

Joyce wanted to tell the girl that her dislike of drugs was something personal, something so demeaning and damaging that no one else could possibly understand. But she didn't know how to put that into words, how to tell them only part of the story without telling all.

She said nothing and simply sipped at her drink. By the time Tony returned from the bathroom, Joyce had made two added trips to the kitchen to refill her glass. She felt warm all over and the rest of the world had taken on a warm glow that made everything look a bit fuzzy around the edges. She giggled when Tony sat down next to her and put his hand on her leg.

"What took you so long?" she giggled. "I thought maybe you fell in."

Tony kissed her and smiled quizzically. "What *are* you drinking?" he asked.

"Kami-kami-kami-whatzits."

"Kamikazes?"

"Uh-huh."

"Joyce, do you know why they're called kamikazes?"

"No. Why?"

"Because they shoot you down real quick, blast you right out-of the sky. They're equal parts vodka and triple sec with a little lime juice thrown in. Drinking a kamikaze is sure suicide."

"I didn't taste any alcohol," Joyce slurred.

"That's because vodka doesn't taste like alcohol or smell like alcohol when it's mixed with fruit juice. How many of those have you had?"

"Three or four."

"Jesus!" Tony turned to Ellie and rudely interrupted her conversation with Sharon. "What the fuck did you do to Joyce? She's shitfaced already!"

"I didn't do anything to her," Ellie glowered. "She did it all by herself. I can't help it if the dumb cunt keeps raiding the refrigerator, can I?"

"You could have stopped her."

"She's *your* date, Mr. Big Man, not mine. If you hadn't barricaded yourself in the john to stuff your nose with joy powder, maybe she wouldn't be soused by now. Don't blame me. Blame yourself."

"I bet you think it's funny? A big joke on little Joycie?"

"Sure. She's a stuck-up little bitch who wouldn't have anything to do with any of us, from the first day she came to our class from whatever private school she used to attend until now—now when high school's almost over and we're all going our separate ways. I thought she needed to learn a lesson about manners. And when I found out she knew nothing about kamikazes, it seemed just too perfect an opportunity to let pass."

"Thanks a lot," Tony said. He put a huge hand on Ellie's bare shoulder and squeezed hard enough to leave a bruise.

"You're a real asshole, Virusso," the blonde said, spitting out the words. "Someday I'll cut your nuts off, grind them to powder, and shove them up your nose. Or maybe," she chuckled, "you'll do that all by yourself before I even get the chance."

Tony hit her. His meaty fist slammed into her soft stomach before she saw it coming, slammed into her left kidney with enough force to knock the breath from her lungs and send sharp pains shooting through her whole midsection. She doubled up and rolled on the floor gasping, unable to get enough breath back into her lungs to cry.

He'd moved so fast that no one else knew what had happened. Or maybe they were simply so stoned that they didn't care. No one came to her aid.

Joyce giggled when she saw Ellie Flanders' left breast pop free of the dangling décolletage. Ellie was doubled over on the floor, twisting and moaning, holding her stomach with both hands. Ellie's motions and moans made no sense at all; but nothing made much sense to Joyce unless she forced herself to think things through. And right now thinking made her dizzy.

All she wanted to do was lie down like Ellie, close her eyes, and go to sleep. She would have stretched out on the floor, but the floor seemed to be moving in waves like an angry ocean in the middle of a storm. She closed her eyes and the floor continued to move beneath her.

And then Tony lifted her from the floor and picked her up in his arms. He was all muscle, and he simply picked Joyce up and carried her the way a father might carry a sleeping infant. He took her to another room and laid her gently atop a big bed that must have been a water bed because it, too, moved in waves. She thought she would soon be seasick if the motion didn't stop.

Tony quietly closed the door and turned on the lights. Joyce didn't like bright lights shining in her eyes even if her eyes were tightly closed. She'd had bright lights shined in her eyes too often before. She didn't like bright lights. But she couldn't think, for the life of her, why not.

She asked Tony to turn off the lights and he did. Then he climbed onto the bed right next to her. He put his arms around her and she clung to him the way a drowning person clings desperately to a floating life preserver. She tried to keep afloat, tried to keep the waves from overwhelming her, but it seemed all in vain.

And then she felt Tony's fingers tugging at the back of her dress. She heard the metallic rasp of a zipper as it separated.

Gently, he peeled the dress from her neck and shoulders. She tried to help by backing her arms out of the sleeves, but she only got all twisted up and made things more difficult for him. Somehow, though, he managed to get the dress down her torso and bunched around her hips. He fumbled at the bow in the pink sash that belted her waist. When the sash came loose, he slipped the dress over her hips, down her legs, and off completely.

Her slip went next. Then her nylons, one at a time. Then her bra. She felt him fumbling with the clasps in the middle of her back. He lifted the cups and his hands squeezed both breasts.

Finally, he slipped the straps from her arms and flung the bra across the room where it bounced from a wall and fell silently to the floor.

His hands were all over her entire body. They fondled, caressed, probed. Then his fingers slipped beneath the elastic of her panties and inched their way down through tangled pubic hair toward their ultimate target.

Joyce was only half-aware when first one finger, then another, entered her wetness. The waves of nausea had passed, replaced by a growing warmth that Tony's closeness generated. But she wasn't fully conscious.

What was happening wasn't happening to *her*, was it? She felt like someone else, someone watching a silent film where every third or fourth frame was missing and the action wasn't at all continuous. Time seemed to jerk quickly from one occurrence to another rather than flow slowly forward in a straight line. Her mind and body seemed intermittently numb and excited, excited and numb. Sometimes both at the same time. She tried to force her mind awake. She was about to lose her virginity and she didn't want to miss a minute of this once-in-a-lifetime experience.

Tony got up from the bed and Joyce could hear him remove his clothes in the dark. She tried to imagine what he looked like naked. Though Joyce had never seen a man naked before, she'd seen plenty of pictures in books. Once, when she was fourteen while waiting in a doctor's office, she'd found a book on the doctor's shelf that showed photographs of men with erections. She envisioned Tony with an erection and a warm tingle began between her legs and quickly spread through her entire body.

Then she felt his lips and tongue on her left breast and she thought she would burst apart with excitement. His hands fumbled with her panties, pulling them down to her knees. As his hands slid up her thighs to probe again at her liquid center, she raised her legs and kicked the panties the rest of the way off so she was free of any encumbrance.

Her mind was racing now, able to fill in the missing frames. She knew when he trailed his tongue across her chest to suck at first one nipple, then the other. She knew when his fingers rubbed her magic button and sent shudders through her lower limbs, tingling her toes. She knew when his erection rubbed against her leg with an insistence she couldn't ignore. She knew when he knelt between her spread legs and aimed his hardness at the heart of her.

And the next thing she knew bright lights filled the room and bathed them both in a horrible glare. And then she heard the laughter.

CHAPTER THREE

That prick, that asshole, that... that goddamned Tony Virusso had humiliated Ellie for the last time.

Everyone had expected Tony to ask Ellie to the prom. Everyone, including Ellie herself. It was only natural, after all, since the prom was the Big Event. Tony and Ellie had dated on and off for almost three years and had fucked at least once a week since. Tony had popped her cherry the summer she turned fifteen. Though they were neither serious about getting married nor even faithful to each other in bed, there was a kind of unspoken obligation that Ellie expected Tony to fulfill.

When Tony asked Joyce to the prom, Ellie was emotionally crushed. Mr. Popularity—Mr. Big Man on Campus—Tony Virusso should have taken Elaine Flanders—class valedictorian and the best fuck a man ever had—to June Moon. Instead, Tony invited that prude... that ignoramus... that twit who didn't know the difference between Coca-Cola and the real thing, and right now they were in the bedroom fucking their brains out while Ellie was in the kitchen nursing both her bruised body and her bruised pride with half a gram of real coke that Keith Carson had just delivered.

"If you're any kind of man at all," she'd raged at Gary Brandt, "you'll break down that damn door and beat Tony Virusso to a bloody pulp. You hear? The fucker hit me! He hauled off and hit me in the stomach. I want you to go in there and hit *him* until he's black and blue and begs for mercy!"

"Whoa," Gary soothed. "Calm down. If you think I'm going to take on Tony Virusso, you're nuttier than a fruitcake."

"You scared?" she hissed. "I thought you were supposed to be tough."

"Not tough enough to take on Tony when he gets mad."

"Then get Tom or John or Jeff to help you beat Tony up."

"No way. Uh-uh."

"Why not?"

"Because they're friends of Tony's."

"Christ!" Ellie was fuming. She wanted that bastard beaten so badly that he wouldn't be able to get it up for at least a month. If nobody would help her, she'd just have to find a way to do it herself.

Gary did help her up off the floor where Tony had left her writhing in pain. He took her to a chair at the kitchen table and poured her a stiff drink. He gave her a wet paper towel and told her to wipe her face. Tears had ruined her makeup and left long smudged lines down both cheeks.

When she'd finished with her face, she opened her dress and examined the bruise growing on her stomach. An area the size of a baseball had turned an ugly purple and was spreading. It felt knotted and hard. It was very painful.

"Look," she shouted. "Look at what that fucker did."

One by one, as the other kids came into the kitchen to see if Keith had delivered the promised cocaine, Ellie showed them the ugly bruise on her stomach. Sharon Davidson thought Ellie should see a doctor immediately, but Ellie refused.

"I want you all to take a good look at what that bastard did to me," Ellie said. "And then I want you to help me get even for what he did."

"I'm with you," said Linda Michaels. "We can't let the bastard get away with hitting a woman."

"What do you want we should do?" asked Tom Torino. Tom seemed more interested in staring at Ellie's naked breasts than the bruise on her stomach. "If you want us to beat the shit out of Tony, you can count me out."

"I'll think of something," Ellie said. "Maybe I can come up with something that isn't as crude as pounding him to a pulp. I want to get him where he lives, right where it'll do the most damage."

"Count me out," Torino said again. "I got no fight with Tony. Do what you wanna do, just leave me out of it." He turned back to the living room where he'd left a joint smoldering in an ashtray.

"I don't want to fight Tony either," said Jeff Schilling. He followed Tom back to the joint.

"I'll stay," said John Grabowski. "Tony shouldn't have hit you that hard."

"Tony shouldn't have hit her at all," Sharon Davidson snapped.

"Okay," John admitted. "He had no call to hit Ellie at all. I think we should make Tony apologize."

"No," Ellie said. "I won't accept a mere apology. I want to teach him a lesson he'll never forget. Give me time to think and I'll come up with an idea. Are all of you with me?"

The remaining five said yes. Idea after idea was discussed and rejected. Ellie favored waiting until Tony fell asleep and then tying him up and threatening to put his balls in a meat grinder unless he begged her forgiveness. Then Keith Carson dropped off the half gram of coke and everything was put on hold while lines were drawn and consumed.

It was probably the coke that gave Ellie her brilliant idea. Tony, she knew, always needed a line or two before getting into bed with a broad. He had some kind of phobia about losing his erection and he swore that coke kept his pecker hard all night long, even after four or five orgasms. Ellie knew that was bullshit. But if Tony believed it, that was all that mattered.

Tony was obsessed with the need to constantly prove his manhood. If Ellie could cause Tony to lose his erection in front of witnesses, she'd have won not only the battle but the entire war.

What a victory!

But how? What would make him lose his erection? He'd certainly snorted enough coke by now to keep it hard for hours, if not all night long.

C'mon idiot, she scolded. Think. Rack your brains. There's gotta be a way.

And then she remembered. Once, when she'd been really pissed at him over something minor, she'd ridiculed his raging hard-on with laughter.

And he'd lost it. It went limp, drooping like a wet noodle. It just shriveled up and shrunk. For a moment she thought his penis would disappear completely. She was so surprised and fascinated by the sight of his withering organ that she stopped laughing and simply stared.

And then Tony hit her right in the face and gave her a black eye.

Would it work again? Would laughter destroy his manhood?

"Listen everybody," she said, already laughing. "This is what we're gonna do…"

Ellie held an empty glass between her ear and the door to amplify sound. She couldn't hear a blasted thing.

And that, she knew, was a very good sign. Though she hated Tony's guts, she had always admired his incredible patience. The bastard was a damn good lover, working his women up to exquisite peaks of pleasure before trying to slip it in. Once inside, he'd bang away like crazy until the girl screamed with ecstasy or until they were both too sore to enjoy it anymore. Ellie had often gotten off just thinking about Tony banging away. And even tonight, as hurt and hateful as she felt, she could barely control a tingle at the thought.

But he wasn't banging *her* tonight. He was banging that red-haired bitch!

Or he would be soon. Since the bedroom still seemed quiet as a graveyard, Ellie surmised that Tony was taking his own sweet time to warm the bitch up good.

"You ready?" she whispered to the others. "On the count of three we enter laughing. One… two…"

Ellie knew none of the doors in Steve's apartment had working locks. All she had to do was turn the doorknob and shove.

She flipped a wall switch to the right of the open door and the harsh glare of an overhead hundred-watt bulb flooded the room. At the same time her five friends burst into the room and laughed.

Tony, she saw, was poised on his knees between the girl's outstretched thighs. His throbbing organ looked like an angry snake about to strike.

As Tony turned his head and body to face the intruders, the snake reared back like a hooded cobra about to spit venom at the intruders.

Then it wilted like a violet that hadn't been watered for months.

Ellie pointed at the shrinking violet and laughed her heart out. Her whole body shook with laughter.

Tony bellowed with rage. He leapt from the bed and knocked John Grabowski to the floor. Though John was clothed and Tony wasn't, Tony pelted Grabowski's body with a series of blows that took a disastrous toll.

Sharon Davidson quickly entered the fray, kicking and clawing at Tony's naked body like a wildcat in heat. Gary Brandt jumped in and grabbed Tony's arms. Gary, a varsity linebacker for three years, was built like a bull. He quickly pinned Tony to the floor while Sharon kicked his stomach and face. A fast foot to the groin made Tony scream in agony.

Ellie winced when Sharon's shoe connected. The poor boy would definitely be out of commission for an indefinite period of time. Ellie made a mental note to forget about fucking Tony again. By the time his balls healed, she'd already be well into her freshman—maybe even sophomore—year at college.

The bitch on the bed sat up and stared stupidly at her ruined lover. Still wiped from the kamikazes, Joyce couldn't seem to comprehend anything that was happening.

Then Ellie saw the scars.

Joyce Roberts's perfectly shaped body was hideously flawed and deformed. Scars ran from her shoulders almost to her ankles. Huge chunks of skin had obviously been removed at various times and there was a crisscross pattern of plaid patches—some as large as two inches square—that hadn't properly healed. Her inner thighs and lower arms were misshapen as well as scarred, almost as though someone had carved out bits of bone from the insides of her limbs.

Ellie's laughter died in her throat.

Claire Kelly's jaw dropped.

Linda Michaels said, "Oh, my God!"

Sharon Davidson said, "You bastard!" and kicked Tony again.

Joyce couldn't see. She blinked her eyes. The glare from the light cut into her vision like cookie cutters cutting circles in soft dough.

Then she heard the laughter. She was sure they were laughing at her, laughing like the thousands of medical residents who had passed through her hospital rooms after the many operations. Though she'd been heavily sedated, she always knew when the residents were making their rounds. They came into her room and lifted her hospital gown, staring at the surgical incisions on her face and naked body while the chief of surgery explained the most recent procedure and the revised prognosis for her recovery. Then that group of residents would leave and another would enter. Later, some would come back on their own for another look at the human guinea pig.

"It's a shame, isn't it?" she'd heard one of them say.

"She'll never be normal. It doesn't matter how many procedures are done on her, she'll always have horrible scars."

"I wonder what'll happen when she grows up. Will she ever find a man who would be attracted to a body like that?"

"Shhhhh. She'll hear you."

"You've got to be kidding, Doctor. She's so drugged up, she couldn't hear if I shouted in her ear."

"Are you sure?"

"Positive. She won't be conscious for hours."

"I think she may be more conscious than we realize."

"That's impossible."

"Not at all. She's undergone twelve separate operations under general or local anesthetic. She's been sedated for long periods of time after each surgery. Don't you think her system has built up an immunity to certain drugs by now? Why, I wouldn't be surprised if she were semi-sentient even under the lights of the operating room, maybe even while the surgeon is using his knife. Can you imagine the horror of having your skin peeled away while you're aware of every incision, every transplant?"

"I still say it's impossible. She'd be unconscious if only from shock, wouldn't she?"

The resident laughed. "Had you going for a while, didn't I?"

The other residents laughed, too. Their laughter was high-pitched and nervous. They laughed a lot, it seemed. These new doctors couldn't afford to cry so they laughed instead.

But now the laughter had stopped.

Joyce sat up in bed and stared incredulously. Her classmates stared back with equal incredulity.

Tony was on the floor, naked. His body was bloody and bruised and Sharon Davidson slammed her shoe again and again into his midsection.

Joyce knew this wasn't a dream. This wasn't a drug-induced nightmare that would someday soon seem like only a half-forgotten memory. This was real. This was happening to her now. Joyce wanted to scream. She wanted to open up her mouth and scream at the top of her lungs. And then she did.

Her screams rocked the room.

Sharon Davidson stopped kicking the fallen football hero, her foot frozen in midair.

Claire Kelly covered her mouth to stifle her own screams.

Tom Torino and Jeff Schilling rushed in from the living room. One look at the scene in the bedroom and both men ran from the apartment. Things had obviously gotten out of hand and neither wanted to be involved when the police were called.

Gary Brandt merely averted his eyes.

Tony Virusso had lost consciousness without seeing a thing. He never knew his beautiful Joyce was less than perfect.

John Grabowski struggled to sit up. He wanted to see what everyone else was staring at. He had a sickening feeling that he didn't really want to see, that he would regret his curiosity, but he had to look. He raised his battered head slowly, finding it difficult to focus his eyes. Tony's flailing fists had caused a severe concussion and John faded rapidly in and out of consciousness. His vision was blurred. His head felt heavy as a rock.

Eventually his head drew level with the edge of the bed and he peered up at the naked body of Joyce Roberts. He blinked his eyes, tried to shake the cobwebs out of his consciousness, and immediately wished he hadn't seen what sat on the bed.

How could anyone so incredibly beautiful when dressed look so hideous naked?

Joyce reminded him of something he had tried unsuccessfully to suppress, something that had haunted his dreams since he was nine years old. John and a friend had visited a traveling carnival that came every summer to a shopping center at the edge of town. They'd gone on all the rides and gorged themselves on popcorn, corn dogs, and cotton candy. They'd tossed balls at stuffed animals, rings at pegs, and darts at balloons. Then they decided to take in the freak show.

They paid their dollars to a seedy-looking man who wore a sweat-discolored straw hat atop a balding head. A brightly painted sign on the canvas tent behind the man showed colorful pictures of snakes with human heads, naked ladies with beards, naked ladies with tattoos, naked ladies who were midgets, and naked ladies who were ten feet tall. The boys nervously entered the tent expecting to get an eyeful. And they did.

Though the tent was purposefully dark, their young eyes quickly compensated for the lack of light. An elaborate maze of canvas flaps divided the tent into separate compartments and the boys moved slowly through each. Several of the exhibits were obviously fake. In one of the compartments they saw what looked to be a dead python with a doll's head glued to the serpentine body. In another room they saw a fully dressed woman with what looked like a fake beard glued to her chin. The woman, supposedly also ten feet tall, wore long trousers that probably concealed a pair of stilts.

The midgets were real, of course. But they, too, were completely clothed.

Only the tattooed lady was naked.

She was definitely real. She sat on a three-legged stool under the harsh glare of a sixty-watt bulb. She was incredibly fat, and layers of flesh bulged around her middle and hid her privates from the prying eyes of the two boys. But her breasts were bare: humongous things that hung from her shoulders and over her enormous stomach. They looked like rotting over-ripe melons left too long on the vine.

Both breasts were covered with blue and red figures, symbols that might have meant something once to someone. But with the woman's weight, they were stretched all out of shape and were completely indecipherable and totally incomprehensible.

Her whole body, not simply her breasts, appeared covered with more of the ugly red and blue splotches.

And then she spread her thighs and showed the boys the secret of her womanhood.

And it, too, was ugly. And deformed. And covered with red and blue scars.

John had fled that tent and never went back to the carnival. Each summer when the carnival returned, John avoided the place like the plague.

But no matter how hard he tried, he couldn't avoid the dreams.

They were recurring nightmares. Every night for nearly nine years, the tattooed lady had entered his dreams and chased him through the long labyrinthine corridors of his unconscious. And the faster he fled, the closer she came, as though they were on an endless treadmill operated by their own expenditure of energy.

He knew what she wanted when she finally caught him.

She wanted to switch places.

She wanted little Johnny Grabowski, his body covered from head to toe with ugly tattoos, to take her place in that lonely carnival tent while she somehow managed to take his place. She would read his comic books, ride his bike, play baseball with his friends, live in his home, and be loved by his parents while people paid good money to view the tattooed boy trapped inside a canvas tent.

Had his conscious mind been able to deal with such a ridiculous concept, the nightmares would quickly have ended. But his greatest fears were all embodied in that single horrendous, revolting image of human deformity. It was simply too terrible to think about.

But now he faced the fact that human deformity sat naked on the bed not two feet away. Somehow the tattooed lady had changed places with beautiful Joyce Roberts when no one was looking.

John's battered brain couldn't handle the overload. He was face-to-face with the fact that human deformity was real and not merely the substance of nightmares.

Slowly, John Grabowski lowered his head back to the floor. He brought his thumb up to his mouth, curled his body into a fetal position, and let his mind go back to that carnival tent.

This time forever.

CHAPTER FOUR

It was Sharon Davidson who had the presence of mind to look for Joyce's clothing. She found the discarded formal on the floor right next to the bed. She didn't bother to look for any undergarments.

"Please get dressed," she whispered, tossing the gown at Joyce.

Joyce reached for the dress and pulled at the sleeves. Twisted, turned inside out, the dress was a mess. It looked too wrinkled to wear.

But she didn't care. She had nothing else to wear.

Nor did she care to take time to hunt for her missing undergarments. She stepped into the dress, slid both arms through the long sleeves, reached behind her back, and worried the metal zipper slowly shut. Her body covered, Joyce slipped silently from the bed. Claire and Ellie stepped aside and let her pass.

Joyce found her purse and shoes on the living room floor. She shoved both feet into the shoes, grabbed her handbag, and ran through the kitchen to the back door. The stairs were dark and Joyce didn't bother searching for a light switch. She plunged head-first into the darkness and took the steps two at a time. Three steps from the bottom, she stumbled and fell. Her right shoe went flying, her body bounced off the last wooden step and skidded across a solid concrete landing into a mass of spider webs, and her dress tore like a stamp separating along the perforations on a roll of postage stamps.

She pushed herself up from the floor, got slowly to her feet, kicked free of the remaining shoe, and ran barefoot out the back door and away from the building. She ran three blocks before she ran out of steam. As her adrenalin levels dropped to near-normal, her lungs began to burn. Every breath she took sent sharp pains stabbing through her sides.

Joyce collapsed in someone's front yard. Her dress—torn,

hiked halfway to her hips—made her look totally defenseless. She lay exposed under the bright glare of a three-quarter moon, a vulnerable teen-aged girl sobbing hysterically in the middle of the night. Anyone passing at that hour of the morning would surely have stopped; or at the very least, they would have summoned the police.

Unfortunately, no cars passed. Nor did any resident stir from a sound slumber. This was, after all, a residential part of Riverdale. No one called the police. No one looked out an open window at two o'clock in the morning.

The town was sound asleep. She could have died there and no one would have noticed.

Instead, she got to her feet and ran. Her dress flapped in the breeze behind her. If she was lucky, maybe she'd be home before daybreak.

"Shit!" Elaine Flanders said. "Shit!"

No sooner had Joyce Roberts run from the room to disappear down the back stairs than an enormous sense of relief seemed to settle over the remaining occupants of the bedroom. They all tried to talk at once.

"Shit!" Ellie muttered again, pacing back and forth in front of the bed. "Shit! Shit! Shit! Shit!"

"I don't believe it," said Claire Kelly. "I honestly don't believe it."

"I do," whispered Sharon Davidson, still in a daze. "I don't want to, but I do."

"Shit!" Ellie said again. She was beginning to sound like a stuck record.

"Joyce looked carved up," Sharon continued, ignoring Ellie. "Like someone took her apart and tried to put her back together again, only they didn't have enough parts left over to finish the job."

"Like Frankenstein's monster," Linda Michaels contributed. "That's what she looked like," Claire agreed. "Like a monster from the movies."

"Oh, shit!" Ellie stopped pacing and sat on the edge of the bed. "Shit! Shit! Shit! Shit!"

"She's no fake monster from the movies," Sharon said. "She's a real person who must have suffered a great deal. I wonder what happened? Why didn't the doctors do to her body what they did for her face?"

"There's nothing wrong with her *face*," Claire said. "Her face is normal, beautiful even."

"Exactly. Her face is perfect, isn't it? Too perfect."

"Are you saying she's had plastic surgery?"

"Think, Claire. Have you ever seen her face without makeup?"

"I can't remember."

"I do," said Linda Michaels. "She wore makeup everywhere. Even to eight A.M. classes."

"Too much makeup. Right?"

"I guess. I'd never wear that much. Especially not to an eight o'clock class. I mean, who's awake to notice?"

"What do you want to bet all that makeup was just to hide scars?"

"Jeeze," Claire said. "I never thought about it before."

"Shit!" Ellie said.

"Can't you say something else?" Sharon asked. "You've been saying 'shit' for the past five minutes and it's getting on my nerves."

Ellie looked her straight in the eye. "Fuck you!" she spat.

"That's better," Sharon said. "If you had the equipment, I'd take you up on the offer."

"Shut up," Gary Brandt whispered. His voice was uncharacteristically soft, barely audible. "All of you, please," he begged, "please just shut up."

Brandt sat cross-legged on the floor, tears running from both eyes. A naked Tony Virusso lay next to him, battered and bleeding. Tony was unconscious.

John Grabowski was curled in the corner next to the bed, his eyes vacant and staring.

Seeing three of West's varsity heroes beaten and submissive, Linda Michaels burst into tears. These were the boys she'd cheered on to victory game after game, boys who'd rallied again and again in the face of defeat to come out winners. Now they looked like whipped dogs. Linda felt disillusioned and betrayed. Her whole world had ripped apart at the seams.

Claire Kelly just stared. Jeff had deserted her, run from the room and disappeared. Tom Torino, too, had disappeared. That meant

Gary would have to drive her home. And Gary didn't look as if he was going anywhere, much less driving.

Ellie Flanders looked at the boys in disgust. Then she turned to Linda and said: "Shit! Damn! Hell! Piss! Fuck!"

Joyce was halfway home when she noticed the car. A late-model, dark-colored Toyota with its lights off. It seemed to be following her.

At first she thought the car was simply parked along the curb, left overnight on the street in front of a yellow two-flat that didn't have a garage. Then she heard the engine roar to life behind her, shattering the predawn silence like a brick hurled through a picture window.

Looking over her shoulder, she saw the car inch slowly forward. It crept past a two-story Cape Cod, past a stone-faced single-story, and finally crawled to a stop at the end of the block.

Joyce ran. Acutely aware that she was virtually naked beneath the shards of lace that had once been her prom dress, she felt vulnerable and defenseless.

After another three blocks, Joyce looked again over her shoulder. The Toyota was parked in front of a vacant lot, less than a block away. Without a doubt now, the car was stalking her.

Joyce dashed across the street and ducked down, hiding in the deep shadows that stretched between two two-story brick houses. Her breath sounded loud and frantic, loud enough to wake the dead and surely loud enough to wake the sleeping inhabitants of both neighboring houses. *Let it,* she thought. *Let my breath be loud enough to wake everyone up. Let them wake up and call the police. When the police get here, they'll at least give me a ride home and I won't have to walk the rest of the way.*

Fresh air, the soothing effects of tears, and two gut-wrenching stops to empty the contents of her stomach on moonlit sidewalks had sobered Joyce completely. No longer did her head swim in circles, her mind unable to concentrate or her eyes to focus. She was, once again, herself.

Let them call the police, she thought. I've nothing to hide from the police.

From her vantage point in the shadows, Joyce tried to see the driver of the Toyota. There was definitely someone in the driver's seat, someone scrunched down behind the steering wheel. Was it a man? A woman? Were there more occupants in the back seat? She couldn't tell at this distance.

Joyce waited and watched, sure that any moment the driver's door would burst open and dark figures would leap out at her. Instead, the motor roared to life. The headlights switched on. And slowly, the Toyota cruised up the street, pausing now and then as though the driver were merely lost in the dark and looking for a house number that maybe he could recognize.

As Joyce watched the car disappear around a corner, she chastised herself for being such a sissy. Surely, she'd acted paranoid over nothing. The Toyota and its driver were lost. Someone, perhaps even another high-schooler, was looking for an all-night party. Perhaps he or she had already had too much to drink and pulled over to the curb to sober up and get his or her bearings. That Joyce happened by was nothing more than a coincidence.

"You mustn't believe, *Liebschen*, that everything that happens in this world is your fault or is directed at *you*," Doctor Joshi had tried to tell her. "You are not the center of the universe. Nor, are you, nor have you been, the center of any plot to harm you. Often we—all of humanity, you included—are simply innocent victims of chance. An infinite number of random factors affect us daily. Some are good. Some are bad. But there is no deliberate conspiracy on the part of the universe to harm any of us. Do you understand, *Liebschen*?"

"Yes."

"But you do not yet *believe*, do you?"

"No."

On a purely intellectual level, Joyce understood perfectly. She'd read Schopenhauer, Kant, Kierkegaard, and every other major philosopher she could come across in the stacks of the public library. Joshi had even loaned her books from his office shelves. She'd read Camus' *The Stranger* and most of Sartre's works before she'd even turned sixteen. But she couldn't bring herself to believe that blind chance could treat her quite so cruelly—never as cruelly as this—without some kind of hidden purpose. She didn't believe it then. And she couldn't believe it now.

Joyce had never believed in blind chance. Nor had she ever believed in the all-knowing, all-powerful deity that Grandma Grace and Grandpa Fred worshipped. At seventeen Joyce sought answers to questions a Christian God either wouldn't or couldn't explain.

No, Joyce knew perfectly well that Joyce Roberts wasn't the center of the universe. Everything that happened didn't happen solely for its effect on a seventeen-year-old nobody. She was merely a tiny cog in a giant wheel, an infinitesimal link in the Great Chain of Being. But she was, nevertheless, a cog, a link. And, as such, her life had meaning and purpose.

It wasn't simply blind chance that had made her life such a mess. She knew in her heart of hearts that she was only a part of something much bigger, a small piece in a giant jigsaw puzzle. But the puzzle would never be completed without her tiny piece in place. The play wouldn't proceed until she'd stepped on the stage and spoken her lines.

And that's why all those terrible things had already happened, why she'd been caught in the middle of death and destruction, why she'd endured insufferable pain, why she could never think of herself as normal despite nearly normal appearances, why Joyce Roberts was unique and different.

"Everyone needs to feel he or she is special, but it simply cannot be," Joshi drummed into her head. "Do you understand? You, me, everyone. All of us are mere victims of chance."

"No. I *am* special. I may a victim of chance, yes. But I'm also someone special. And nothing you'll ever say, doctor, will convince me otherwise."

But I will admit, Joyce thought as the Toyota turned the corner, that coincidences are possible. Not everything that happens in the universe is directed at me. Sometimes I very well might be merely a victim of chance.

And sometimes, she thought glumly, I'm the victim of sinister design.

She walked the rest of the way home without wanting to think any more about anything.

Gary Brandt squeezed Linda Michaels and Claire Kelly into the back seat of his Chevy. Elaine Flanders slid into the front seat. Gary climbed behind the wheel.

Only Sharon Davidson had stayed behind to care for John

Grabowski and Tony Virusso. Sharon didn't really mind staying behind. She was an only child, daughter of divorced parents, and she lived at home with her mother and a stepfather she couldn't stand.

If she went home, she'd surely be the center of another argument. Eldon and Joanne were already both falling-down, rip-roaring, irrational drunk at this hour on a Sunday morning and going home now would be worse than staying out all night. She was better off waiting until noon when Mommy and Stepdaddy were fast asleep.

Eldon Andrews, her stepfather, wasn't a bad man when he was sober. But Eldon was seldom sober, especially on weekends.

Eldon had a good job as plant manager at one of the city's larger tool and die works. He'd worked his way up from apprentice machinist to setup man to supervisor. Nineteen years after he'd left subsistence poverty in his native Arkansas, he made plant manager. He seemed like an ideal husband for an over-the-hill divorcée with a teenage daughter.

Nobody, not even Mom, knew the truth. Eldon came home from work and went straight to the liquor cabinet. He liked his martinis very dry — 99 and 99/100 percent pure gin—and he was drunk on his ass before the six o'clock news had halfway finished. Passed out in his overstuffed chair in front of the TV, Eldon was seldom a problem on weeknights.

But weekends were sheer hell. Eldon started drinking right after work on Friday, stopping off for a few with the guys and cashing his paycheck at the local bar. He was good and drunk before he even got home.

Knowing he didn't have to work on Saturday or Sunday, Eldon drank the entire weekend. By nine o'clock on Friday night, he was drunk enough to slap Joanne around. Sometimes he beat her black and blue. Sometimes she locked herself in the bathroom and escaped without a scratch.

Sometimes Joanne outdrank Eldon and turned out to be twice as mean. When that happened, Eldon left Joanne alone and came after Sharon.

Sharon had tried to fight back. But Eldon was older, stronger. He beat the shit out of her every weekend, regular as clockwork.

No. Sharon Davidson didn't want to go home. Instead, she

climbed the wooden stairs to the second floor. She walked through the kitchen and sat on the living room floor. She looked around for a rolled joint, found one, and lit it. She wished for a toot or a Valium or anything stronger than homegrown grass. This was a start, though. Later she'd look for something else to help her through the night.

She finished the joint and felt too mellow to move. She closed her eyes and floated in space. Never once did she hear footsteps on the stairs. Nor did she notice when the backdoor opened and someone walked quietly across the kitchen linoleum.

And when the hammer hit her head, she noticed nothing.

Except the pain.

CHAPTER FIVE

Stephen Virusso felt so incredibly tired that he seriously contemplated using toothpicks to prop his eyes open. As the night manager of a twenty-four hour restaurant, Steve had been on duty since before midnight. His watch now read 10:23.

Joe Hendricks, the Sunday morning assistant manager, had overslept as usual and Steve had to cover. Every Sunday was the same, and Steve was getting real sick and tired of having to wait for Joe to haul his ass out of bed and come in to work. Steve made up his mind to get Joe fired as soon as he could find a suitable replacement.

Refilling his coffee cup from the twin fifty-gallon stainless steel urns behind the counter, Steve headed to his office in the back of the kitchen. The morning rush was over, thank goodness, and the restaurant was nearly empty. Two couples from the adjoining motor lodge still sat at tables finishing late breakfasts and a lone trucker sipped coffee at the counter, but the hungry hordes that flooded the restaurant from six till ten had all been fed. His three waitresses could certainly handle the dining room alone until Joe came in.

Sipping his black coffee, Steve tackled the morning's mountain of paperwork. Normally, he'd have finished the daily accounting summary by nine, and been home in bed by nine-thirty. But last night's business was heavier than usual. And Joe, scheduled to come on duty at seven, had screwed everything up by oversleeping again.

Steve cursed softly under his breath. He hated paperwork almost as much as he hated Joe Hendricks. But both, he realized, were necessary evils.

Weekend assistant managers were too hard to find, and reliable people were next to impossible to find. Hendricks worked another job during the week, partied hardy Friday and Saturday nights, and seldom, if ever, made it to work on time on Sunday. But Joe, Steve had to admit, at least was honest and a hard worker, rare qualities these days. And, although Steve had put up with Joe's tardiness in the past, he didn't like it—or Joe—one bit this morning.

Joe showed up at a quarter to eleven, clean shaven, freshly showered, and smelling of English Leather. "Sorry, I'm late," he said.

Steve lashed into him with a volley of four-letter words that made Joe actually blush. Joe took two steps backward and Steve was sure the kid would bolt straight out the door and never come back. That, unfortunately, would mean Steve would have to do double duty on weekends until Joe's replacement was found.

If a replacement could be found.

"Forget it," Steve said quickly. "I'm tired and irritable and I want to go home and sleep. Finish up the paperwork for me and I won't tell the GM. Okay?"

"Okay," Joe said.

Since Joe worked the rest of the week as an accountant, Steve knew Joe would balance the summary sheet in no time at all and be out on the floor to cover the noontime rush. Sunday noons were busier than hell with senior citizens who stopped for lunch on the way home from church. Steve didn't want to be around when the rush started.

Fifteen minutes later he parked in the alley behind his apartment and wondered why Tony's car was still parked at the curb.

Oh shit, he thought. Don't tell me that asshole's passed out with a broad in my bed again. Every time I let my kid brother use the pad, he takes advantage of me. Well, screw it! I'm in no mood this morning to put up with Tony and his girlfriends.

Intent on throwing everyone out of the apartment, Steve didn't notice that the downstairs door was unlocked. Nor did he notice that the kitchen door was left ajar. He burst into the apartment, swore at the mess in the kitchen, got royally pissed over the illegal pot left in the living room, and was ready to kill his brother by the time he reached the bedroom door.

And then he saw the blood on the carpet.

And even before he opened the bedroom door, he knew someone had beat him to it. Someone else had killed little brother Tony. Literally.

Steve didn't want to look, didn't know how he'd ever be able to explain to Papa or Mama that Tony was dead, didn't know how he'd be able to explain to the police that Tony just happened to get killed in Steve's apartment while Steve was at work. And then he did look… and his breakfast spewed out his mouth and down his chin.

Detective Sergeant Carl Erickson shook his head. It wasn't fair, he thought. Three good-looking kids with bright futures ahead of them, star pupils at West Riverdale High, struck down before their lives really (yes, Virginia, there *is* life after high school) began.

It wasn't fair. Not fair at all.

But then death was never fair. Erickson had been a cop fifteen years now; a homicide detective almost twelve. He'd seen hundreds of victims. And not one of those victims, in his expert opinion, had ever deserved to die.

Certainly not like this.

Grisly, the newspapers would call it. Grisly. Gruesome.

Two boys, Anthony Virusso and John Grabowski, both age eighteen, lay dead on the bedroom floor. Pools of blood ruined the carpet and flecks of blood and brains stained the wallpaper. Both boys were faceless. Whoever committed this atrocity didn't stop with just murdering the victims. Long after both boys were dead, the killer continued to pound at their heads until the faces were unrecognizable.

Pounding and hacking, hacking and pounding. Until the skulls cracked wide open and brains oozed out like runny yolks from cracked eggshells. Until it was impossible to put Humpty Dumpty back together again.

"Bloody mess, isn't it?"

Carl looked up, started to hear a human voice. A female voice.

"I'm Dr. Wade," she said, entering the bedroom. "I'm the lucky pathologist who gets to do autopsies on these kids."

Carl couldn't help staring. She didn't look like any doctor he'd ever seen. She looked more like someone's teenage daughter, a blonde-haired girl in a ponytail. She wore Adidas athletic shoes, Calvin Klein designer jeans, and a too-tight T-shirt that showed off her tits. Obviously, the doctor didn't believe in bras.

"You got any identification that shows you're a doctor?" he asked. "I gotta see an ID, doctor. Everybody at a homicide scene has gotta show an ID card. Even my own men."

While she reached into a black purse strapped to her shoulder, Carl added, "Just regulations, nothing personal. You understand, don't you?"

"I understand completely," she said. She fumbled in the purse and found what she wanted. "Here," she said.

She handed Carl three cards. One was an AMA membership card. The other two showed she was a Fellow of both the College of American Pathologists and the American Society of Clinical Pathologists. Marsha Wade, M.D., *was* a licensed physician with board certifications in both anatomic and clinical pathology.

"These don't have your picture on them," he said. "I need to see a picture ID."

She fished in her purse again. This time she came up with a Maryland driver's license. Marsha Wade was thirty-two, according to the DOB on her license. But the photo, taken more than two-years ago, made her look nineteen.

"Still live in Baltimore?" Carl asked.

"Not anymore. I completed my residency in DC and did postgraduate fellowships at Johns Hopkins. I'm a new staff pathologist at Bryson Memorial."

"Got an Illinois driver's license?"

"Not yet. But I can legally drive on my Maryland license, can't I?"

"Only for ninety days. You been here ninety days yet?"

"Oh." She pouted. "Are you going to arrest me if I have?"

Carl wanted to laugh. Instead, he handed back the IDs.

She dropped them into the purse.

"Okay, doctor. You're who you say you are. What the hell are you doing here anyway?"

"The coroner's office asked Memorial to do the autopsies. Since it's Sunday and I'm new and on call, I got the page."

"And you came directly here? You should have gone to the hospital and waited for the meat wagon to deliver the corpses."

"Professional curiosity, Lieutenant. I thought it'd be a good idea to see the bodies before they were moved. I'm not a forensic pathologist, but I have taken a couple of courses in forensic pathology. The coroner or medical examiner is supposed to visit the scene and take charge of the bodies and all personal possessions of the victims."

"We provide color photographs, doctor. You could have saved yourself the trouble of the trip."

"Listen, Lieutenant…"

"Sergeant," he corrected.

"Sergeant. Okay. Now listen, Sergeant. I have studied forensic medicine with some of the best forensic scientists in the country. They taught me that it's vitally important for pathologists to visit the death scene and see the body before it's disturbed. Pictures never do justice…"

"Our boys are pretty good," Erickson interrupted. "I've got my best men assigned to this case."

"And you don't want a woman getting in your way. Right, Lieutenant?"

"Sergeant."

"Okay. *Sergeant!*" She spat the word from her mouth with obvious distaste.

"Listen, lady. I'll take whatever help I can get and I don't care if you're male, female, or something in-between. If you can tell me who did this and why, I'll kiss your ass in the center of State and Main at twelve noon."

"Don't get testy, Sergeant. I'm not after your job."

"That's good, lady. Because if you were, I'd give it to you. After I get through here, I've got to tell the parents of these kids that their little pride and joys are now nothing more than pieces of dead meat on metal slabs in the morgue. I gotta tell them that they can't claim the cadavers until after Dr. Marsha Wade takes them apart and sews them back together again. You want my job? You can have it."

Carl was steaming. This little slip of a girl had walked in here and sent his blood pressure soaring. His face was bright red. He didn't dare say anything more for fear he'd literally explode.

The girl—her driver's license said she was thirty-two, but she didn't look that old—turned her attention to the victims. She bent over the bodies, carefully examined the extent of trauma, and went through many of the same motions Carl's techs had gone through previously. He'd meant what he said about accepting any help he could get. Maybe Marsha Wade would turn up something his own boys had missed. If she did, he'd certainly be grateful—not grateful enough to kiss her behind in public, of course—but certainly grateful enough to kiss her.

The idea of kissing her was definitely appealing. She wasn't bad looking. And she had great tits and didn't seem to mind showing them off in a T-shirt.

At thirty-seven, Erickson was still single. His adult life, devoted to law enforcement, had allowed little time for romance. Since most murders happened at night, he found it nearly impossible to keep a date. Lasting relationships were quite impossible. Few women were willing to compete with a badge for time and attention. When he'd turned thirty-five, he'd given up all hope of marriage and family and concentrated on his career.

But something about Marsha Wade attracted him, made him want to become involved with a woman as a long-term investment. And that frightened and thrilled him like nothing else had in a very long time.

After completing a preliminary examination of both of the boys, Marsha moved into the living room to look at the Davidson girl. Carl followed.

"Did any of your men move this body?"

"No."

"Look here. There's a trail of dried blood smeared on the carpet. Either the girl crawled from the center of the room after she'd been struck, or someone moved the body. Why would her assailant—or assailants—take the trouble to drag her clear across the room and into the bedroom?"

"I don't know."

"And notice that the girl's face is still intact. Why were the males mutilated with multiple blows to the face while the female was murdered with a single blow to the back of the head?"

"You tell me, doctor, and we'll both know."

"Obviously, Sergeant, the assailant—or assailants—must have entered the apartment via the kitchen door. Finding the female sitting on the floor—over there by the drugs on the mirror—the assailant killed her and quickly moved the body out of sight before proceeding to the bedroom and the intended victims."

"You mean the girl was killed merely to get her out of the way?"

"Precisely. The intended victim was one or both of the boys."

"What makes you so sure?"

"The brutality perpetrated on the male victims seems excessively cruel and unusual, don't you think? Why was the girl spared the same treatment?"

"Chivalry? Male chauvinism?"

"Maybe it was simply to get her out of the way quickly. And you may be making a mistake, Lieutenant, in thinking the assailant was male. More than half the world's population is female."

"Sergeant, doctor. Remember? I'm a sergeant."

She smiled. "All right. Sergeant. I guess I must think you deserve a promotion, Sergeant."

"Are you telling me a woman killed these kids?"

"It's possible, Sergeant. Women are capable of anything and everything a man can do. And women are often more brutal than a man when it comes to murder."

"But what makes you think the assailant was a woman?"

"Number one: no signs of sexual assault on the female victim. Number two: no signs of homosexual assault on the male victims, though one of the boys is naked and was severely kicked and beaten antemortem. Number three: excessive cruelty perpetrated on both males. Number four: the lack of excessive cruelty to the female victim. Number five: the nature of the assault itself. All three victims were bludgeoned to death. Although it is certainly true that more men than women commit murder, most men would have chosen a gun as a preferred instrument of death. Women usually use common household implements of some kind: a kitchen knife, a fireplace poker, poisons. Shall I continue?"

"What about the signs of a struggle in the bedroom? How could a woman fight off two high school football players?"

"The struggle occurred earlier. Both boys were asleep or drugged at the time of assault. I won't know for certain until autopsy, but I suspect the contusions and bite marks on Virusso were hours old at the time of death."

"You mean to tell me that he was in a fight, then he fell asleep, and later he was murdered? In his sleep?"

"That's how it appears. We'll learn more at autopsy."

"Christ!"

"You see, Sergeant, I might have missed something if I hadn't examined the actual scene. Pictures and diagrams are helpful, of course. But they aren't the same as being here, are they?"

Carl shook his head.

"I've seen everything I need for now. If you'll ask your men to bag the bodies, I think were ready to call the meat wagon. I want to get started on the autopsies as soon as possible."

It was already late afternoon when Grandma Grace roused Joyce from a sound slumber.

"You've slept most of the day away," the old lady scolded. She threw open the drapes and flooded the room with bright sunlight. "Get out of bed, lazy bones. When you're dressed, I expect to hear all about the wonderful time you had last night at the prom."

"Go away, Grandma. I don't feel good."

"What's the matter, dear?" Grace felt Joyce's forehead with the back of a hand. "You don't have a fever, do you?"

"No. It's my stomach. And I ache all over."

"You just need something to eat, dear. I'll fix some soup."

"I'm not hungry, Grandma."

"Nonsense. You've missed both breakfast and lunch. No wonder your stomach's upset."

"It's not just my stomach. I ache all over."

"Your head's all right, isn't it?"

"My head's fine," Joyce lied.

"Thank God," the old lady whispered. "If anything happened to your head..."

"My head's fine. I just need more sleep. Please leave me alone."

"Now, you know I can't let you go back to sleep, Joyce. Your grandfather wouldn't stand for it."

Damn him, thought Joyce. She said instead, "I'll be down soon as I shower and dress."

"That's my good girl," Grace said, relieved. "Soup'll be ready when you are."

Joyce waited until Grace had left before throwing off the covers and getting out of bed.

Her head hurt. Some of the pain she could attribute to a hangover. Though she'd never had a hangover before, she'd heard about the aftereffects of alcohol. She had a classic case of morning-after headache.

And some of the pain, she knew, was psychological. She'd suffered a terrible shock to her ego, something that required time and distance to overcome. A little hair-of-the-dog wouldn't help the hurt stares and laughter had caused.

But most of the pain was something familiar. It was an old pain, something she'd grown used to.

Her head throbbed.

She walked to a corner closet and snatched her cotton robe from a hanger. Slipping the robe over her shoulders, Joyce walked down the hall to the bathroom. Adjusting both faucets, she let water fill the tub. She dropped the robe on the floor. She peeled her pajamas from her body.

Naked, she settled into the warm bath.

She couldn't remember. Try as she might, she couldn't remember much that that had happened after her first drink. What she could remember were the stares and laughter.

"Selective recognizance," Doctor Joshi termed it. She racked her brains for clues. Sooner or later it would all come back to her. Sooner or later.

"Please, God," she begged. "Make it sooner."

Outside, the day was gorgeous. Bright afternoon sunlight made colors clear and vivid. Temperatures were somewhere in the eighties, warm enough for short sleeves.

Detective Erickson removed his suitcoat and tossed it to the back seat before entering the car.

"Where's your gun?" Marsha Wade wanted to know. Carl had asked if she needed a ride to the hospital, and she'd accepted his offer.

"Good detectives never show their guns until they're ready to use them."

"But you do have a gun, don't you? Aren't police officers required to carry a gun?"

"Yes to both questions. Does it make you feel safer?"

"I just thought you'd wear your gun in a holster," she said. "I don't see a gun belt. You're not wearing a shoulder holster. I guess I'm just curious. Where's your gun?"

Carl laughed. "Listen, doctor," he said. "I've never had to use a gun—other than for target practice—in fifteen years on the force."

"So you don't have one?"

"I've got one. Let it drop at that, won't you?"

Carl held the door and Marsha slipped into the passenger seat of his unmarked squad. He couldn't help staring at her T-shirt. He'd watched her move about Virusso's apartment, her tight ass sheathed in Calvin Klein denim, her tits encased in thin cotton that left little to the imagination.

He was surprised how much he wanted her. Like he'd never wanted anyone or anything before in his entire life. Carl slammed the passenger door and walked around to the driver's side. Getting in beside Marsha Wade, Detective Carl Erickson knew he was in lust and suspected he might be falling in love.

Slowly, very slowly, some of it came back. She remembered going to bed with Tony. She remembered Tony's fingers tugging at the back of her dress. She remembered her bra bouncing from the wall. She remembered Tony's fingers probing her wetness. His hands, all over her body, caressing and probing.

She tried to force her mind awake. A warm wetness flooded her thighs.

She felt his lips, and tongue on her breasts. His hands fumbled at her center. She was ready. He was ready.

And then she heard the laughter.

Erickson dropped the doctor at the emergency entrance. She slid smoothly across the seat and out the door. And then she bent down and stuck her head through the open window and he could see her bare tits through the neck of her T-shirt. He felt his face turn red.

"I'll call you," she said. "After I've finished the autopsies."

"Do that," he said.

"I'm on page," she said. "If you need me, just call the hospital and ask them to page Dr. Wade."

"I'll be in touch," he promised.

He watched her disappear through the hospital doors before he put the car in gear and drove off.

"I'll be in touch," he said again. "That's a promise I intend to keep."

CHAPTER SIX

They were waiting for him. The entire surviving Virusso family—Tony's father, mother, two sisters, one brother, an uncle, and two aunts—waited in the living room of Stephano Virusso's split-level brick ranch to hear that Tony's killer had been captured.

"What kinda cop are you?" the elder Virusso demanded. "What kinda cop can't catch the killer of seventeen-year-old kids?"

"I will catch your son's murderer," Carl promised. "But I'll need a little more time."

"More time? How much more time do you need?"

Like his sons, Stephano was a giant. He stood six-six, half a head taller than Erickson. His arms and chest were massive. His neck was thick as a bull's. His stomach, however, showed signs of a middle-aged paunch from too much pasta and vino and not enough exercise. His hair, what little was left of it, was graying. He wore a pencil-thin mustache on his upper lip and his teeth were tobacco-stained from three cigars a day.

Handsome in his youth, he hadn't aged well.

Carl also knew that Virusso was an alderman, an intimate friend of both the mayor and the police commissioner. One word from Virusso and Carl would be taken off the case. Detective Carl Erickson was expected to feel intimidated. But Carl didn't intimidate easily.

"As long as it takes, Mr. Virusso," Carl told the grieving father. "As long as it takes. But I'll get him. That I promise you. I'll get whoever killed your son and make him pay dearly."

Virusso, towering over the detective, seemed to soften.

"You promise?"

"I promise."

For what seemed like an eternity the two men faced each other, their eyes locked in a battle of wills. Neither man blinked nor turned away.

"I believe you," Virusso said at last. His eyes had begun to fill with tears, and he had to blink or cry. He chose to blink.

"Thank you," Carl breathed.

"Sit down," Virusso offered. "Gloria, bring the officer a drink."

"I'm on duty," Erickson said. "Thank you, but I'll pass on a drink."

"Nonsense. Gloria, bring the officer whatever he wants. You want coffee? You can drink coffee, can't you?"

"Coffee would be fine."

"Take cream or sugar?"

"Black," Carl said. He sat on the couch next to Virusso's son, Steve.

"Bring two black coffees," Virusso told his daughter. "Put a little cognac in mine, please. Will you do that for us, Gloria?"

The girl disappeared into the kitchen. The rest of the family remained seated in the living room. Virusso sat in a leather armchair and put his feet on a hassock.

"Stevie told us some of what happened," the old man said. His voice was raspy as a hacksaw. "But I'd like to hear the details from you, if you don't mind. One of my sons has been *murdered*. How the hell could that happen?"

"Someone pounded his head until nothing was left."

"Why?" The old man looked defeated. "I ain't got no enemies. None who'd do something like this anyway."

"But you do have enemies?"

"I've been in business in this town for thirty years. You can't be in business without making *some* enemies. I've been in politics, too, and beaten the pants off all my opponents. But no one kills your kids because they don't like the way you do business or can't agree with your political views."

"Stephano's got lots of friends," his wife said. "No real enemies, but lots of real friends."

"No friend did this," Virusso snapped.

"Are you sure?" Erickson asked.

"I'm sure."

Gloria came from the kitchen and handed her father a steaming cup of black coffee. Then she passed a cup to Carl.

"Why?" Virusso asked with tears in his eyes. "Why would, anyone want to murder my Tony?"

"I had hopes you could give me some leads," Carl said. "Did Tony have any enemies?"

"Everyone loved Tony. He was a very popular boy."

"That's what the school said."

"He had scholarships to three colleges. I coulda paid his way, but he earned three scholarships on his own. Everyone wanted Tony to play ball for them. He was a good ballplayer. A good student, too."

"He made the honor roll last semester," Mrs. Virusso said. "He was supposed to graduate on Friday. Next fall he was going to Madison, to the University of Wisconsin."

"I wanted Stevie to go to college," Virusso said. "But Stevie had to prove he could make good on his own, without his old man's help. He's the manager of a hotel restaurant out near the bypass. I'm proud of him, whether he knows it or not. Both my boys made me proud."

"You have a right to be proud," Carl said.

"But Tony was gonna go far. I could tell already."

"How far?"

"Maybe become a lawyer. Or maybe he'd go into business like his old man."

"Maybe even take over the old man's business," Steve interjected.

"Shut up!" the father rasped.

"You're a furniture manufacturer. Is that correct, Mr. Virusso?"

"A furniture retailer. I've got showrooms all over town. My father manufactured furniture, but we closed down the plant in '88 when the old man retired. It's cheaper to import the stuff from Europe or the Far East than it is to make it here in America."

"You expected your sons to follow you in the family business?"

"What man doesn't?"

"Steve didn't. Do you hold that against him?"

"Naw. I already told you. I'm proud of my boys. Both of 'em. Stevie can do whatever he damn well pleases."

"Tell me about Tony's friends," the cop urged. He took a notebook and pen from his pocket. "I'd appreciate complete names and addresses, if you know them."

"Stevie, who'd Tony hang around with? You know any names?"

"You didn't care, did you?" Steve suddenly shouted. "You didn't even care enough about Tony to know who any of his friends were."

"I couldn't keep up with all the friends he had. You know that. When he got to high school, he was always palling around with someone. Or going to games or parties with someone. Shit! He was named the most popular kid in the whole damn school, for Christ's sake! How could I keep up with all his friends?"

"That isn't the point, Dad. You didn't even try."

"Of course, I did."

"Did you even once see Tony play varsity ball? Did you? Hell, no! You were always too damn busy. You spent all your time down at that furniture showroom of yours or you were over at City Hall playing big-shot alderman. You never had time for your kids. Either of us. If you had given Tony more of your time, maybe this wouldn't have happened."

"Are you trying to lay the blame for my son's death on *me*?" The old man was livid. "Tony was killed in *your* apartment. If anyone's to blame, you are for letting him use your apartment."

"I know," Steve said. He began to cry. Huge sobs wracked his body. "I should never have let him use the apartment."

"Whoa," Carl said. "Blaming yourselves won't bring him back. Let's see if we can put the blame on the killer. I need names. Can you think who else might've been at that party last night? Do you know who Tony took to the prom?"

"Some girl from his class," the elder Virusso said. "Sharon Davidson maybe?"

"Uh-uh," Steve shook his head. "Tony took some girl he'd never dated before."

"And he had gone out with Sharon Davidson previously?"

"Once or twice," Steve said.

"Do you know the new girl's name?"

"No."

"Do you know what she looked like?"

"Never saw her. Tony said she was a real looker, though. Had to be special for him to go to all the trouble he did just to set up the date."

"What kind of trouble?"

"He followed her around for months on end trying to get her to go out with him. He could have had any girl in the class just by asking. But this girl was different. She turned him down at first. That sent him for a loop. When she finally said yes, Tony went all out to impress her. He borrowed the old man's new car, rented my apartment, paid for a ton of booze, and invited a bunch of friends to watch him score."

"Do you know the names of any of those friends?"

"Besides Sharon and John? Yeah. Let's see. He would have invited Gary Brandt—they were best friends. Probably Tom Torino and Jeff Schilling. And they all would have had their own dates with them."

"Do you have addresses or phone numbers for any of those people?"

"I do," said Gloria, trying to be a helpful teenager. "Want me to get them?"

"Please," Carl urged. "I need to talk to everyone who was anywhere near that apartment last night."

A minute later Gloria returned with an address book. She was also carrying a high school yearbook.

"This was Tony's annual," she explained. "He had all of his friends sign it. Maybe it'll help."

"Mind if I borrow the yearbook?" Carl asked. Gloria looked at her father.

"Take it," Virusso said. "And don't bring it back until you've caught my son's killer."

"I'll bring it back," Carl promised. "Maybe not tomorrow, but someday soon."

"Then I look forward to seeing you again," Virusso said. "Real soon."

Tom Torino wasn't home.

Tom had phoned his parents and told them he was spending the weekend with Jeff Schilling. Jeff Schilling wasn't home either. Jeff had told his parents he was spending the weekend at Tom Torino's home.

Gary Brandt was home. Erickson broke the news gently, careful to say no more than was necessary to get the Brandt boy to talk

"You're kidding, aren't you?" Gary asked.

"I wish I were. Three of your friends were murdered this morning. Tony Virusso, John Grabowski, and Sharon Davidson are all dead. When did you last see them alive?"

The sense of shock on the boy's face was real. Erickson immediately ruled out Gary Brandt as a suspect.

"I can't believe they're dead. I mean, I saw them—all three— just this morning. I don't know the exact time. Just before dawn, I guess. I dropped off the girls and got home just as it was setting light."

Erickson jotted notes on a pad of paper. "What girls?" he asked.

"Ellie—uh, Elaine—Flanders. She was my date to the prom. And Claire Kelly and Linda Michaels."

"Three girls?"

"Yeah. Well, Ellie was *my* date. Claire and Linda went to the prom with Tom and Jeff."

"Tom Torino and Jeff Schilling?"

"Yeah. You talk to them already?"

"Not yet. But I intend to."

"You don't think they did it, do you?"

"Why do you ask?"

"Well, they just disappeared. I mean, they could still have been in the apartment, for all I know. Or they could have come back after we left."

"Do *you* think they did it?"

"No. Of course not."

"Then who do you think committed the murders? Any ideas?"

"I don't know." Brandt looked disoriented, frightened. "I still can't believe this is real."

"I'm sorry to say it is real. Very real."

"You don't think *I* did it, do you?"

"Did you?"

"No," Brandt said. He stared Erickson in the eye while saying it, too. Just like he knew the detective was testing him.

Brandt seemed suddenly nervous.

This kid watches too much TV, Carl thought. I bet he's seen every episode of CSI and all the reruns of Columbo.

"Relax, Gary," Carl said. "I'm not here to haul you in on a murder warrant. All I want is your side of what happened last night in Steve Virusso's apartment. Just tell me, in your own words, what happened. Tell me everything you can remember. I want to know everything that happened from the time you left the prom until I rang your doorbell ten minutes ago. And I mean *everything.* Do you understand? I'm not here to judge you. I know you didn't kill those kids. All I want is information that'll lead me to apprehend whoever did kill your friends."

"Shit." Brandt ran his fingers nervously through his hair. "If I tell you everything, you'll bust me for possession."

Carl laughed. "I'm a homicide dick," he said. "I'm not interested in nailing you for petty misdemeanors. I already know about the dope and booze. I'm not going to bust you for smoking a few joints or underage drinking,"

"You swear?"

"I swear. Anything you say will not and cannot be used against you. I'm not after you, kid. I'm after a killer."

Brandt looked relieved. "OK," he said. "What do you want to know?"

"Everything," Carl said.

While Brandt talked, Erickson listened.

And every once in a while, the cop wrote down a name or incident in his notebook for future reference.

Grace served up a steaming bowl of homemade chicken noodle soup. She set the bowl and a box of crackers on the kitchen table in front of Joyce.

"There's some mail for you, dear, from yesterday. It's on the desk in the den."

"Anything important?" Joyce crumpled a cracker and added it to the soup.

"Something from the University of Illinois."

Joyce dropped her spoon. It sank beneath the surface of the soup, and when she tried to retrieve the spoon, she burned her fingers.

"The soup's still too hot," she told Grace. "I think I'll check the mail while the soup cools."

Joyce tried not to run. Though absolutely certain she'd been rejected by the university for the fall, she still harbored hopes they might admit her in the spring. This was the first official response she'd had from a college or university and she couldn't wait to see what they had to say.

Her letter was buried at the bottom of a pile of bills. Obviously, Grandpa Fred had already gone through the mail. She was surprised to find her envelope still sealed, the only one in the entire pile that hadn't been ripped open.

Fred had a habit of prying into everything that happened in his house. He claimed that Joyce was no more than a guest under this roof and he felt he had a right to read her mail, rifle her drawers, monitor her phone calls, and control her life as long as she lived here.

She knew she had to get out of the house before the old bastard ruined any chance she had of ever being normal. And this letter from the university just might be her ticket out of the hated house and away from her stodgy old grandparents forever.

She tore at the envelope. Inside were several sheets of paper embossed with the University of Illinois at Chicago logo.

Before she could begin reading, the patio door opened, and Fred came in from the backyard where he'd been trimming hedges.

"Something there from the university," he said. "You find it already?"

"Yes."

"What'd they have to say?"

"I haven't had a chance to read it."

"You aren't thinking of going away to school, are you?"

"Maybe."

"You wouldn't fit in."

Joyce gave the old man a look that should have killed any ordinary mortal. Fred didn't even flinch.

Her grandfather was sixty-eight, four years older than Grandma Grace. He'd been a mechanic all his life. Two years ago his arthritis had grown so bad be couldn't manipulate his tools with any kind of precision, and he'd had to retire. He still took odd jobs, and he loved to tinker with anything that seemed out of alignment or out of adjustment. He had little tolerance for people or objects that didn't meet his rigid specifications of performance.

Joyce could never—not in a million years—come anywhere close to his high expectations. She was permanently flawed. Yet Fred persisted in his attempts to toy with her life. Fred was a man who couldn't accept failure. Unfortunately, he looked at Joyce as a kind of personal failure. She was out of alignment, warped. And she was something he didn't have the ability to fix with his own two hands.

He had to send her out to be repaired. He'd sent her to bone mechanics, skin mechanics, and even brain mechanics. But none of them had known what they were doing.

Oh, they'd taken the dents out of her fenders and even patched some of the holes in her undercarriage. They'd put in a whole new windshield and rubbed some of the dents and rust out of the chrome.

But they hadn't known beans about fixing the engine or aligning the steering. Underneath that fancy new exterior, Joyce was still seriously flawed. What kind of mechanic was that Joshi fella? He'd tinkered with her engine twice a month for eleven years and still hadn't fine-tuned her wiring so the cylinders would fire in sync.

In his younger days, Fred would have fixed her himself. He'd done lots of things when he was younger that he couldn't do now. And having his teenage granddaughter around was a constant, uncomfortable reminder of his own failing health, own failures as a man, and his failure as a father.

Failures he didn't like to face.

Fred knew Joyce hated him. She probably thought he hated her, too. But he didn't hate her.

He loved her.

Almost as much as he'd loved Leona, Joyce's mother.

But he didn't dare show his love. All he could do was watch and wait. And watch he did. Like a hawk. Maybe his joints were fouled up with arthritis, but here was nothing wrong with his eyesight.

He knew everything she did from the time she got out of bed in the morning until the time she went back to bed at night. He'd seen her holding hands with that wop kid after school. He'd followed her to and from the high school every day for the past year and a half, driving a different car when he had one he was working on for a friend, or simply using his beat-up old Jeep when nothing else was available. But Joyce had never seen him, never known he was following her. If she had, she would have said something by now.

He wasn't born yesterday. No, sir! Fred knew the score. That damn wop had wanted to get into his granddaughter's panties. But Fred hadn't let him. He wouldn't let anyone get into Joyce's panties. Not even the doctors.

That's why he'd had to put a stop to their tinkering.

They'd said she needed still more surgery. They wanted to do a different procedure every six months just as soon as the trauma of their last cutting and probing had subsided and her body could stand the shock of another operation. They wanted to take all her clothes off again and leer at her naked body with their hungry eyes. They wanted to touch her thighs with their sweaty hands and their sterile instruments. And Fred wouldn't let them.

Not anymore.

They'd had their chance. When Joyce was younger, it didn't matter much. But when she filled out and began to be a woman, Fred couldn't stand the thought of all those doctors examining her, touching her, doing things to her body....

Things Fred wanted to do, but couldn't.

So he'd stopped them by refusing to sign consent forms. And since Joyce was a minor and Fred was her legal guardian, the doctors could do nothing. They needed his written permission to toy with her body. And he'd be damned if he'd give it.

Now he faced his granddaughter and wondered if he'd been wrong. Fred had made his share of mistakes in his life. He was man enough to own up to most—though not all—of them. Perhaps it had been a mistake to deny her the medical treatment that might have made her whole. The doctors claimed they'd be finished with her body by the time she turned eighteen, less than one week from today.

Her last operation had been two-and-a-half years ago. They'd peeled the skin from the insides of her tender thighs to do the final graft on her forehead

They'd shaved her pubic patch to prevent infection and Fred had been appalled when he saw what they'd done. But the real kicker was the residents—young men barely old enough to shave themselves. The doctors had let residents come into her room at all hours of the day and night to lift her hospital gown and stare at her naked body. Fred had seen it! He'd even seen one resident touch her thigh, running a finger the length of her leg.

That was when he made up his mind. No more operations.

Money had nothing to do with his decision. Gordon's estate, valued at well over a million dollars, covered most of the medical expenses. And even though most of the money had run out, money had nothing to do with his decision.

It was a matter of principle. She was *his* now, she belonged to *him*. And if he had any say in the matter, no other man would ever be allowed to touch her.

Marsha Wade went to work on the bodies as soon as the meat wagon—a police van with MARS lights blazing—had delivered all three cadavers to the emergency room entrance and orderlies had wheeled the bodies downstairs to the morgue at the far end of the basement.

Doctor Wade signed for the bodies, got two medical assistants to help, and wheeled the carts into the autopsy room where she would do the dissection.

Unlike many pathologists who performed autopsies, Marsha Wade possessed a bundle of high-quality surgical steel blades. Most doctors, cost-conscious in light of budgetary constraints that fixed fees, bought their autopsy blades at a hardware store or K-Mart. Any cleaver, butcher knife, or straight razor would do the job. Only an amateur would waste good blades on cutting up cadavers.

But Marsha Wade didn't consider herself an amateur. She was a skilled surgeon and anatomic pathologist who knew the value of precision instruments. Her teachers at Memorial Sloan-Kettering Cancer Center in New York and Johns Hopkins in Baltimore, had taught her the subtle advantages of using surgical steel. And she'd studied the techniques of many of the best forensic men in the country. As a resident, she'd taken advantage of every ASCP seminar that had free standby space available for residents. She'd listened to every word of the experts, studied every slide diligently under the microscope, and asked enough questions to drive the instructors crazy.

Now her training would pay off. She laid the body of Anthony Virusso on the autopsy table and began a Y-incision from the sternum to below the navel. As the flesh parted and muscle and sinew separated, she smiled to herself. This was what her extensive and expensive education had prepared her for. This was what she'd practiced again and again under the watchful eyes of the distinguished faculty of some of the finest medical schools in the country.

Marsha Wade excised Tony's liver and placed it on the scales. She removed his heart, lungs, and kidneys and measured their gram equivalent. She took samples of blood and bodily fluids and sent them off to another part of the lab for analysis. She used a rotary Styker saw to open the cranial cavity and examined and removed Tony's brain. When she finished examining Virusso, she began on Grabowski.

Three hours later she finished with Davidson.

Now she had to wait. DRGs and prospective payment limits hampered medical technologists from running routine tests on Sunday. There was no money in the hospital's budget to pay overtime for weekend work.

Wade removed her bloody gloves and scrubs. She stepped into an adjacent shower room reserved for male surgical personnel because it was handy and she didn't think there were any surgeons working this late on a Sunday. She let warm needles of hot water remove tension from her neck and shoulders.

Three autopsies took more concentration than she was used to these days.

When Dr. John Eickmann joined her in the shower, she didn't notice.

And he, having seen his share of naked bodies in the past seventeen years of practice, seemed not to notice either.

CHAPTER SEVEN

Armed with the information Brandt had supplied, Detective Erickson talked to Elaine Flanders.

Ellie, wearing a white two-piece string bikini, was lounging on a deck chair near an Olympic-size backyard swimming pool. Her parents, a handsome couple close to Carl's own age, were on their way to a matinee concert when Carl arrived. They showed him to the pool and left him alone with their teenage daughter. They said they didn't want to be late for the concert. They didn't seem at all curious why a detective wanted to question their only child.

Though Elaine Flanders wore dark sunglasses that hid her eyes and greasy suntan lotion had stained the cloth of her bikini, the strips of cloth that covered her private parts seemed almost transparent in the bright afternoon sunlight. She couldn't have looked more naked if she'd been nude. The only part of her torso that seemed adequately covered was the left side of her stomach hidden beneath part of a beach towel.

"Tony?" The girl sat up and removed her sunglasses. "Someone killed Tony?"

"Tony and two of his friends were murdered this morning in Stephen Virusso's apartment."

"John and Sharon? They're dead too?"

"All three."

"Oh, God! Then I could have been killed too." The horror on her face looked genuine. "I didn't leave the apartment until four this morning. How long after I left did it happen?"

"The bodies weren't discovered until early this afternoon. They could have been killed anytime between four and nine. We won't have a better guess for time of death until autopsies have been completed. Can you account for your whereabouts during that time period?"

"Gary and I drove Claire and Linda home. Then we came back here and necked for a while."

"Necked?"

"Necked, played around. You know. Okay, so we fucked our brains out." The girl smiled coyly. "Is that what you wanted to know, Sergeant?"

"Gary's your boyfriend?"

Ellie laughed. "I've got lots of male friends. Gary was my date to the prom. I guess we were both horny this morning so we got it on in the back seat of his car."

"Got it on?"

"Fucked."

"Oh. How long were you together?"

"How long did we fuck?" The girl seemed to enjoy using the word. Was she trying to embarrass him? Saying "fuck" sure wouldn't do it. Carl used the f-word a lot himself.

"Listen, lady," Carl said. "This isn't a game. You look older than eighteen and in this state that means I can haul you down to the station and keep you there as a material witness until I catch the killer of your friends. But I don't want to do that unless I have to. Cooperate with me now, and I'll let you stay here and enjoy the sun for as long as you like."

The girl squirmed in her chair. Her fingers tugged the top of her halter to cover her breasts and she moved the towel to cover her entire stomach. Her demeanor changed from sexual suggestion to deadly serious.

"What do you want to know?" she asked.

"Everything," he said.

She told him everything.

"I'll be eighteen next week," Joyce said. "I can go away to school if I want."

"Sure," the old man said. "But don't expect me to pay for it."

"If I go," Joyce said, slipping the opened envelope and unread sheets of paper into a back pocket of her Levi's, "I'll pay my own way."

"You do that," said the old man. He opened the cellophane on a pack of cigars. "I won't pay a penny for such foolishness."

"You can't stop me, Grandpa. I'll get away from you yet."

"Sure." He stuffed a cigar into his mouth and bit off the end.

"And I'll never come back!" she taunted.

"Do that," he said, striking a match. He lit the tip of his cigar and dropped the match into an ashtray. Joyce ran from the room sobbing.

"You'll be back," the old man said. He puffed on his cigar and expelled bellows of smoke from his tight lips. "Soon as they see what you're really like, you'll be back. Mark my words. You're damaged goods, girl. You don't belong in no college."

He dropped into his favorite overstuffed easy chair and sucked on the cigar. "Mark my words," he said again, an ugly smile curling his lips. "You'll be back."

And under his breath he whispered, "I'll be here, right here in this house, when you come back. Sooner or later, you *will* come back. And when you do, I'll be here."

Without having to say it again, he thought: *I'll be here waiting for you to come back. And when you do…*

"You can rule out robbery as a motive," Dr. Wade dictated. "The injury pattern is indicative of a single claw hammer—one hammer with two sharp claws—repeatedly used as a bludgeon. There are repetitive imprints of the weapon on all three skull fractures. Toolmark analysis will show—I'm fairly certain—that the same weapon was used to cause all three deaths. Only the head of the hammer was used on Sharon Davison, but both the head and the claws were used on the two boys. Cause of death, therefore, is determined as blunt force trauma evidenced by subdural and subarachnoid extravasions with cerebral contusions. The wounds show abrasions and underlined margins indicative of a crush injury with tearing of tissue as the tissue is compressed against the hard bone beneath the surface.

"Notice the parallel marks in the bone on Tony Virusso and John Grabowski, indicative of sharp force trauma caused by the claws.

"There's evidence of excessively violent multiple blows to both of the male victims. The brutal and personal nature of the crime suggests a sexual or psychotic element. The lack of theft or household damage corroborates this suggestion.

"The designation of the psychological status of the assailant at the time of the crime is left to the psychiatrist or forensic psychologist, not the pathologist.

"The manner of death is homicide. Proximate cause of death: cerebral contusions and multiple lacerations of the brain; primary traumatic injury of the internal carotid artery caused by repeated blows with a fabricated instrument, most likely an ordinary claw hammer. The metabolic rate of blood ethyl alcohol varies substantially from person to person. Though all of the victims showed signs of alcohol consumption, none was legally intoxicated at time of death.

"All three victims showed signs of recent cocaine ingestion prior to death. Anthony Virusso appeared to be a chronic user, probably to the point of dependency.

"The mechanism of death for all three victims: hemorrhagic shock.

"The mode of death: violence.

"Cause of death: blunt force trauma.

"At this point both motive and instrument are officially unknown.

"I suspect the instrument of death was an ordinary claw hammer.

"I suspect the motive for death was psychosexual."

Marsha Wade made several duplicates of her autopsy recording. She e-mailed one to the pathology department secretary for transcription on Monday. She copied a duplicate onto a flash drive and set it aside to personally give to Detective Erickson. She listened to it again and made notes. Final lab results wouldn't be available for seventy-two hours. Neither histology nor hematology techs worked weekends anymore, and the blood, urine, and tissue samples wouldn't be processed until after stat tests for living patients were run on Monday and Tuesday.

Though Marsha knew the procedures for running blood and urine tests, she wasn't sufficiently familiar with some of Bryson Memorial Hospital's more advanced and sophisticated analysis equipment to try to do the work herself. Sometimes she thought medicine had become too technical for its own good, depended too much on technology and machinery to do the work that human minds should be doing.

She had to wait.

Unfortunately, every hour that passed increased the likelihood that the killer or killers would strike again. Mass murderers and serial killers, both playing out a fantasy game with their victims until they were caught or inevitably killed or killed themselves, kept on killing. Mass murders were usually committed by spree killers who, once they began, didn't stop killing until they killed themselves. Serial killers, on the other hand, stopped and started up again as the mood struck them. They disappeared for a while, then reappeared. They didn't want to be caught, and they rarely committed suicide. They had to be relentlessly pursued until they were captured or killed by law enforcement.

Crimes of passion—psychosexual crimes of violence—were usually committed by persons who had somehow known their victims, either quite well or just barely, prior to the commission of the crime. All three of the recent victims bore the marks of a crime of passion. They weren't random killings. Each of the victims was someone the killer already knew or who knew them or knew of them.

Sooner or later, a pattern would emerge from the killings. After more people had died, a distinctive pattern would finally emerge that law enforcement officials should have recognized earlier but usually didn't. Part of the pattern was already there—planted in the evidence from the first murders—and it was up to Marsha to discover the pattern before the killings continued. Time was already running out. There was a time bomb ticking away somewhere in the city and Marsha and the police had to find the time bomb and disarm it before it exploded. If they didn't, a lot of people would die before this nightmare ended.

Marsha racked her brain for clues. There'd been a thousand similar cases in the literature of forensic science that provided examples she could examine. John Wayne Gacy, Richard Speck, Charles Manson, the Hollywood Stranglers came immediately to mind. Jack the Ripper, Lizzie Borden, and the Boston Strangler were others in the same league. What was it that tied them all together?

Multiple murders.

But why?

What made them select their victims? Why did they kill some

people and not others? While Marsha Wade sought answers to her questions, the time bomb continued to tick.

"Your soup's getting cold, dear," Grace called from downstairs.

Joyce didn't bother to reply. She'd run from the den right to her bedroom, slammed the door, and threw herself on the bed.

She couldn't control the tears.

Her grandfather was right. Even if she were accepted into a college, she couldn't afford to go. She had no way to pay tuition, much less pay for room and board and books.

So sure she'd be stuck in this house forever, she even considered suicide. She knew her grandfather kept a straight razor in the medicine cabinet above the bathroom sink. The thought of walking into the bathroom, taking the razor from the second shelf of the medicine cabinet, running water in the sink or bathtub, sliding the razor across her wrists, and bleeding to death before anyone found her held a certain appeal.

But she knew she couldn't do it.

"Oh, God!" she cried. "Didn't you die on the cross to take away all this suffering and pain? Why must *I* suffer too?"

Suicide was a sin. The kind of sin God could never forgive.

And besides, it *hurt.* And Joyce had already been hurt enough. No. She couldn't do it.

But she couldn't go on the way she'd been going, either. Her only chance at happiness, she knew in her heart, was to get out of this house as quickly as possible.

She'd seen the way her grandfather had watched her ever since she'd come to live in this house. He'd never let her go. He wanted to keep her here, keep her forever locked in the confines of this house, keep her within his grasp and control.

Maybe she'd never get out of this house alive. Not unless *he* was dead.

And he wasn't about to die soon without a little help.

Now that, she thought, *has possibilities.*

"Joyce did it," said Elaine Flanders suddenly. "I know she did."

"Who?"

"Joyce Roberts. She killed Tony. It's as plain as the nose on your face. Joyce came back and killed them all."

"Who is Joyce Roberts, and what makes you think she's capable of murder?"

Elaine had just finished telling Sergeant Erickson, in great detail, all about her torrid love affairs with Tony Virusso and Gary Brandt. Carl had let the girl ramble on, hoping to gain some insight into the complexities of modern romance. He was shocked to learn that sex, not romance, dominated the teenagers' lives almost to the exclusion of all else. If the girl had tried to embarrass him with her daring language and vivid descriptions of intimacy, she may finally have succeeded.

Then, suddenly, she said she knew. She knew who'd killed Virusso and the other kids.

Joyce Roberts.

Brandt had mentioned that Flanders was insanely jealous of the Roberts girl, literally livid that Tony had taken Joyce to the prom instead of her. Flanders had led the others to play a prank on Roberts and Virusso, a prank that caused the altercation that ended the party for everybody and left Virusso beaten and bloody. Anything that Flanders said about Roberts needed to be examined in light of her jealousy and taken with a grain of salt.

"She's crazy. She seems normal, but she isn't."

"Joyce Roberts? What makes you think she's crazy?"

"You haven't seen her yet, have you?"

"No."

"You should. Go see her next."

"I will."

"You'll have to take her clothes off."

"Why?"

"To see what kind of a monster she is."

"Monster?"

"She looks perfectly normal with her clothes on. You've got to take her clothes off to see what she's really like."

"She's still a minor, isn't she?"

"She's seventeen."

"Then I have no authority to ask her to disrobe."

"Can't you get a policewoman to check her out?"

"No. Not unless I have enough evidence to arrest her. If she's booked and incarcerated, then the juvenile authorities will be able to examine her."

"She did it. I know she did. She killed Tony."

"Can you prove it? Were you an eyewitness to the actual murders?"

"No."

"Then how can you be sure Joyce Roberts is a killer?"

"She hated us, all of us. She killed Tony to get even."

"Why did she want to get even?"

Flanders shifted uncomfortably on the deck chair. Beads of perspiration dotted her tanned body. Carl wondered if the girl was sweating from nervousness or merely from being in the sun too long.

"We interrupted their fucking," Flanders said.

"She killed Tony because you interrupted their lovemaking?"

"Yes."

"I find that hard to believe."

"It's true."

"Why? Why do you think she'd kill her lover because someone interrupted their lovemaking?"

"Because she's crazy." Flanders picked up a towel and rubbed the sweat from her face, revealing a purple bruise on her belly the size of a fist. "And because," she said, "that's what I'd want to do if anyone interrupted me having sex. I'd kill them." She threw the towel to the patio tiles and stared Carl straight in the eyes. "Wouldn't you, Sergeant? If you and I were fucking our brains out and someone interrupted us, wouldn't *you* want kill them? Kill every single one of them?"

"But why did she kill Tony?"

"I already told you. She killed Tony because she's crazy."

"Joyce!"

Joyce lay curled in a ball on the floor in a corner of her bedroom.

"Joyce!"

There was something familiar about this position, something that brought back memories.

She saw him raise the hammer over her head.

"No, Daddy! No!"

Her throat was raw from screaming.

"No, Daddy!"

And then she was on the bed, naked. And everyone was laughing....

Her head hurt.

"Joyce!"

She was right at the, edge of remembering....

"Joyce!"

She opened her eyes and stared.

"Joyce!"

And then the spell was broken and the image faded, and she returned to reality. As though awakening from an ordinary dream, her mind remained momentarily disoriented. A vivid vision of her father—a horrible look in his eyes and a terrible grin on his face—lingered in her memory like a ghost. She tried to snatch at the memory, to bring it back into focus. But by reaching for it, she made it less tangible. She felt it slip away like smoke escaping through a tall chimney until it was gone and she was back in the upstairs bedroom of her grandparents' house and her head was pounding like a bass drum and she heard someone calling her name.

"Joyce! Answer me!"

"What is it, Grandpa?"

"Why wouldn't you answer me? I've been callin' you for five whole minutes!"

"I didn't hear you."

"Are you deaf? I suppose you didn't hear the doorbell either?"

"The doorbell?"

"Come down here, young lady. Come down right now! There's a man here to see you."

"I ... I'm changing my clothes, Grandpa. I'll be down as soon as I'm dressed."

"Hurry up!"

Joyce went to the dresser and sat down in front of her makeup mirror. She'd been crying a lot lately and her eyes looked simply terrible.

As she deftly wiped her face with cold cream and applied fresh makeup, her heart began to beat wildly in anticipation. She was sure the man downstairs was Tony Virusso. It *had* to be Tony. Who else could it be? She rushed to her closet and selected a new sweater, an orange acrylic she'd bought on sale at J. C. Penney. Within seconds, she'd changed.

Back at the mirror, she ran a comb quickly through her hair and checked her makeup again.

"Joyce!"

"I'm coming, Grandpa."

Eager to see Tony again, yet hesitant over a possible confrontation, Joyce began the slow climb down the stairs. What had happened last night? Try as she might, she couldn't remember.

But Tony would know. He'd be able to fill in the missing pieces. He could tell her what had happened after the lights came on and the laughter started. And what she'd done.

She was sure they'd never consummated what they'd begun on the bed. They'd been interrupted at the crucial moment. But then what happened?

Tony would know. He'd be able to tell her. At the bottom of the stairs she hesitated one long moment to gather her nerve before entering the living room. Then she walked in. "Tony," she said, "I'm glad you—"

But it wasn't Tony who sat on the couch.

He wasn't nearly as tall as Tony, his hair was cut differently, his shoulders weren't as broad. And he looked almost old enough to be Tony's *father*.

"Joyce?" the man asked. "Won't you please sit down?"

"Who are *you*?"

"I'm Detective Sergeant Erickson," he said. "And I'm afraid I'm the bearer of bad news...."

CHAPTER EIGHT

As Carl climbed the steps to the Foltz house—noting the freshly mowed lawn, neatly trimmed hedges and sidewalk edges, newly painted exterior and trim—he wondered what kind of a man was so compulsive that he kept all his possessions in such perfect repair.

And when Fred Foltz answered Carl's ring, the answer was obvious.

Fred was in his sixties but as lean and mean-looking as a Marine Corps drill instructor. His gray hair was painstakingly trimmed in a buzz cut. His dark blue cotton-twill shirt and pants looked freshly starched and pressed. Even his shoes were highly polished.

"Yes?" the old man asked through the screen door.

Carl produced his badge and ID. "I'm Detective Sergeant Erickson," he said. "Does a Miss Joyce Roberts live here?"

"What do you want her for?" The old man looked scared. Obviously, he didn't like the police coming to his house. Did he have something to hide?

"I'd like to speak with her, if I may. It's regarding some friends of hers."

"Joyce don't have no friends."

"May I speak to her, please? It's important I speak to her in person."

Reluctantly, the old man opened the door. "Come on in. I'll call her down from her room."

The inside of the house was just as immaculate as the outside, maybe more so. The walls, painted flat white, were spotless. The carpets, too, were spotless; they'd evidently been vacuumed and raked within the hour. The house even smelled clean, more like a hospital than a home. It positively reeked with disinfectant and cleanser.

"Joyce!" the old man bellowed.

When she didn't answer, he bellowed again.

"Are you sure she's home?" Carl wondered.

"She was a minute ago." Foltz took three steps up the carpeted stairs. "Joyce!"

A woman wearing a pale blue housedress came out of the kitchen. "She's in her room, Fred. If you'd like, I'll go up and get her."

"If she's in her room, then she should answer me."

"I'll go up and get her. Please don't shout anymore, Fred. You know how your shouting upsets me."

"I want the girl to answer me." Foltz took another step up the stairs. "Joyce!" he shouted. "Answer me!"

"What is it, Grandpa?"

"She'll be down in a minute," the woman said, sounding relieved. "Won't you step into the living room and sit down, Mr.—?"

"Erickson. Detective Erickson. I'm with the city police."

"I'm Grace Foltz," she said. "Joyce is my granddaughter. She isn't in any sort of trouble, is she?"

"I don't think so." Carl sat on the sofa and Grace faced him from a straight-backed chair. "I just want to ask a few questions regarding some friends of hers from school."

"Perhaps I could answer your questions. Must you bother Joyce?"

"Do you know what time Joyce came home from her date last night?"

"I'm not certain. Why do you ask?"

"Were you already asleep when she got home?"

"Well, yes. I tried to wait up for her, but I'm not used to being up later than ten o'clock."

"What about your husband?"

"He went to bed earlier than I did."

"So neither of you know what time Joyce got home after the prom?"

Fred came into the living room. He sat on the couch next to Carl. "Joyce got home about six-fifteen," he said.

"This morning?"

"Yes. Grace was still asleep, but I'm used to getting up at five-thirty, whether weekday or weekend. I heard her come in about six-fifteen."

"Does she stay out all night very often?"

The old man's face grew red with anger. "What kind of grandparents do you think we are? No, of course not. Last night was the first time we'd let her out alone since she came to live with us nearly twelve years ago. I argued against it, but Grace insisted that I let her go to the prom. Joyce'll be eighteen next week, and then I won't have a say in what she does anymore. So I let her go this one tine, just to keep peace in the family, and look what happens!"

"What happened?"

"Well"—the old man seemed taken aback—"something must have happened, didn't it? Else why would you be here?"

Before Carl could answer, Joyce stepped into the room. "Tony," she started to say, "I'm glad you—"

Carl got up from the couch. "Joyce?" he asked. "Won't you please sit down?"

"Who are *you*?" The girl looked disappointed. She'd obviously expected Virusso to be alive.

"I'm Detective Sergeant Erickson," Carl said softly. "And I'm afraid I'm the bearer of bad news. Please sit down."

Carl waited for the girl to bring a chair from the corner of the room. As soon as she was seated, he hit her with both barrels. "Anthony Virusso, Sharon Davidson, and John Grabowski were murdered last night. Their bodies were found in Stephen Virusso's apartment earlier this afternoon."

Grace Foltz gasped.

"You were Tony's date for the prom, weren't you?" Carl continued. "When did you last see him alive, Joyce?"

Joyce didn't reply. Her eyes, filled with tears, seemed a million miles away.

"Answer the man," Fred Foltz demanded.

But Joyce Roberts just stared at the old man as though he weren't there at all. Her eyes—very beautiful, well-made-up eyes—seemed *so* far away. Carl thought for a moment that the girl had gone into shock and might require medical intervention.

"Tony picked her up around eight," Grace interjected. "They left for the prom shortly after nine."

"Let the girl answer," Fred snapped. "She's got a tongue of her own. If she expects to go away to college, she'll have to learn to do things herself."

"Go away?" The grandmother looked bewildered. "Joyce isn't going away. She can't go away."

"She got a letter from the University of Illinois that says she's been accepted. They expect her to start in September."

"I've been... accepted?" The girl looked startled. Her eyes suddenly came back into focus.

"Didn't you read the letter?"

"No." Joyce glared at the old man with hate in her eyes. "But obviously *you* did. You've been reading my mail all along, haven't you?"

The old man blanched. Carl thought Fred Foltz looked a lot like a Peeping Tom who'd just been caught in the act. Caught with his pants down, too.

"Your letter was in with all the bills," the old man mumbled. "I must have opened it by mistake."

"And then you sealed it up again, didn't you?" The girl wasn't about to let the subject drop. In fact, she seemed to enjoy the old man's discomfort. "You pried open the envelope, read my letter, and sealed the envelope up so I wouldn't know what you'd done. I bet you read every piece of mail that's addressed to me, don't you? You treat me like I'm a child and don't have any rights, Grandpa. But I'm not a child anymore. I'm almost eighteen. And I don't want you spying on me anymore. Do you hear?"

"Excuse me," Carl interrupted. "You can continue your family disputes later, if you want. But right now I need Joyce to answer some important questions. Do you feel up to it, Joyce?"

"I think so." She grimaced as though fighting off physical pain. "I'll try, anyway."

"Tell me—in your own words, please—everything that happened from the time you and Tony left for the prom until you returned home this morning. Take your time. Try to remember all the details—anything and everything."

Though Joyce couldn't wait to get back to her room and read the letter from the university, she forced herself to sit in her chair and answer the detective's questions. Now that Tony was dead, Joyce was sure she'd never learn all that had happened after the lights came on and the laughter started. Maybe talking about it would help her remember.

She told the detective the truth: she couldn't recall anything that happened to her after she finished her third kamikaze.

"How did you get home?" he asked.

"I don't know."

"Tony didn't drive you?"

"I don't think so." She brushed back a strand of hair that fell from her forehead to cover her eyes. "I think I walked, but I'm not certain."

"You walked all the way home and don't remember?"

"I'm sorry. I really don't."

"Do you know what time you reached your own house?"

"No. The next thing I remember was when Grandma Grace woke me this afternoon."

"We found drugs in the apartment. Did you or any of the kids use drugs? Don't worry, I'm not trying to bust anyone. I need to know if the drugs were related in any way to the homicides."

"Some of the kids smoked marijuana."

"Did you?"

"Yes," she said. It wasn't a lie. She did try to smoke.

Grace gasped and Fred got an I-told-you-so expression on his leathery face.

"What about coke?"

"Coke?"

"Cocaine. Did you see any of the kids doing cocaine?"

So that's what Ellie really meant about liking coke! The sudden insight made Joyce blush at her previous stupidity. "Someone named Keith was supposed to bring some *coke* later," she said, sounding disgusted at the word. "At the time, I thought they meant he was bring Coca-Cola. I guess they meant he was bringing cocaine. I don't know much about drugs."

The detective smiled. He had a nice smile, and Joyce smiled back.

"Do you remember a fight between any of the boys?"

An image of Tony, naked, flashed through her mind. He was held on the floor while someone kicked his naked body. "There *was* a fight," she recalled. "Tony and... and..." She pressed her hands to her head. "Darn! I almost had it."

"Take your time."

"I'm sorry," she said. The image had vanished just as quickly as it came. "Maybe I'll remember later."

The detective asked other questions which Joyce answered, questions about the other kids at the party, the marijuana left on the floor, the exact locations of certain objects in the living room, the female undergarments found in the bedroom, the broken shoes in the stairway. Joyce glanced periodically at her grandfather, expecting the old man to interrupt at any minute. But Fred didn't say another word.

Joyce knew what that meant. As soon as the detective left, the old man would be all over her.

"So you drank alcohol and smoked dope, hmmmmm? So you went to bed with a boy, hmrnmmm? Didn't I warn you? Didn't I tell you what would happen if you did those things?"

And then he'd beat her with his belt.

And if Grace tried to stop him, he'd beat Grace, too. Joyce recalled her embarrassment each time the old man had forced her to lift her skirt, pull her panties down, and bend over to be punished. As she grew older, her embarrassment had grown proportionately. She realized that she had submissively bared her sex to the prying eyes of this hateful old man. She had felt his lecherous eyes violate her body as his belt beat her naked buttocks black and blue.

Not this time, Joyce promised herself. *If he lays a hand on me, I'll kill him. I swear. I'll kill him.*

When the cop finished his questions, Fred had a few questions of his own for his granddaughter to answer. But Fred could wait. If patience was a virtue, then Fred Foltz was a very virtuous man.

The detective handed Joyce a business card. "If you remember anything else, please call me. There's someone at my office number twenty-four hours a day. If I'm out, just leave a message with the duty officer and I promise to return the call as soon as possible."

Fred waited until he saw the detective drive away. Then he made his move.

Joyce was halfway up the stairs on the way to her room before Fred caught up with her on the staircase. His huge hand grabbed the girl's shoulder and spun her around. When he saw the hate in her eyes, he went berserk. How could she hate him after all he'd done for her? How dare she be so ungrateful? All his pent-up anger erupted like a volcano.

His hand lashed out at the girl's face, catching the side of her head before she had a chance to duck. *Whap!*

The blow knocked her to the carpet. Fred raised his fist again.

Grace rushed up the stairs, screaming, "No! For God's sake! Not her head! Don't hit her head! Please, Fred. Don't hit her head."

Fred turned around to face his wife, and the upraised fist Fred used to hit Joyce smashed into Grace's nose and dislodged her dentures. Her glasses flew from her face and shattered against the wall.

Before he could hit her again, he came back to his senses.

Fred hadn't meant to hit either of them, and he certainly hadn't meant to hit either of them so hard they lost consciousness. He was shocked by the results of his own violence. "My God!" he wailed in a pitiful voice. "My God, what have I *done*?"

Fred had inadvertently knocked Grace completely off the stairs. She lay on the carpet at the bottom of the stairway. Her head and neck were positioned at an awkward, unnatural angle. Blood dripped from her broken nose and pooled in the toothless hollow above her chin. Fred worried for a moment she might be dead, but the rise and fall of her bosom quickly allayed his fears. He knew she was still alive.

Joyce lay on the stairs halfway to the second floor. The hate was gone from her eyes. She stared vacantly into space as though her mind had fled.

"*Oh, God! I'm so sorry!*" The old man sank to his knees. "I didn't mean to hurt you. Really, I didn't. Please believe me."

In the quarter century since Fred Foltz had foresworn alcohol, he'd been careful to keep his temper under control. Praise God, he hadn't hit anyone in anger for more than twenty-five years! Although he had disciplined his wife and his granddaughter many times, those blows had been deliberate and never in anger. A husband had a right to discipline his wife. And the Book of Proverbs said, "withhold not correction from the child: for if thou beatest him with the rod, he shall not die. Thou shalt beat him with the rod, and shalt deliver his soul from hell."

But today, Fred had lost control completely. He was acting like the alcoholic he'd been before Christ—acting through Grace—had saved him and forgiven him for all his past sins.

Obviously the Devil—working through this teenage slut of a granddaughter—had engineered this evil act. Fred wasn't responsible, surely, for things the Devil made him do; just as Fred couldn't be held responsible for any of the despicable things he'd done under the influence of demon rum, one of the Devil's most powerful tools.

The Devil was in this girl, no doubt about it, just as the Devil had been in the girl's mother. And in the girl's father, too.

The Devil had infected these people and visited them like a plague upon Fred in much the same manner as the Devil had visited plague upon faithful Job in the Old Testament. It was always the righteous, the chosen, who had to suffer such trials. It was God's way to test his chosen few—to test them constantly as even Christ was tested in the desert and at Gethsemane. In order to be an instrument of God's divine will, one must first prove himself worthy.

At first Fred had failed God's tests. He hadn't been able to recognize the Devil at work because he had allowed his eyes to be blinded by demon rum. And blinded by demon rum, he had allowed that Jezebel—that Devil-inspired harlot begotten of his own loins—to lure him into sin.

But God works in mysterious ways, His will to be done. God had saved Fred from his folly when Grace caught them in the Devil's act. At first, Fred had thought his life—to say nothing of his marriage—was over. He was certain Grace would tell the authorities and Fred would have to spend the rest of his life in jail.

Instead, Grace had forgiven him. She had helped him to see the errors of his ways.

It was rough at first to make it through a day without alcohol. But Grace had made him promise to give up the bottle in return for her silence and forgiveness and he kept his promise because the alternative was too terrible to think about.

Eventually, his mind free of the influence of the Devil's drink, he was able to see God's plan and his own part as an instrument of God's will. And when Gordon Roberts took a hammer to the head of that Jezebel Leona and the heads of her three children, Fred knew this, too, had come to pass as part of God's plan.

Even when the youngest daughter—the spitting image of Leona—survived, Fred accepted it as God's will.

But now he knew that Joyce's survival was really the Devil's doing. Joyce had survived and come to live with Fred and Grace as another test of Fred's steadfastness, his worthiness.

And, Fred had to admit, the Devil's temptation was strong. During the first six years, while the girl was constantly in and out of the hospital, Fred had been just as strong, able to cast temptation aside with little or no effort. But as the girl grew older and her body healed and developed, Fred had to fight to stay in control.

By the time Joyce was fourteen, she looked exactly like her mother at that age.

Maybe it wouldn't have happened if Grace had had another child. Maybe if Leona hadn't grown up and become so damned independent, if Grace hadn't spent so much time going to church meetings and thinking it was God's will she couldn't get pregnant again, if Grace hadn't denied him that which was his right as a husband, if Leona hadn't been so damned beautiful, if Fred hadn't run out of whisky and hadn't switched to brandy and then to vodka and become so blind drunk he didn't know what he was doing... maybe it wouldn't have happened.

But it *did* happen.

Fred had gone upstairs to use the bathroom and discovered his daughter masturbating. Naked, Leona sat on the edge of the toilet seat with her legs spread and her eyes closed. One hand massaged her young breasts. The other hand moved up and down over the thin patch of pubic hair below her belly. She didn't hear him enter the bathroom until it was too late.

He should have left the moment he saw her. He should have turned right around and gone back downstairs and had another drink. But he couldn't take his eyes off her.

She was so damned *beautiful*.

He knew now that it hadn't been his daughter he saw, but rather a *goddess*. A pagan goddess. A wood nymph. A witch. Her beauty cast a spell over him, bewitched and compelled him to perform the unspeakable act.

He unzipped his pants and played with himself in front of her. And then... then...

Oh, God!

She let him. She didn't do anything to stop him.

It was all *her* fault. He could see that now. She'd tempted him. And demon rum had made him too weak to resist the temptation.

And when she came to him again, on Sunday morning while Grace was at church and he was nursing his hangover with vodka and tomato juice, he was filled with guilt and remorse. His eyes filled with tears and he begged her forgiveness.

"I've been thinking," she had said, sitting on his lap like she used to as a little girl. Only she wasn't little anymore. And she wasn't wearing *anything* beneath her nightgown. "I've been thinking a lot," she said, squirming her bottom against his crotch.

"About what?" he asked nervously.

"Oh, *things*. You know. About what we did last night." Her lips curled into a smile and her eyes grew bright. She stroked his whiskers with the tips of her fingers. "You'd like to do it again, wouldn't you?" He couldn't answer. "If you take me to the store and buy me lots of nice things," she whispered in his ear, "I'll let you do it again."

"Oh, God, no!" He tried to push her off his lap.

"You don't want to?" she asked incredulously.

"It isn't right!" he shouted, shoving at her. "Don't you understand? It isn't right!"

She stood up defiantly and faced him. "I'll tell Mom," she said simply, her smile turning hostile and vicious.

He bought her ninety-three dollars' worth of "things" at the department store.

And when they got home, she insisted on trying on all of them while he watched.

He was surprised to learn they even made black lace bikini panties to fit fourteen-year-olds.

Within a year, Leona had a whole new wardrobe. Dresses, jeans, blouses, sweaters, whatever she wanted. Twice a week, whenever Grace went to church, she'd come to her father and model for him, show him something new. When she turned sixteen, she started going out with boys her own age and Fred could do nothing to stop her. He'd wait jealously for her to come home from dates, and he drank more and more.

Their twice-a-week sessions became once a week. Then once a month. Then they stopped entirely.

She was always too busy, having too much fun, to think of her father anymore. Except when she needed money. And then she simply asked for money and didn't even thank him.

It was after she had turned eighteen, during the last week of her senior year in high school, the night of Leona's senior prom, that she went too far. She was wearing a low-cut strapless evening gown covered with sequins that must have cost a fortune. When she paraded in front of him for his approval, he demanded to know how much she'd paid for the dress.

"Don't worry about it," she said. "The money didn't come from *your* pocket."

"Then how could you afford that dress?"

"Can't you guess?"

He grabbed her arm and squeezed until it hurt. "Tell me!" he demanded.

Her smile turned hostile and vicious. "You bastard!" she spat.

He squeezed harder. "Tell me!"

"Let go of my arm first, you bastard!"

He wanted to smack her, to hit her, to throw her to the floor and beat her senseless. Instead, he released the grip on her arm.

"You really want to know?" she asked.

He nodded his head, dreading what he was about to hear.

"Some boys bought it for me, Daddy dear."

"What boys?" he asked, his voice weak.

"Lots of boys. I've forgotten their names, there've been so many."

"And what'd you have to do to get those boys to buy you that dress?" His voice was barely audible now, no more than a whisper.

"I fucked 'em, Daddy dear. Just like I fucked you. And each time I fucked them, they gave me money."

Fred's world seemed to topple. His legs grew weak and he was about to fall. It was almost as though, without warning, the rug had been pulled from beneath his feet, causing him to lose his balance.

"Sweet dreams, Daddy dear," Leona called as she went out the door and left the house on the arm of a date she didn't even bother to introduce to her father.

Fred killed a fifth of Jack Daniel's that night. When Grace came home from Saturday evening services, Fred was passed out on the floor. She left him there to sleep it off. He was still on the floor the next morning when she left to teach Sunday school to fourth graders.

Shortly before noon Fred picked himself up off the floor and opened a new bottle of bourbon. After swilling four or five swigs of sour mash, the terrible taste in his mouth went away, the pounding in his head subsided, and he sat down in a chair to sip his booze and feel sorry for himself.

Everything would have been fine if Leona hadn't returned from her all-night date just at the very moment Fred felt his sorriest. No sooner had his hate and anger reached the boiling point than his daughter entered the house. "What're you doing up?" she asked. "I thought you'd be sleeping off your hangover."

"I've been waiting," he said, trying to keep control of his voice. "Waiting for *you*."

"Sorry, Pops, I'm all worn out. You waited up for nothing."

"Puh-le-e-e-e-a-s-e!" he begged.

"Uh-uh," she said, not trying to hide the disgust in her voice. "I'm tired. I'm going up to bed and get some sleep."

"You *whore!*" he screamed, springing at her from his chair. She turned to run, but he was on her before she could take two steps. His huge hands ripped her dress to shreds, tore the fabric off her breasts, and mauled her naked flesh. She tried to kick at him but he pushed her to the floor and pinned her to the carpet so she couldn't move. His foul breath blew in her face as he grunted and groaned and whispered obscenities.

And then he was in her, moving his body in and out with such force that she screamed in pain.

It wasn't until after he had finished that he realized Grace was standing in the doorway staring at him in horror.

Of course, Leona claimed it was all *Fred's* fault, that Fred had raped her and *forced* her to become a fornicator. Fred tried to deny it, naturally, but Grace refused to listen to a word he said.

Leona moved out of the house that afternoon, moving in with some boy she knew who had an apartment clear across town.

Leaving Fred to face Grace all alone.

Grace cried, of course. She went to her room and cried her heart out. Though Fred stayed out of her way, he could hear her sobs throughout the house.

She sat up half the night, crying and praying, praying and crying. And sometime after midnight, she came downstairs holding her well-read Bible in her trembling hands. She asked Fred to kneel and pray for forgiveness.

And he did.

He had no choice.

"This is stupid," he nearly said aloud. Instead he said, "Lord, forgive me for I have sinned, and I am sorely sorry for my sins."

Under the careful tutelage of his wife, Fred prayed. He uttered every prayer he'd ever heard on television, recalled the Lord's Prayer from childhood Methodist Sunday school lessons, and even made up a few prayers of his own.

He stayed in a position of supplication for hours, his eyes closed, hands folded, until his knees ached and his bent back throbbed with pain. Bright-colored lights flashed across his eyelids like bolts of lightning and a ringing, then a roaring, filled his ears with sounds unlike anything he'd ever heard before.

His body shook as though palsied, his heart beat like a drum. He peed in his pants.

"I forgive you," he heard God say. "You were weak and foolish, but henceforward you shall be strong and righteous. You are born again, Fred Foltz."

When Fred told her what God had said, Grace shouted, "Hallelujah!" Then she cradled his head to her breast as a mother would cradle a newborn. Together, they praised the Lord and cried tears of joy.

Grace made Fred promise to attend church twice a week, to give up booze entirely, and to walk in the ways of righteousness for His name's sake forever. Fred gave his promise. And he had kept it, too. Until now.

Leona moved to Chicago, where she landed a job as a ticket agent at O'Hare International Airport. It was there that she met Gordon Roberts, a young business executive who traveled a lot.

Though Fred and Grace received invitations to the wedding,

they didn't attend. Grace sent a polite note and a twenty-dollar bill as a wedding gift. She wished the newlyweds well and promised to pray for their marriage.

Thirteen years later, Gordon used a carpenter's claw hammer to shatter the skulls of his wife and children. Then he blew his own brains out with the blast from both barrels of a twelve-gauge shotgun. When Fred and Grace were told of the terrible tragedy, Grace insisted on visiting Joyce at the hospital. One look at her sole surviving grandchild—only six years old, fragile, helpless, hooked up to machines that barely kept her alive—and Grace promised God that if it were His will to heal the child, then Grace and Fred would take the girl into *their* home and raise her as their own.

Fred objected, of course. But when Grace told him of the almost two million dollars in real estate, stock certificates, and insurance Gordon's estate had left Joyce, Fred was willing to concede that adopting the girl could indeed be part of God's plan.

Especially since Gordon's parents wanted no responsibility for the child and were willing to waive any and all claims to the estate.

Within nine years most of the money was gone, eaten up by greedy physicians hungry for the almighty buck. There was always another operation, another procedure, the doctors said they needed to perform; experts flew in from New York and Los Angeles and recommended this or that new technique; surgeons cut and sewed, cut and sewed, and the bills mounted up, multiplying like rutting rabbits, until Fred finally put his foot down and refused to give permission for another operation.

Now Fred knew that the girl was part of the Devil's plan, not God's. The money had been another of the Devil's temptations, a way to get the girl into this house so she could work her evil on Fred Foltz.

And work evil she had. Right from the first, the girl's very presence caused a rift between Grace and Fred. Grace spent all her time doting on the invalid, coddling the girl until it made Fred sick to watch. Later, when the girl was well enough to get into mischief and Fred tried to discipline her, Grace would try to intervene. During family arguments, Grace would side with Joyce to make Fred feel like a fool. It was the Devil's doing, all right. The Devil did his foul work by turning husband against wife, wife against husband.

Was it not written, "If a house is divided against itself, that house will not be able to stand"?

Thank God, it wasn't too late. Grace was alive and Fred had come to his senses in time to save them all. He heard his arthritic knees pop as he lifted his unconscious wife from the stairs. He carried her up the steps to their bedroom and laid her comfortably on her own side of the bed. Then he went back for Joyce.

Not wanting to touch her upper body, fearing that one touch would contaminate his soul beyond any hope of redemption, he grabbed the girl's feet and dragged her slowly upstairs to her own room. He left her on the carpet at the foot of her bed, her eyes staring vacantly up at the ceiling as though she could read some invisible writing etched on the roof.

As he closed the door to her room, he pulled a key from his pocket and locked her in.

CHAPTER NINE

Carl intuitively sensed that something was very wrong. He had to fight a sudden urge to whip his car around in a U-turn and drive straight back to the Foltz house with his siren blaring and MARS lights flashing

Why? What was there about that girl and the old man that just didn't jive? Why did he have this uncomfortable feeling that something was wrong— very, very wrong—in the Foltz house?

Good detectives had an instinct, Carl knew, a sixth sense that worked overtime. It sorted out what the eye saw, what the nose smelled, what the ear heard—sorted, filed, stored for future reference things the conscious mind missed. Consciousness was selective, picking up only what it could concentrate on at the moment. But the subconscious acted like a giant sponge, soaking up everything indiscriminately. Later, when the subconscious had time to sort things out, it sent messages to the conscious mind. "You missed something important, didn't you, dummy?" the subconscious would taunt, "I know what it is, but I'm not telling. If you're so all-fired smart, you can just figure it out by yourself!"

Carl parked the car at the curb and left the motor running. He pulled a cigarette from the half-empty pack in his pocket and jabbed the dashboard lighter with his thumb. He had to wait a full minute for the coil to get red-hot before he could light the cigarette.

It was the first cancer stick he'd allowed himself all week and it tasted terrible, stale. But he forced himself to inhale anyway, nearly choking on the smoke.

"No good," he said, flipping his cigarette out the open car window. He pulled the pack from his pocket, crumpled it up in his fist, and dropped the crushed pack and the broken remaining cigarettes to the floor behind the driver's seat. Carl had been trying to quit by limiting the number of cigarettes he smoked. This system was supposed to work because, by the time he got around to smoking the last half of the pack, the remaining cigarettes had dried out and tasted terrible. Cigarettes were a nasty, dirty habit he had tried to break many times and discovered he couldn't. He told himself he didn't need another cigarette. But he wanted a cigarette. He wanted it so bad he could taste it. He told himself he couldn't think without a cigarette. He knew it wasn't true, but he told himself he couldn't think without a cigarette and so all he could think about were cigarettes and it became a self-fulfilling prophecy that he couldn't think about anything else until he had a cigarette.

He cursed himself as he slammed the car into gear and drove directly to the nearest gas station and purchased a pack of cigarettes and a cheap Bic lighter. He called himself every name in the book as he tore the cellophane top from the fresh package of Camels, but he breathed a sigh of relief as he drew a deep drag from the dreaded cancer stick and slowly exhaled a lungful of smoke.

Something was nagging at him. Now that he'd satisfied his craving for nicotine, maybe he could think straighter. He climbed back in the car and drove around the block, unable to make up his mind. Should he return to the Foltz house? Why? What was it that nagged him as incessantly as a hound tailing a rabbit? Was it something about the girl? The grandmother? The grandfather? The house? What?

He focused on each in turn, pulling as many details as possible from his memory, sorting, collating, analyzing. As thorough and efficient as a computer, his mind recalled images, smells, sounds. His mind's eye saw the girl, beautiful, young, naive, standing out in stark contrast to her surroundings. She certainly didn't belong in that house with the old man. Carl was glad she planned to go away to college. The sooner she got out of that house, the better off she'd be.

Carl felt sorry for Grace Foltz, the fragile-looking old lady. When the girl did leave for college, Grace would likely wither away and die. He'd seen it happen before—quite often, actually—to older women of her type. Married to men like Fred Foltz, such women lived only for their kids. When the kids grew up and moved away—severing the umbilical cord that had tied them to mother's apron, the vital umbilical that somehow had reversed itself and eventually nourished only the mother—such women searched desperately for something, *anything*, to keep them alive. If they had more than one child, perhaps there would already be grandchildren by the time the youngest child moved out, and they survived then by transferring affection to their grandkids. They doted on the grandkids at every opportunity, clinging like vultures to any tiny form of love they could salvage.

Or, without grandchildren to sustain them, some women nurtured at the trough of religion. Their daily bread became the body of Christ, and they clung like vultures to the tenets of the church. They became dogmatic, even evangelical. Their professed duty was to save all of God's children, to bring souls to Christ, to feed the starving children of the world, especially those in faraway lands. Such women usually drove their husbands to drink, turning their home life into a living hell.

Men, like women and children, wanted and needed nurturing, too. It was quite natural for husband and wife to nurture each other during courtship and the early years of marriage; but with the arrival of children relationships often changed. Husbands, starved for affection, were forced to forage outside the home for sustenance while mothers and children grew fat on each other. Carl had seen it happen hundreds of times: to his own family and to friends, to neighbors, to victims and suspects alike. He vowed it would never happen to him.

And it couldn't. Not if he stayed single.

Carl's job nurtured him the way no woman ever would, ever could. Not even his mother (God rest her soul) meant as much to him as his silver shield.

"You didn't come around to visit me until you knew I was definitely dying," Carl's mother had accused him from her deathbed in the nursing home. "You're my only child, Carl. I worked and slaved to bring you up after your dad died, to make sure you got everything you ever needed. And when I needed you, did you even remember I was here until it's too late?"

"I couldn't get away, Mom. Honest."

"Is that job of yours more important than your own mother? It must be, or you would have found a way to visit me before now."

"Mom, I don't want to argue."

"You'd rather be off playing cops and robbers than be here with your poor old mother. Wouldn't you?"

When Carl didn't reply, his mother smugly continued: "I'm right, Carl. You know I'm right."

"Yes, Mother. You're right."

She'd slipped into a coma that very same afternoon and died three days later. Doctors could find nothing physically wrong with Carl's mother despite years of expensive tests and various diagnostic procedures, but her health continued to decline until she was unable to take care of herself and had to be placed in a nursing home. Carl suspected she was simply tired of living, had nothing more to live for, wanted to die, and so she eventually did die. She was only fifty-three when she died. Carl was twenty-nine.

The burden of guilt was almost unbearable. Carl took a two-week leave of absence from the force and tried to drink himself to death.

Until he remembered his father.

Edgar Erickson was a chain-smoking alcoholic womanizer who'd run off with another woman when Carl was five. Three years later, word arrived from San Francisco that Edgar Erickson had been murdered by an unknown woman in some rundown hotel in the tenderloin district. The killer was never caught.

"Watch out you don't become like your father," his mother had warned during Carl's wild adolescence. "I worry that you'll grow up to be just like *him*."

Carl worried about it, too. Two weeks after his mother died, Carl quit drinking, threw out all the bottles of booze he had in the house—even the full ones—and as soon as he sobered up, returned to duty and began attending local Alcoholic Anonymous meetings.

But Carl had never completely broken the cigarette habit.

Suddenly Carl knew what was bothering him, nagging at him. It was the old man, Fred Foltz. The old man was obviously a reformed alcoholic and his behavior was typical of what people in AA called a "dry drunk." Carl recognized in Foltz all the signs of a recovering alcoholic turned workaholic—obsessive cleanliness, neatness, orderliness, unreasonably demanding of both himself and others, strict adherence to a rigid schedule—traits Carl had fought most of his life to overcome or modify in himself. Although he was no longer as compulsively obsessive about most things, Carl certainly remained so about his job. Some things were impossible to change.

Why did the old man's compulsiveness seem such a threat? Was Foltz involved in the murders of his granddaughter's friends? Could Foltz be the killer?

Didn't Dr. Wade say the preliminary evidence pointed to a woman? Was it possible that Grace Foltz had helped her husband kill those kids?

Or was Joyce Roberts the killer, as Ellie Flanders claimed?

Carl compulsively turned his car around and headed for the hospital. Only one person might have answers to his questions, and that person was Marsha Wade.

There were days when Carl Erickson wished for a nice dull nine-to-five, Monday-through-Friday, paper-pushing job. And then there were days—like today—when he knew such a job would simply bore him to tears. Erickson thought of himself as a people person, not a paper pusher. And in his official capacity as the city's chief homicide investigator, he had an unequaled opportunity to meet and interact with every type of person imaginable.

He knew he was the right man for the job, and this job was right for the man Carl Erickson had become. Not everyone was able to say the same about *their* jobs. Erickson had met hundreds of people who hated their own jobs, who found themselves trapped in an uninteresting occupation that bored them to death and meant nothing more than a regular paycheck. They were the kind of people who wouldn't work at all unless they had to, and many of them simply punched clocks and collected their pay, did as little as possible until eventually they were fired, and then stayed at home and collected their unemployment checks until their eligibility ran out.

He'd also met men like Stephano Virusso, men who busted their butts to build a business and a reputation that they could pass on to their sons. Such men became pillars of the community and were active in church and politics. They claimed that everything they did was for the benefit of their family or their community, never for themselves. They were able to provide their family with a big house, fancy cars, expensive clothes, and college educations. When they died, they left behind an inheritance their kids didn't always want.

Very rarely, however, did a detective meet someone like Dr. Marsha Wade.

Most doctors, Carl had long ago discovered, belonged to the "pillar of the community" category. Either they hated their jobs and remained in medicine merely for the money, or they were out to build a reputation that would make them respected members of the community so they could hobnob with politicians and financiers and donate large sums of money to favorite charities. Few, if any, really cared about patients.

Marsha Wade seemed different.

Like himself, Marsha Wade loved her job. She wasn't in medicine just for the money. Nor did she give a damn about building a reputation in order to become a pillar of the community. Pillars of the community didn't run around in bra-less T-shirts and tight jeans.

Carl had watched her closely as she'd gone over the crime scene with a fine-toothed comb. He was impressed by her thoroughness, something he hadn't expected from an on-site medical examiner. Most MEs never bothered to visit an actual crime scene, preferring to let technicians and police do all the dirty work. But Marsha Wade was definitely different. Not only did she appear to know what she was doing, she also seemed to care.

The way Carl cared. Not only about a job, but about everything.

Carl hoped Marsha Wade had finished all three autopsies by now and could offer information that would point a finger at the killer or killers. He didn't want to admit that the real reason he wanted to see Doctor Wade again had nothing to do with this case.

"Oh, Christ, what do I do now?"

Fred Foltz sat on his own side of the double bed and wrung his hands with worry. He'd already tried everything he could think of to revive his unconscious wife and nothing had worked.

He hadn't meant to hit her, had he? No, of course not.

She'd done it to herself when she fell, hit her head first against the wall and then against the floor. She couldn't blame him for this, could she? No, of course not.

He knew he should phone for an ambulance and get Grace to the hospital. She needed professional treatment, something he couldn't provide.

But Fred Foltz was scared. If he brought Grace to the hospital, the doctors would *know* she'd been hit by a *fist*. They'd ask all kinds of probing questions he didn't want to answer. Then they'd call the cops and he'd be arrested for assault and battery. The cops wouldn't understand when he told them that it was all the *girl's* fault, that she was an agent of the Devil. No. They wouldn't understand at all. They'd lock Fred up in jail. Then they'd come to this house and release the *girl*, set her free to do more of the Devil's work while Fred went to prison for the rest of his life.

No. He couldn't take Grace to the hospital. Not yet, anyway.

First, he had to take care of the girl

Although the Lord God didn't approve of killing, surely He'd look the other way this one time. Wouldn't He?

Of course God would. Didn't the Bible say, "Thou shalt not suffer a witch to live." If Joyce Roberts wasn't a witch, she was at least the daughter of a witch. She deserved to die.

Killing Joyce was necessary. If the girl ever got free to work her evil on other men, there was no telling how many souls would be lost. Hundreds, perhaps thousands, of men would succumb to her charms.

She would seduce them all. Just like her mother.

Fred would put a stop to it. He'd been chosen—hadn't he?—to be the instrument of God's will. He had to destroy this terrible evil before it got free and destroyed the world.

But how?

The solution came to him—unbidden—in the image of a claw hammer that flashed suddenly before his tired eyes. It looked exactly like the picture of a hammer that he'd seen recently in a hardware store flyer. He remembered thinking at the time that $19.95 was a lot of money to pay for a new hammer, especially since he already had three perfectly good, though old, claw hammers in his toolbox in the basement.

Fred stood up and walked to the door. Once he got an idea in his head, he was like a bloodhound who'd whiffed a scent. Nothing could pull him off the trail till he'd caught his prey.

"When I get back, everything'll be set right," he told his wife.

"Everything'll be just fine."

He walked slowly to the stairs. The swollen joints at his knees throbbed with arthritis pain and he was forced to limp, one step at a time, down two flights of stairs. Had Fred Foltz seen a doctor about his arthritic condition, he might have learned that mental stress always aggravates arthritis. But Fred didn't believe in doctors; he remained painfully unaware of the integral link between pain and stress.

By the time he reached the basement, the evening sun had already set. The room was pitch black. Fred fumbled in darkness for a metal chain that dangled from a light fixture, finally found the chain, and pulled. Bright light flooded the room and Fred was momentarily blinded, his pupils contracting to mere pinholes.

Even before his vision cleared, he'd located his toolbox. Being a methodical man had definite advantages. Fred had a specific place for everything in his life, and he did his damnedest to keep everything in its place. The toolbox was right where it belonged.

But when he opened the lid, he couldn't believe his eyes.

He blinked, rubbed both eyes with his knuckles, and looked in the box again.

The toolbox was completely empty. Three claw hammers, four flat-tipped and two Phillips-head screwdrivers, two pairs of pliers, and a set of socket wrenches had been in that box Saturday morning. Now they were gone.

He looked around the room for his missing tools. Had Grace borrowed them? No. Grace had no need to use his tools. What about Joyce? Would Joyce take them? Why?

It had to be Joyce. Perhaps hiding his tools was her way of getting back at him. But when had she taken the tools?

All three claw hammers, along with the other tools, had been in the toolbox yesterday morning. Joyce had spent yesterday afternoon getting ready for her date. She'd been out all night and had slept all morning. Could she have slipped down here, unnoticed, sometime earlier this afternoon?

Possibly.

And then he spotted the tools. The handle of a hammer protruded from a pile of dirty laundry in the far corner of the basement near Grace's washer and dryer.

Fred grinned from ear to ear. The stupid bitch wanted to play hide and seek, did she? Well, now that he'd found a hammer, he'd tag her good.

And then he'd hide her where nobody'd ever be able to find her.

Both his knees made painful popping sounds as he bent to retrieve his tools. Tossing the clothes aside, he recovered the screwdrivers, pliers, and socket wrenches. But look hard as he might, he could find only one hammer.

Two of his large claw hammers were still missing. Damn that girl! What'd she do with the other hammers?

Fred wasn't about to waste any more precious time looking for them. They'd turn up sooner or later.

One hammer was all he needed for *this* job. He hefted the hammer in his hand and felt the tremendous power of the tool, the same power that his cave-dwelling ancestors must have felt when hammers were first invented by tying a rock to the end of a stick with animal sinew. *With this in my hand*, he thought, *I could conquer the world.*

Smite my enemies.

Build a new world upon the broken bones of my smitten enemies.

He straightened his painful knees and was about to turn around and head upstairs with the hammer in his hand when the ceiling light suddenly shattered and the world plunged instantly into darkness. It happened so fast that he felt as though the rug had again been pulled out from beneath his feet and left him without a foundation to stand upon.

And then something hard and sharp hit him across the face and tore away his nose.

Fred Foltz fell to the floor. His disoriented mind was unable to grasp that he was about to die.

The second blow caught him squarely on the chin and pulverized his jaw and false teeth. Blood flooded his mouth and trachea and he nearly choked to death before the third blow drove jagged claws into his left eye and mercifully ended his miserable life.

The fourth blow cracked his skull in half, but Fred was already dead and it didn't matter. The fifth blow tore flesh away from his face in huge hunks. The sixth and seventh blows cut into his neck and nearly severed his head from his torso. The eighth and ninth ripped away his scalp and laid bare his ruined brain. The tenth blow missed, slamming into the cement floor and cracking the concrete, sending a shower of sparks flying through the darkness.

The deadly hammer was set aside for a moment while a gloved hand fumbled for the light chain that dangled down from an unbroken ceiling fixture.

Then the gloved hand picked up the hammer and set to work again, hacking away at the body, deliberately dismembering the limbs, ripping flesh from bone, pounding bone into powder, neglecting nothing.

Not a single part of Fred Foltz remained untouched.

Satisfied that the deadly claws had done their job, Leona Roberts left the hammer lying on the floor in a pool of her father's blood.

Then she picked up the other two hammers and walked upstairs.

CHAPTER TEN

Carl Erickson hadn't touched his steak at all.
Instead, he leaned back in his chair, sipped at his coffee, stared appreciatively at Marsha Wade, and lit another cigarette. When Carl had asked Marsha to sit outside on the restaurant patio where smoking was permitted, she hadn't objected.

"You'd live a lot longer if you gave up cigarettes," she said.

"God knows I've certainly tried to give up cigarettes. But I've smoked two packs a day since I was fourteen, and now I'm hooked worse than a damn junkie."

"If you'd really like to quit, maybe I can help."

"How?"

"Give me your cigarettes. Keep the one you've lit, but hand me the rest of the pack."

He passed the pack across the table.

"Now watch," she said. One by one she pulled the cigarettes from the pack and dropped them into Carl's water glass. At first the cigarettes merely floated in the clear liquid. Then, slowly, the water began to turn brackish.

"See how brown and yucky the water gets? Imagine your lungs looking like that."

"It's not the same," he argued. "I don't ingest raw tobacco. I don't have whole cigarettes floating around in my body. I don't swallow the damn things. I smoke 'em."

"You're right," she said. "Only it's worse—much worse—to ingest the smoke from cigarettes. Do you know how many carcinogens are created when tobacco burns? Just breathing in that particular combination of gasses causes cellular changes to the lungs that can maim or kill a man as easily as a loaded gun. After dinner we'll go back to the lab and I'll show you tissue samples taken from the lungs of deceased smokers. You'll think this water is almost pretty by comparison."

"I'll go back to the lab with you," he said, stubbing out his half-finished cigarette in an ashtray, "simply because I need to go over the autopsy report with you. I'll take the time to look at diseased lungs after I've caught whoever murdered those kids."

"We," she said.

"What?"

"After *we've* caught the murderer."

"That's what I said. *We.*"

Carl leaned back in his chair and, despite the doctor's demonstration that had turned the water in his glass an ugly dark brown, wished for another cigarette. When he'd accepted Marsha's suggestion to grab a quick bite to eat at this steak house around the corner from the hospital while they talked about the case, he thought there'd be no harm in mixing a little pleasure with business. Now he knew he'd made a mistake.

Every time he tried to talk about business, Dr. Wade effectively redirected the conversation. She smiled a lot and seemed genuinely friendly; and Carl had been gullible. Between the time they placed their orders and the time their dinners arrived, she'd pried into Carl's personal life by offering tit-for-tat tidbits about her own. She was single, the daughter of a doctor, and she'd never considered anything other than medicine for her life's work. She'd deliberately chosen pathology as her specialty because, she said, laboratory medicine was the basic tool upon which modern medicine relied. It was the pathologist who offered the clinician a proof-positive diagnosis of most illness and it was the pathologist who told the surgeon when to cut, where to cut, and what to cut. And, she added with an enigmatic smile that Carl found incredibly attractive, it was the forensic pathologist who pointed the finger of guilt at most murderers and rapists. Without forensic pathologists, she claimed, more than half of all crimes would remain unsolved. Detectives needed pathologists, she insisted, much more than pathologists needed detectives.

Carl admitted he needed all the help he could get on this particular case. He asked her to tell him anything she'd learned from the autopsy of the victims, anything at all that might finger the killer or killers.

"I've ordered *stat* hematology, microbiology, cytology, and histology tests on fluid and tissue samples from all three victims. But I won't have final lab results back until Tuesday."

"What can you tell me now? Anything? What are your preliminary findings?"

"I saved a copy of my report on a flash drive. Here," she said, handing him the flash drive.

"Doesn't do me any good without a computer," he said.

"We can go back to the lab after dinner. You can bring it up on my laptop."

Then she switched the conversation again, suggesting, since they'd be working so closely together to solve this case, they should call each other by their first names. "I'm Marsha," she offered. "You don't mind if I call you Carl, do you?"

That was when he started to get suspicious.

Without a cigarette to keep his hands occupied, Carl poked his steak with a fork. "Still think the killer's a woman?" he asked.

"Maybe," she said.

"This afternoon you seemed fairly certain."

"Nothing's certain until the test results are finished."

"Look, Doctor..."

"Marsha."

"Marsha. I need some straight answers."

"You'll get them."

"Ok. Was it a woman who killed those kids?"

"I don't know. I won't know until all the evidence is in."

"What's your educated guess?"

"I think we've got a psycho on our hands."

"Doctor, look..."

"No. You look, Carl. Look at it from my viewpoint. I want to catch this nut as badly as you do. Maybe worse."

"Then why won't you tell me all you know?"

"Because I don't know *everything*. Not yet. And because what little I do know is enough to scare the hell out of me."

Carl looked at her with sudden concern. "You think the killer's after *you*?"

"No," she said.

He threw his fork on the table. "I don't see why you can't give me a straight answer."

"Can I tell you a story?" She watched his eyes for his reaction. "It's a true story," she added, as though that made a difference.

He breathed an exasperated sigh. "Go ahead. I have this crazy feeling you won't tell me anything else unless I listen to your story. Am I right?"

She smiled. "You're very perceptive."

"It's my business to be perceptive."

"Once upon a time," she began, "in a medium-sized city not too different from this one, there occurred a series of murders. Sixteen killings in less than three weeks. Each victim suffered multiple stab wounds to the genitals that castrated the males and violated the females. Fear spread through the city like a plague. People became paranoid and accused their neighbors, and the police wasted valuable time following up false leads. You with me so far?"

"Go on."

"The medical examiner in that county was kept busy day and night. When he wasn't doing autopsies, he was writing autopsy reports. He never got out of the lab. Homicide investigators worked day and night, too. They combed crime scenes for clues, interviewed thousands of people, and finally arrested a man who admitted to the murders after police interrogated him for several days. Everyone relaxed when an arrest was announced. Everyone, that is, except the killer.

"The killings continued. But the killer, though psychotic, was clever. He decided to hide each of the bodies of this new batch of victims after the innocent man was arrested. Neither the police, nor the public, was aware of the danger, believing the killer to be incarcerated and awaiting trial.

"Homicide investigators were also unaware of the dramatic increase of missing persons reported in that city. Specialization and compartmentalization within the police force kept vital information from reaching those who most needed it.

"The real killer was never caught. He simply, inexplicably, committed suicide. No one knows why. Maybe he finally felt guilty. One night he put a loaded pistol in his mouth, pulled the trigger, and blew his deranged brains out the back of his head and all over the walls and furniture of his house."

She paused and took a sip of coffee.

Carl waited for her to continue, but she merely sipped her coffee, smiled coyly, and left lots of questions unanswered.

"How'd they ever determine that this man and not the other—the one who confessed—was the real killer?" Carl asked, suspecting he already knew the answer.

"Police found seventy-four bodies buried in the real killer's basement," she said softly, barely more than a whisper. "They decided to dig around in the basement after discovering one half of a broken pair of blood-stained scissors that tool mark analysis proved to be the murder weapon of the original sixteen victims. ABO typing and DNA linked dried blood on the scissors to two of the early victims. Dried blood on one pair of the man's shoes linked him to other victims. I don't think there's any doubt he was the real killer. Do you?"

"Why'd he do it? What was his motive?"

"He was nuts." Marsha took another sip of coffee and set her empty cup on the table. "He was psychotic, deeply disturbed, bonkers. Call it whatever you will. A mentally stable person simply doesn't kill another human being." Her eyes had a faraway look that reminded Carl of the way Joyce Roberts had looked when Carl had told Joyce Tony was dead. "I can't understand why one human being would ever want to take the life of another person. Murder doesn't make any sense at all to me. Yet it happens all the time, doesn't it? People kill each other every day. Nations wage wars and thousands of people are killed and we all know war is insane, but still war still happens. Sometimes I think the whole world's nuts."

"Maybe it is," Carl said. He shoved his chair away from the table and stood up. "Will you excuse me a moment? I'll be right back."

He felt her eyes on his back as he walked to the cashier and asked for change for a twenty. She was still watching, he knew, as he fed dollar bills into the cigarette machine and pushed the button marked *Camel*.

"Why'd you do that?" she asked when he returned to the table.

"If the whole world's nuts," he said, "then I guess I have a right to be nuts too." He ripped open the pack and pulled out a cigarette.

"I thought you were different," she said, sounding disappointed.

"But you're not. You've got a death wish just like everyone else."

"You sound a lot like my mother," he said, lighting the cigarette. "She claimed I became a cop so crooks could take potshots at me. Maybe she was right. But I've been a cop for fifteen years and I've never been shot or even been shot at."

"You could be, though."

"Yes. And I could be run over by a truck while crossing the street, too. Should that stop me from crossing the street?"

They stared silently at each other across the table. Her eyes were light blue, almost the color of a clear sky. Her golden hair, held back from her face with a pair of tortoiseshell barrettes, seemed to glow in the soft light of the restaurant. She still wore the same T-shirt she'd worn that afternoon and he felt almost guilty watching her breasts move up and down every time she took a breath. He couldn't stop looking at her.

She looked back. Her eyes seemed to caress his face, his ears, his neck, his shoulders. Was she examining him as a doctor would examine a patient? Did she have X-ray vision to see cancer cells growing inside his lungs even as he inhaled smoke from his cigarette?

"I don't *want* to die," he said, breaking the silence. "But I'm not going to hide from death, either. When my time comes, I'll fight death tooth and nail. But I doubt it'll do any good."

"That sounds too fatalistic," she said. "As a doctor, I don't believe in fate. I fight death and disease every day with science and reason, not with bullets and guns. Nine days out of ten, I win a temporary victory and hold death at bay another day. I don't see how anyone with an ounce of intelligence can believe in fate. It is true that death reaches everyone sooner or later, but I prefer to think we do have the power to make it later rather than sooner."

Carl found himself staring again at her eyes. Marsha's eyes twinkled as she talked. Whenever she seemed passionate about a subject, her eyes actually twinkled. She was as passionate about life as she was about death.

"I know we can stop this killer," Marsha said. "If we work together, we can!"

There she goes again, he thought. Saying "we." "We" can catch the killer. "We" can stop the killer. "We."

Didn't she realize that catching killers was a cop's job, not a doctor's? Other pathologists he'd worked with understood their respective roles and were content to stay in their laboratories; none ever voiced a desire to play cops and robbers with the big boys; none ever got in the way of an investigation.

But Marsha Wade was different.

He had the feeling that she wanted to be intimately involved in the entire investigation. She would never be content simply to confine her contribution to laboratory analysis. She wanted to do field work, to visit the scene of the crime while the body was still warm. She wanted to interview suspects, to cross-examine them, to confront them with bits and pieces of evidence to test their reactions, to doggedly pursue all leads until she had the killer cornered.

And then what? Did she plan to call the cops after she had cornered the killer?

By then it would be too late. She'd corner the killer and inevitably get herself killed, wind up a victim on her own autopsy table.

And Carl couldn't let that happen to her, wouldn't let that happen.

"Look," she said, her eyes still twinkling. "I'm not trying to get in your way. I don't want to impede your investigation. I want to *help*. If we work together, maybe we can catch the killer before she strikes again."

"She?"

"She."

"Then you do think the killer's a *woman*?"

"I'm not certain."

"Okay," he said, throwing up his hands in resignation. "Okay. You win."

"I win?" Her mouth spread into a surprised grin and her eyes not only twinkled but virtually danced. "What do I win?"

He lit a second cigarette from the butt of his first and made her wait in suspense while he stubbed the butt out in the ashtray, deliberately grinding the cigarette slowly to shreds. Then he said, "Me."

The grin faded from her face. "I don't understand," she said.

"You understand perfectly, doctor. You've been working on me all evening, haven't you? Buttering me up at the same time you buttered your rolls. You tell me a story about a mass murderer—a serial killer—who was never caught, a man who was allowed to murder again and again simply because the authorities screwed up and didn't exchange vital information, a man who was a nut case just like the man or woman who killed those three kids this morning. You want me to know that the same thing could certainly happen here if you and I don't work together hand in glove to catch the killer. And you want me to let you talk to any suspects—especially anyone who admits to the murders—before booking him or her. Am I right so far?"

"Go on," she said as the twinkle came back into her eyes.

"I've told you before that I'll accept all the help I can get on this case, and I meant it. I do need your help, doctor. I won't withhold *any* information, regardless how irrelevant it may seem, provided you withhold nothing from me. Sound fair?"

"Yes. Continue."

"I'll let you come with me when I interview suspects. I'll tell you which ones are my prime suspects and you can ask them whatever questions you'd like."

"Go on."

"But I want you to promise one thing: you won't investigate a crime scene or talk to a suspect unless I'm with you. Will you promise me that?"

"Are you afraid I might solve the case all by myself?"

He exhaled a long stream of cigarette smoke through his nostrils. "No," he said, shaking his head. "No, not at all."

"But why? Why should I have to promise that I won't investigate on my own?"

"It's quite simple, really. If you think about it, you'll know I'm right."

"I don't see…"

"Sure, you do." He pulled a pistol from his pocket and laid it on the table next to the polluted water glass. "To put it plainly, doctor, I'm armed and you're not."

He could see the dawn of realization in her eyes. It began slowly and then her eyes got gradually bigger and bigger until he thought they'd pop out of their sockets. Somehow it had never occurred to her that she could place herself in mortal danger, that the killer might come after her with deadly claws and tear her apart like those three kids had been torn apart, that Marsha Wade could be killed as quickly and easily as anyone else.

"Look," he said, "we're after a psychopathic killer who's already killed three people and won't have any qualms about killing either of us if we get in her way." He put the .40 caliber Glock back in his inside coat pocket. "So, if you want to play cops and robbers," he said, grinning, "I advise you take along a bodyguard."

"You? You want to be my bodyguard?"

"The city pays me to protect the lives of its citizens."

She laughed. She laughed so hard that tears came to her eyes. He laughed, too, and together they laughed and, for a moment, they forgot about killings and killers and just enjoyed laughing.

"Okay," she said at last. She reached across the table and offered him her hand. "You've got a deal. You promise to guard my body and I'll promise to go nowhere unless you're with me."

After shaking on the deal, she didn't withdraw her hand. He felt her thumb lightly caress the hairs on his fingers. The fear that had transformed her eyes only a moment ago had vanished. In its place he saw trust, respect, and… and… something else.

The twinkle was back, brighter than ever.

And—though he couldn't see it—he knew there was a twinkle in his eyes, too.

Later, when they were in the lab going over the autopsy report together, he told her about Joyce Roberts and the strange feeling he had about Fred and Grace Foltz.

"They're my prime suspects," he said. "Is it possible they're in this together? Could there be two murderers?"

"Anything's possible," she admitted.

"I plan to go back there first thing in the morning and talk to them again. Would you like to come with me?"

"Yes," she said. "What time?"

"I'll pick you up at eight. Will you be at the hospital, or should I pick you up at home?"

"At home," she said. She wrote her address and phone number on a napkin and handed it to him. "I'll be ready at eight."

Her head hurt.

Joyce Roberts sat up in bed and held her head with both bands, pressing her fingernails into the soft flesh of her temples until she wanted to scream. But the throbbing didn't dissipate, the ringing in her ears didn't lessen, the dizziness didn't abate, and the pain wouldn't go away.

It was already completely dark when she began to regain her senses, and even with her eyes wide open she couldn't see an inch beyond her nose. She sat in the darkness and listened to the sounds of the old house. A clock ticked in the hallway outside her room, a faucet dripped in the bathroom at the end of the hallway, an occasional car drove by on the street in front of the house, and she heard footsteps slowly climb the stairs from the basement to the main floor.

Then the footsteps started upstairs to the second floor, getting louder, coming closer.

She knew instantly they weren't her grandfather's footsteps. His arthritis made him limp. She could recognize Fred's footsteps a mile away. Nor were they Grace's footsteps. Grace walked so softly that Joyce had often remarked that Grandmother Grace had cat blood flowing in her veins. Though the footsteps belonged neither to Grandpa Fred nor Grandma Grace, they were nevertheless familiar to Joyce. Each step reminded her strongly of something in her past, something she should easily recognize. But what? Who?

Memories began to flash, unbidden, before her eyes. As if the room were suddenly filled with dazzling light so she could see—as if the events were actually taking place *now* rather than then—images and hear voices and sounds. It was as if she were *there* reliving the experience, as if it were happening now for the very first time.

Ka-thunk!

Robin's skull cracked. Deadly claws cut into her scalp, gouged out deep furrows of flesh, and tore her left ear loose. The ear dangled from the side of her ruined face like a rotten pear from a broken tree branch.

Joyce screamed.

"You're supposed to be asleep," she heard her father say. His voice was surprisingly soft, calm. "Go back to bed."

Joyce screamed again.

"I told you to go back to bed, Joyce," her father whispered. "Do what I say. You wouldn't want to make Daddy mad, would you?"

Joyce couldn't stop screaming.

"Dammit!" Daddy said. "Dammit all to hell!"

Then be raised his hand and the hammer's claws caught the light and Joyce realized what her father was about to do to her and her mind moved faster than his hand and she spun around and ran and ran and ran. She had to find a place to hide where Daddy couldn't find her, someplace where he wouldn't think to look for her, someplace where he couldn't find her and tag her and make her "it" forever.

But where?

This was no ordinary game of hide-and-seek, not like any of the hundreds of hide-and-seeks she'd played with Trevor or Robin or even one of the teenage babysitters Mommie used to hire before Robin became old enough to take over babysitting duties, not like any fantasy she'd innocently concocted in her very vivid six-year-old imagination. This was real. This was not a game. This was playing for keeps.

How her six-year-old mind was able to discern fantasy from reality in such a situation—at such an age—she never knew. As she thought back on it now, she was simply astounded that she'd been able to tell at that vital moment what was real and what wasn't. Surely, no normal person would have expected her father to become a homicidal maniac in the middle of the night. Yet from the moment she saw him raise those deadly claws, she *did* know. Had a single doubt remained in her mind, she would never have survived that night. She'd have been slaughtered like the rest of her family.

Perhaps the shock of having seen her sister's face torn away…

Whatever the reason, she ran and ran until she was out of breath. Her father's footsteps followed her down the hallway, down the stairs, around the corner to the kitchen, down the stairs to the basement. He didn't run. He didn't need to run. He was six feet tall and had a thirty-inch stride. He wasn't even breathing heavily when he reached the bottom of the basement stairs.

"You can't escape, Joyce," he said, switching on all the fluorescent lights in the basement rec room. His voice was self-assured, normal. "Daddy's gonna catch you…"

Oh, no, he isn't! Joyce told herself. I'm not gonna let him find me.

I'm gonna hide so Daddy can't ever find me.

She slipped behind the furnace and worked her way slowly, crawling on her hands and knees, to the safety of her secret hiding place. It was dark and damp and filled with cobwebs, but she didn't care. This was *her* place, the place where no one else could go 'cause they were all too big to fit in the foot-wide, two-foot-high space between the furnace and the cement-block wall at the far end of the basement.

While her father searched the rec room, Joyce had headed straight for her hiding place behind the furnace. She lay in the dark listening to his footsteps.

"Come out, come out, wherever you are," he called.

Joyce was sure her father would eventually find her, but she was equally sure he couldn't reach her with the hammer. Her hidey-hole behind the furnace was barely big enough for a tiny six-year-old. Never in a million years could a grown man squeeze his body through that crawl space. She didn't try to hide her heavy breathing—couldn't, even if she'd wanted to. Her side hurt from all her running and her mouth was dry as cotton from her screaming. But she was still alive and still breathing, and for now that was all that mattered.

Years later, when she was in her early teens, she came across a book by Piaget in Dr. Joshi's office. Piaget, a child psychologist, called six the "magic" age. Sometime around six, he claimed, a child's cognitive development reaches a critical stage. Thereafter, a child can know right from wrong abstractly; a child can reason; and a child can see the relationship between present actions and future consequences. Prior to six, Piaget suggested, the human mind hasn't matured—developed physically—enough to conceptualize such thoughts; infants are more mimics than true thinkers. But around six, something magical happens in the human mind. And Joyce was almost six and a half on the night her father went mad.

She heard his footsteps coming closer and she knew it was only a matter of moments before he found her hiding place. But those moments seemed like hours to the six-year-old.

And then he was there in front of the furnace, his body blocking out what little light seemed to filter back to the far corner of the basement. He was big and powerful and dangerous. She was small, scared, and helpless. But she was six and he wasn't. And that made all the difference.

"Come out," he ordered, waving the hammer. "Come out and I'll give you a present."

She held her breath. Maybe she could make herself invisible and he wouldn't see her.

He turned his back to the crawl space and waved the hammer at shadows in the opposite corner. "Come out, come out," he said again, "wherever you are. Come out and Daddy'll give you a present. It's something special. Something..."

She'd done it! She'd made herself invisible simply by wishing it! He hadn't seen her! She nearly cried aloud with relief.

His footsteps faded as he searched the rest of the basement. From time to time she heard his voice, growing fainter and fainter the farther away he went. "Come out, Joyce. Come and see what I have for you. It's a present. Something you've asked for."

She suddenly realized that her father still thought of her as an infant, someone who could be tricked with the promise of presents. She was still a child, yes. But she was no longer an infant.

Somehow, unbeknownst even to her, she had grown up almost overnight.

Just as her father had gone crazy almost overnight.

Though still unable to verbalize such thoughts, a teenage Joyce Roberts waited in the dark for the sound of footsteps to fade. Only instead of fading, they came closer and closer. Finally, they stopped at the top of the stairs. Right in front of her bedroom door.

Now she was no longer six but almost eighteen. She had played this game before and knew what to do and what not to do. She stayed quiet as a mouse. Her breath stuck in her throat and she thought she'd choke. She wanted to scream, but she didn't.

And then she heard the doorknob on her bedroom door turn, first one way and then, inevitably, the other.

But the door didn't open. It was locked.

For what seemed like an eternity, but could not have been more than merely a minute, Joyce listened to the door being tried again and again.

Then the footsteps moved away from her door. She heard

them—softly, so softly on the hall carpet—walk toward her grandparents' room.

A door creaked open. Joyce thought it sounded more than a little like a coffin lid being closed on a corpse.

And then she heard the one sound she dreaded most in the world, the one sound she had prayed night and day that she would never hear again.

Ka-thunk!

And Joyce began to scream. She screamed and screamed and couldn't stop screaming....

Neighbors called the police.

Because the night was unseasonably warm and windows were left open to catch what little breeze there was in the night air, the girl's screams were heard up to two blocks away.

When ordinary people are awakened from a sound slumber in the middle of the night by the sounds of screams, they naturally call the police. Four black-and-whites immediately responded. All four were on the scene within five minutes of the first call.

By that time the screams had already stopped.

One uniformed officer who entered the house through a basement window stumbled over something in the dark. When he turned on the overhead light and saw the mess splattered on the floor, he couldn't hold back the bile that rose in his throat and spewed out his open mouth like oil from a gushing well. He was violently ill for a long time, unable to control any of the dozen or so spasms that convulsed his body from head to foot. Two of the officers who entered by the unlocked back door rushed upstairs to the second floor, their guns drawn. Two other officers followed closely behind, providing cover and backup.

There were three rooms on the second floor, two bedrooms and a bath. The bathroom door was wide open and one of the officers quickly checked it out, looking behind the shower curtain and searching the linen closet. He signaled to the others that the bathroom was empty.

They split up into two teams, two men to each of the bedrooms. One officer would go in while the other covered the door. Teamwork. Two men to a team. Two teams. That was the way they'd been trained.

One of the bedroom doors was locked. The other one wasn't.

The first team penetrated the unlocked room, found the light switch on the wall next to the door, and flooded the room full of bright light with a simple flick of the switch. They saw a frail-looking old lady lying in a blood-soaked bed. The woman's skull was cracked wide open. Blood and brains still oozed from the wound and it was quite evident she hadn't been dead more than a few minutes, five at the most.

The killer or killers were likely still in the area. If not on the premises, then they were somewhere in the neighborhood.

The second team kicked in the locked door and rushed into the darkened room with their weapons at the ready.

Then the screams began again.

BOOK TWO

A man's dying is more the survivors' affair than his own.

Thomas Mann

CHAPTER ELEVEN

He'd been over every inch of that basement and hadn't seen hide nor hair of his daughter anywhere.

"Come out, come out," Gordon called again and again. "Daddy's got a present for you."

But Joyce didn't come out

He knew she was scared. Who wouldn't be after witnessing what the hammer had done to Robin's no-longer-pretty face?

Gordon decided to leave her alone for a while, give her a chance to cool her heels. Sooner or later she'd have to come out on her own.

Meanwhile, he had other things to do.

Joyce heard his footsteps going upstairs. Was this a trick? Was he trying to make her believe he'd left her alone when he was really waiting patiently at the top of the stairs? If she came out of hiding, would he rush down the stairs and grab her?

She thought she heard the door to the basement slam shut. Then she *did* hear her father's footsteps on the kitchen floor, above her head.

He was really gone. She was safe. Still, she waited ten minutes more before she dared budge from her hidey-hole.

Ever so cautiously she slid from the shadows and crawled forward, ready to retreat at a moment's notice. She finally emerged and was glad to be able to stand up straight again. She stretched the kinks from her arms and legs. She was almost too big to fit into her hidey-hole anymore. Were she a year older, she'd never have made it into the womblike safety of the secret crawl space that had just saved her life. Neither Trevor nor Robin could fit anymore, and soon Joyce wouldn't be able to fit, either.

Barefoot, wearing only a short cotton nightie, she felt naked and vulnerable. How she wished to be able to go back to sleep and simply forget this nightmare!

But she knew she couldn't do that, knew if she went to sleep she'd never ever wake up again. So she rubbed all the sleep out of her eyes with her knuckles, walked softly to the other end of the basement, where the door to Trevor's room was left slightly ajar, and peeked in.

At first she was sure Trevor was sound asleep. His nine-year-old form, curled up quietly beneath the bedsheets, looked no different from that of a dreaming child. Trevor had always been a sound sleeper and nothing short of a bomb blast would wake him in the middle of the night. What little light there was in his room came from a Mickey Mouse nitelite plugged into an outlet near the foot of his bed.

She didn't notice the blood until she had stepped in a puddle pooled on the carpet.

Any hope she'd had of Trevor being able to help was suddenly dashed apart when she saw what little was left of his face. Blood had streamed down both cheeks like tears. His pillow was covered with a gray slime that looked a little like puke in the dim light.

His forehead was dented and cracked like a broken toy.

The top of his head was completely crushed. It was as though a giant had stepped in the middle of Trevor's head and crushed the skull with its oversized foot.

One eye had been gouged out. A pool of blood had collected in the empty socket. Trevor's other eye was wide open. Joyce thought for a moment that Trevor might still, miraculously, be alive. Then she saw that there was no muscular control left in the eye, the eyeball had rolled back, and only a bloodshot white bulged obscenely beneath his brow like a golf ball set on a tee awaiting a number two wood to send it flying.

Joyce didn't doubt that Trevor was dead.

She suddenly remembered the dozens of times she'd seen her brother deliberately step on ants that crawled across their driveway in the summer. Trevor loved to crush them beneath his shoe to hear them crunch. Then he ground them into the concrete with a back-and-forth scraping motion that tore their frail carapaces apart like tissue paper.

"Watch," he'd command. "Watch them squirm. They know they're gonna die. They know they can't get away from me because I'm bigger 'n smarter. All they can do is squirm. And when I'm ready"—he'd lift his foot and bring it down hard—"I crush them and they die."

Joyce would run to Robin's room, squealing in horror at what Trevor had done.

"He's an asshole," Robin would say. "Don't pay any attention to Trevor. He likes it when he can upset you and make you mad."

Joyce was mad at Trevor now. How dare he be dead? How dare he die just when she needed him most? She hoped Trevor had squirmed like an ant before he'd died.

The door from the kitchen to the basement squeaked open and Joyce heard footsteps on the stairs.

There was no place to run, nowhere to hide. She was trapped in Trevor's room, trapped with her brother's hideously mutilated body, cut off from any avenue of escape.

"Daddy has a present for you," she heard her father taunt as he reached the bottom of the stairs.

Her bladder let go and she felt a warm trickle on her leg. She'd wet her pants! She hadn't wet her pants in over a year. She was so embarrassed she could die.

She began to cry.

She was acting like a baby. She hated herself when she acted like a baby.

But Daddy was at the bottom of the stairs now and she could see him standing in the doorway with the hammer in his hand, and she knew she was about to die from something more than embarrassment.

Joyce would die like Robin and Trevor. Her head would be ripped to shreds and her brains would spill out.

But before Daddy could swing the hammer, there was a sound at the back door upstairs in the kitchen. Someone had put a key in the lock and was turning the doorknob.

Mommie! It had to be Mommie!

Then she heard her mother's footsteps on the kitchen tiles. Mommie had come home just in time!

Bad timing, Gordon thought as he brought the hammer down as hard as he could on his six-year-old daughter's head.

Ka-thunk!

He raised the hammer and brought it down again.

Chunk!

And again.

Ka-thunk!

And again and again and again.

"Trevor?"

Gordon could tell Leona was drunk from the tone of her voice. *She's falling-down drunk,* he thought. *That will make things easier.*

"Trevor? What are you doing awake? And what was that noise?"

"I gave the kids a little present," Gordon said. "Want to come down and see?"

"Gordon? What're *you* doing home?"

"Waiting for you. Where were you?"

"I… I had to go out," she said from the top of the stairs.

"At three in the morning?"

"I've been out for awhile."

"Where'd you go?"

"Irene and John's."

"Irene's out of town, isn't she?"

Leona didn't answer.

"Isn't she?" Gordon asked again.

"That's right."

"And you left the kids all alone and went over to John's in the middle of the night?"

"John called and invited me to a party."

"And you went?"

"Yes."

"You left the kids all alone to go to a party?"

"Yes… but Robin was here. She's big enough now to take care of the others by herself."

"Is she?"

"Of course."

"But what if something unusual came up? What if, say, a homicidal maniac wanted to kill the kids? Would Robin know what to do?"

"Don't be a fool," she snarled. Her voice had that nasty edge Gordon had only recently recognized as the real Leona. "I'm tired and I'm going to bed."

"Mind if I join you?" he asked, already knowing the answer.

"I've a headache, Gordon."

"And it's late," he finished for her. "I know. It's always late and you've always got a headache."

She laughed. "You should know by now, dear, shouldn't you? We've been married almost…"

"Thirteen years," he said. "Thirteen long years."

"Yeah," she said, her voice, sounding distant. "Thirteen long years." She paused as though trying to remember. "I guess," she said, "if anyone should know me, you should by now."

"Oh, I do. I do know you, Leona."

"Well, good. Let me go to sleep, then."

"I will," he said. "I'll let you go to sleep. I'll even help you sleep."

He heard her use the bathroom. Water ran in the sink and he knew she was brushing her teeth. Then she leisurely stepped across the floor to where he knew the bed would be. He envisioned her throwing clothes on the floor, taking off her bra, unhooking her nylons from the garters that dangled from a red lace garter belt, rolling the nylons down her legs one at a time, dropping the nylons and her garter belt and soiled panties to the floor by the bed, and crawling naked beneath the sheets.

Gordon had waited long enough.

He looked at his daughter. Her face was a bloody mess. Chunks of her hair had been pulled from her scalp and still clung to the deadly claws of the hammer Gordon held in his hand.

"You're mine," he whispered. "Mine."

He walked out the door and started up the stairs. "No one else will ever have what's mine."

Leona Roberts could barely keep her eyes open. She had been awake since noon, running her fool ass off trying to get everything accomplished before Gordon came back from his business trip.

In the three-and-a-half days since he'd left, she'd managed to sell off most of their investments, turning long-term securities into quick cash. She'd raided safe-deposit boxes, cashed in savings passbooks, and even pawned the diamond necklace her husband had given her for their anniversary. She had a fair-sized nest egg stashed away for the day she left her husband and children behind and ventured off on her own.

That day was going to be tomorrow.

Gordon's coming home early had surprised her. He wasn't due to return from his business trip until next Tuesday. But nothing would stop her now. Not even Gordon.

Especially not Gordon.

When she'd married the bozo thirteen years ago, Gordon Roberts was still a fun-type guy. He loved to party almost as much as she did.

Then she got pregnant and everything changed.

They gave up their single-bedroom Gold Coast condo, bought this Tudor-style monstrosity in the suburbs, and settled down to a boring life that drove Leona right up the walls of the house.

Gordon continued his business travels while Leona was left behind, trapped at home with first one, then two, and eventually, three screaming brats.

None of which were really Gordon's kids.

Her first pregnancy was the result of a trip to Los Angeles. While Gordon was tied up day and night for two weeks of contract negotiations, Leona was left alone in a fancy first-class hotel with lots of free time to try to get into trouble.

And she did. Bored and lonely from sitting alone in her room, she went to the hotel bar for excitement. There she met a man who wined and dined her and took her to his room, where they shared a bottle of French champagne and then a heart-shaped king-size bed.

After she'd worn him out and still wanted more, he introduced her to several of his associates, who took turns trying to satisfy her. Leona never knew which of the six or seven men she'd met in San Francisco was Robin's real father. But the timing had been perfect and she knew it hadn't been Gordon.

Robin looked nothing like Gordon.

And Trevor? Trevor must have happened when Gordon went to New York for that week-long hardware convention ten years ago. Robin was two, old enough to leave with a sitter while Leona spent a night out on the town. She'd made a round of the clubs and singles bars on North Rush Street, looking to get lucky. When she did get lucky, she brought the man back to this house, this bed, and fucked his brains out. Again the timing was perfect. Nine months later, almost to the day, Trevor was born.

Joyce, on the other hand, had to be John's child. John was Gordon's business partner, the man who stayed home to mind the store while Gordon was away on company business. Though John was married, he'd had his eye on Leona for years before he got up the nerve to make a move. While Gordon was in Vegas for another hardware show and Irene—John's wife—was visiting her mother in Dallas, John invited Leona over for a friendly drink.

Leona, of course, was always glad to accept a friendly invitation.

Eventually, she could make John do almost anything: send Gordon out of town when Leona wanted to party, rent a suite at a downtown hotel when Leona wanted to get lucky, watch the kids while Leona went barhopping, give her a loan whenever she needed some mad-money, and keep her company when she got lonely or horny.

John was almost as good-looking as Gordon and Leona liked John a lot. But only in small doses. No one man could ever satisfy her completely. Men were nothing more than play toys, objects Leona used and abused and then discarded.

Just as she was about to discard Gordon after thirteen years of living hell.

She'd married Gordon Roberts because he was handsome and had lots of money, certainly lots compared to her miserly father.

When she told Gordon she was pregnant, he immediately gave up smoking and drinking and demanded that she do the same.

"You've got to be kidding," she told him.

But he wasn't. Next, he required her to stay at home while he continued to travel. During the second trimester she didn't feel much like traveling anyway, so she stayed at home, watched her diet, exercised as much as possible, and delivered a healthy seven-pound-four-ounce baby girl that Gordon adored to pieces.

She never had the heart to tell him the kid wasn't his. God, but Gordon could be naive! But then, all men were. Weren't they?

And women were, too. Look at Irene, dear sweet Irene. John had been screwing around behind her back for years and she never even suspected. Or how about good old Mom? Grace would never have known of Fred's infidelity if she hadn't happened home at just the wrong moment and caught him with his pants down. Women could be just as naive as men, and Leona had to laugh at the whole human race. People believed only what they wanted to believe. They operated on the principle that what they didn't know wouldn't hurt them half as much as what knowing might.

Gordon didn't know that none of the kids were his. And he hadn't been hurt, had he?

And he didn't know that Leona was planning to leave—had planned this for months. She was going to leave him and the kids and head out to sunny California, where she could live high on the hog off the money she'd siphoned from his savings. When she boarded an American Airlines 737 at O'Hare tomorrow afternoon, she'd have more than a hundred thousand dollars tucked in her purse. She'd be free again, free to do whatever she wanted whenever she wanted. No husband. No kids. No responsibility. Just little old Leona and a hundred thousand dollars. And Gordon didn't need to know until after she was long gone. He'd never be able to find her even if he tried.

She heard his footsteps on the stairs and knew he'd soon try to join her in bed. He wouldn't let her sleep. He'd simply rub himself against her body until she responded.

Not tonight. Tonight she wouldn't respond. Tonight she needed to rest up for tomorrow. She'd planned to be gone before Gordon returned from his business trip, wanted to leave with as little hassle as possible; here today, gone tomorrow; no muss, no fuss, no bother. Gordon's surprise homecoming was something she hadn't planned on and didn't want to deal with. Somehow, it reminded Leona of that day Grace came home early from church and found Fred fucking Leona on the floor. It seemed like a bad portent.

But what could go wrong now? Nothing. She'd still be able to sneak out of the house tomorrow afternoon even if Gordon was home. There was nothing he could do to stop her. Was there?

When Gordon entered the room, Leona kept her eyes shut and pretended to be asleep. He approached the bed. She felt his presence towering over her. He stayed standing.

"Are you awake?" he asked.

She didn't answer.

"Aren't you curious why I canceled the rest of my trip and came home two days early?"

Still she didn't answer.

"Irene Koster phoned me today in New York. We had a nice long chat."

Leona tensed. Why would Irene call Gordon in New York? Don't tell me she…

"Irene suspected John of having an affair," he said. Gordon's voice was calm, cool, and emotionless. "Maybe more than one. She hired a private investigator to follow John around. Can you guess what that private investigator reported he saw?"

Leona almost laughed. Maybe Irene wasn't quite so dumb after all.

"He saw you and John spend the night together every time I was out of town and, coincidentally, Irene was away visiting her mother. On several occasions you went to a hotel or motel together. Usually, though, you didn't even bother. You either went to John's house and stayed overnight in his bedroom or you brought him here."

Gordon, it seemed, wasn't quite as dumb as he pretended either. Obviously, he wanted to play an elaborate game of cat and mouse. He wanted to toy with her before he pounced.

"When Irene confronted John with the evidence, John broke down and admitted everything. *Everything*, Leona. He told Irene that you've been blackmailing him."

Gordon's voice had begun to crack. Gone was the cool, calm, self-assured voice with which he'd started this conversation.

"John claims you seduced him. You set him up to become a virtual slave to your every whim by getting him drunk and taking advantage of his vulnerability. Then you blackmailed him, made him pay you a small fortune that he had to steal from the business. I worked hard for that money, Lee. I busted my butt so my family would always be financially secure. And what do you do? You try to steal me blind when I'm not looking."

Gordon was crying now, sobbing like a hurt child.

"Know what else John told Irene? He told her that he'd fathered Joyce. You deliberately got pregnant so you could use it to blackmail him. Is that true?"

Everything had fallen apart. She had to get out of there quickly, had to get dressed and get to the airport and make her getaway. Leona's only way out was to lie, to convince Gordon that John had lied to Irene to save his own marriage. But what about the detective? What kind of evidence did the private investigator have? And had Gordon seen that evidence too?

"Answer me, Lee." Gordon shook her. I know you're awake. If you don't answer, I'll know it's all true."

She was about to speak, to lie. She opened her eyes and saw him standing right next to the bed. He held something in his hand. She squinted her eyes to see what it was.

In a sudden blur of motion, Gordon lifted the object over his head and brought it down directly at her face.

An instant before it hit, she saw what it was.

CHAPTER TWELVE

"We're going to have to stop meeting like this, Carl," Marsha Wade said as she arrived at the crime scene. "People will begin to think we're in love. Where are the bodies?"

"One's in an upstairs bedroom and the other's down in the basement."

"Anybody touch anything?"

Dennis Gustafson, a police department physical evidence specialist, laughed. "You're a day late and a dollar short, doctor," Dennis said. "The beat boys tromped over everything before we got here. Plus, the ambulance boys came and mucked things up even more before Carl arrived to seal off the scene or I got here to snap pictures and look for prints. The ambulance boys carted off our only witness to the hospital about an hour ago."

"A witness? A live witness?"

"She's alive," Carl said. "But maybe she'd be better off dead."

"What?" Marsha stared incredulously at Carl. "I don't believe you said that. If she's alive, we can help her get better. And she can help us, too. When can I see her?"

"When the girl recovers from shock," Carl said. "If she recovers from shock. She was screaming her fool head off but otherwise being unresponsive, acting almost catatonic, when the beat boys broke down the door and barged in."

"She should be out of shock in twenty-four to forty-eight hours," Marsha said. "Sooner, with competent professional care. What hospital did they take her to?"

"Memorial," Dennis offered.

"Then I can check on her at the hospital in the morning. Now, where are the bodies?"

"You can't see them now," Carl said, sounding angry. "You're gonna have to sit down and shut up like the rest of us until the boys upstairs are through with their part of the investigation. Do you understand what I'm saying?"

"No." Marsha stared at Carl as though he were crazy. "I don't understand. I thought you and I had an agreement."

"We did," he said. "But everything's changed."

Marsha sat on the living room sofa and looked as if she were about to cry. "Jesus Christ, Carl," she whispered. "I thought I could trust you."

Carl sat sideways on a straight-back chair in front of her. He pulled a cigarette from his pocket, stuck it in his mouth, and thought twice about lighting it. "Uh-uh," he said, talking around the unlit cigarette dangling from his lips. "Wrong attitude. You can't trust anything or anybody anymore."

"Listen, Carl. You called me at home. You woke me up, got me out of a nice soft bed, asked me to come down here and examine a death scene, and when I get here you tell me to sit down and cool my heels because everything's changed and I can't *trust* you anymore. *What the hell's going on here?*"

She started to shout, her own anger about to reach critical mass. "I've got a right to see those bodies before they're moved. I'm a duly appointed deputy coroner and I have a legal right to keep those bodies from being moved before I examine them."

"Not anymore," Carl said, almost in a whisper.

"Will you please tell me what's going on?"

"The state's attorney took jurisdiction," Dennis said. "The DA's got his own boys bagging the evidence, the county coroner himself is upstairs examining the bodies, and we're out in the cold until they've finished posing for the press."

"Oh, shit!" Marsha looked suddenly pale, as though the blood had drained from her face.

"Grace Foltz, one of the victims," Carl said, still speaking around the unlit cigarette dangling from his lower lip, "went to church with the DA's wife. They'd been friends for twenty years, and Mrs. DA demanded her husband take over the investigation and find the killer."

"In the middle of the, night? How did she know Grace had been killed?"

"Grace missed church services tonight, the first time in twenty years that she didn't make Sunday night services. Mrs. DA was convinced Grace was ill or injured. She tried to phone, repeatedly, and when she got no answer at the house, she called nine-one-one. She kept calling the house, and finally one of the police officers picked up the phone about an hour ago and told Mrs. DA that Grace was dead."

"Then all hell broke loose," Dennis said. "The DA stormed in here and took over the investigation. He called the state crime lab and asked them to send out a team of forensics specialists, guys with Ph.D.'s. Then he got Doc Johnson, the county coroner, out of bed and demanded the old boy do what he'd been elected to do. Can you guess what Johnson did first when he saw the body in the basement?"

"He became ill."

"Yeah. How'd you know?"

"Lucky guess," Marsha said.

"Johnson took one look at the body and threw up over everything. He wasn't the only one to throw up. A rookie cop beat him to it. They contaminated vital evidence by puking in the victim's blood, splattering on footprints, making a mess. Can you believe it?" Dennis shook his head disdainfully. "Guy's supposed to be a *doctor*, for Christ's sake. You'd think a doctor'd be used to the sight of blood."

"Johnson's a politician," Carl interjected. "He used to be a pediatrician before he went into politics. He's been county coroner for eighteen years and hasn't practiced medicine since the day he was elected. He usually leaves the dirty work to assistants and signs off on the reports without ever having to examine a victim himself. This is the first time I've seen him actually at a homicide scene in the twelve years I've been a homicide dick."

"If he's as incompetent as you say, perhaps he'll welcome my help," Marsha suggested.

"I'm sure he'd love to have help," Carl said. "But the DA simply won't allow it. Doc Johnson's stuck on this one. If he admits that he needs help, the DA'll dump him from the party ticket in the spring primary coming up. Without his party's endorsement, Johnson can't get re-elected; and that'd mean he'd have to go out and do an honest day's work again to earn his living, something he doesn't know how to do. No, Marsha. Johnson doesn't dare ask for your help."

"And the real reason," Dennis said sarcastically, "that the DA's here is the election coming up. Otherwise the DA'd simply tell his wife to go to hell, let us locals handle this routinely, and he'd be in bed getting a good night's sleep while we did his dirty work. *But* multiple murders just before an election generate lots of press coverage. The DA wants to give voters the impression he's a take-charge guy and on top of everything. He'll try to milk this for all it's worth." Dennis suddenly slapped his forehead with the palm of his hand. "Oh, shit," he moaned. "I just thought of something."

"What's that?" Marsha asked.

"I bet he'll charge the girl with the murders."

"What girl?"

"Joyce Roberts," Carl said. "Our one and only living witness."

"Do you think she did it?"

"Killed her grandparents?" Carl shook his head. "No. Nor do I think she killed those three kids you already did autopsies on, either."

"Then why would the DA indict her?"

"Because there's sufficient circumstantial evidence to point a quick finger at her. She was found alone at the scene of the crime. And because the DA will prove in court that Joyce was mentally ill at the time of the killings and belongs in a mental hospital rather than jail, he doesn't need to ask for the death penalty. He'll be able to sleep nights even if the girl was innocent because the state will put her away someplace and pay for treatment. And as soon as the doctors declare she's well enough, she'll be released from custody as a free woman."

"Does she belong in a mental hospital?"

"Probably." Carl finally lit his cigarette. "The paramedics said she'd gone into some kind of paranoid withdrawal. They couldn't get her to respond at all."

Marsha sighed "That fits the pattern. Mass murderers are normally either sexual sadists or paranoid schizophrenics. Sometimes they're both."

"Do *you* think the girl's guilty?" Carl asked.

"I don't know. But if she isn't, then there's apt to be other murders.

What will the DA do if someone else is killed the same way?"

"He'll say it's a copycat killer," Dennis chimed in. "He won't admit he's made a mistake. He'll say the murders aren't related, that someone else is trying to get publicity by copying what Joyce Roberts did, and he'll say he's turning the investigation over to us in order to avoid any more publicity that might induce additional murders. Then he'll put the pressure on us to find the killer and to keep everything quiet—put a lid on the whole thing—when we do."

"You don't like politicians, do you, Dennis?"

"No, ma'am. I don't like politicians, I don't trust politicians, and I don't want to be anywhere near them when an election's coming up."

"Doesn't look like you have any choice," Carl said. "You and I are caught in the middle."

"I can quit," Dennis said, holding his chin firm. "I can give them my resignation and look for a job somewhere else."

"Sure you can," Carl said softly. "So can I. But who'd protect the good people in this community if you and I up and quit? The politicians? Don't make me laugh!"

"Maybe it'd serve the people right."

"Maybe," Carl said. "And maybe a lot of those people will die because you and I didn't stop the killer. Think you could live with that?"

"Now come on, Carl. Are you trying to make me feel guilty? I didn't kill anyone."

"But you could help stop the killings." Carl looked around for an ashtray. When he didn't see one, he walked to the front door and tossed the cigarette out to the sidewalk. "And if you don't help stop the killings, you *will* be guilty. Just as guilty as the murderer herself. Just as guilty as the DA and Doc Johnson. Maybe you can't be indicted as an accessory after the fact, but you'll still be guilty in *my* book. If you think you can live with that, then get the hell out of here *right now!*"

Dennis stared in astonishment. Then he clapped Carl on the back and broke out laughing.

"See why I like working with this guy?" Dennis asked Marsha. "He's got his head screwed on straight."

"And this guy's the best tech in the business," Carl said, clapping

Dennis on the shoulder. "We need his help if we're going to catch the killer."

"How do you propose to catch the killer," Marsha asked, "when we're kept from assessing evidence at the scene?"

"We wait," Carl said. "Then, after the DA and his boys have left, we go over everything again with our own fine-tooth combs." Carl leaned closer to Marsha, his lips barely inches from her ear. "I bet we find something, doctor, something that'll lead us to the killer. Some clue that the politicians missed, perhaps. Something the state forensic experts overlooked as unimportant."

Marsha Wade turned her face toward Carl and her lips nearly touched his.

"What makes you so sure?" she asked.

"Because the politicians don't really care," he whispered.

"And we do," Dennis Gustafson said.

"And that makes all the difference, doesn't it?" the doctor said, looking into Carl's eyes.

"All the difference," he said.

Marsha Wade couldn't sleep.

Though she was dead on her feet, her physical reflexes slowed nearly to nonexistence, her mind was racing a mile a minute.

She hadn't felt like this since the early days of her residency. Then she would go three days and three nights without sleep before she collapsed.

Other residents depended on drugs—Dexedrine or Benzedrine—to stay awake and alert. But Dr. Marsha Wade didn't need to do drugs. A naturally hyperactive pituitary stimulated her body and mind and drove her to obsessive excesses of performance that earned praise from her professors and opened doors that normally were closed to women. Someday, she knew, the terrible toll on her body would manifest itself. She'd grow old before her time, be worn out and used up at forty-five or fifty. But for now, she was belle of the ball and the best in the business and she was capable of doing things that others couldn't and her mind was racing….

Her body demanded sleep, literally ached for it. Her mind knew sleep was necessary, that the human machine couldn't run at high speed for more than fifteen hours at a time without burning itself up.

But she couldn't sleep.

After State's Attorney Randall Drew held his news conference on Fred Foltz's front lawn and announced that Joyce Roberts would be charged with killing her grandparents, the press, politicians, state forensic specialists, and uniformed police officers finally called it a night and left.

Both bodies had been bagged and removed to the county morgue.

Detective Sergeant Carl Erickson was responsible for securing the house until midmorning when the state boys would be back to reexamine the crime scene. Meanwhile, he had the whole house to himself.

While Carl locked the doors, Marsha and Dennis went right to work. They combed the basement for clues, took specimen samples of congealed blood, noted the broken light bulb in a ceiling fixture, photographed a bloody hammer found near a pile of clothes in a corner, dusted an empty toolbox for prints, and found that the area had been so contaminated by footprints and vomit that they couldn't determine what prints or body fluids were the victims', the killer's, or the previous investigators'.

Carl met Dennis and Marsha on the stairs and all three examined the bedrooms together.

"The door was broken by the first officers on the scene," Carl said. "The door was locked when they arrived."

"This is the girl's room?"

"Yeah. They found her huddled in the bed, completely incoherent. She was in such a state of shock that she mistook the investigating officers for her father."

"Her father?"

"Her father's been dead for twelve years. He killed himself."

"Killed the rest of the family, too," Dennis said. "According to the DA, the father went bananas and hacked his entire family to pieces. Then he shot himself in the head with both barrels of a shotgun."

"Hacked his family to pieces? With an ax?"

"With a hammer," Carl said softly. "A claw hammer."

"He hit the girl, too," Dennis added. "But somehow she survived."

"Disfigured?"

"Not that I could tell when I met her," Carl said. "In fact, she was a rather good-looking girl, if I remember correctly. But Elaine Flanders claimed Joyce Roberts had ugly scars all over the rest of her body."

"The DA said she'd had plastic surgery," Dennis interjected. "He claimed she'd suffered terrible psychological trauma induced by the nature of her injuries. Extensive psychological counseling and cosmetic reconstruction were necessary to make her appear normal. She was in and out of hospitals for almost ten years. Her grandmother home-schooled her until two years ago. The DA claimed the trauma of seeing her family murdered and then being hit on the head with a hammer herself eventually drove her crazy and caused her to do this terrible thing to her grandparents. Anyway, that's what the DA told the press."

"It's entirely possible," Marsha admitted. "Maybe the DA is right. Maybe he already has the real killer in custody, and we're only wasting our time looking for someone else."

"Maybe," Carl said. "But we've got to be sure, don't we? Wasn't that what you wanted me to learn from that story you told? If the DA's wrong, then the real killer is still on the loose. And if the killer's already struck twice, he or she will probably strike again. Can we let that happen? Can we even afford to take the chance?"

They worked for nearly six hours, going over everything in detail. When the crime lab boys returned, Carl stayed at the house and followed them around.

Dennis drove Marsha home.

She undressed and showered. It was Marsha's fourth shower in just under twenty-four hours, and the water revitalized her tired body better than any magic elixir ever invented.

Wearing a cotton terrycloth bathrobe, she sat at the tiny desk in her living room and made notes on long sheets of a yellow legal tablet. If there were patterns to the murders, she knew she had to find them and tell Carl. The killer had struck twice in one day, and it was only a matter of time before he or she struck again.

What Marsha had seen in the Foltz house had convinced her that Carl was right. Joyce Roberts wasn't the killer.

The killer was still at large.

Leona Roberts slept like a baby.

Curled up in a fetal ball, her thumb just inches from an open mouth oozing spittle, Leona dreamt of her childhood.

Mother was there, of course, in Leona's dreams. Grace Foltz had been a beautiful woman in her youth. Soft, warm, beautiful, and happy.

Dad was there, too. He was young and handsome, the muscles in his strong arms rock-hard as he held her. His hair was short and blond and still all there. He looked more like a Teutonic demigod than a truck mechanic. Even he was happy, and he didn't drink much then—certainly, never enough to get drunk.

Oh yes! Those were happy times. The happiest of all times. Leona liked to return to those times in her dreams. Life was so simple then and so beautiful. Leona herself was young and innocent and cute and the center of attention. She could make Mother and Dad do anything she wanted simply by crying or cooing or crawling. Life was just that simple.

And then, slowly, everything began to change.

This was the part of the dream she hated. She grew up, Mommy and Daddy grew older, Daddy worked lots of overtime so they could afford a new house, Leona spent all day in school, Mommy spent Sunday morning in church and made Leona go with her, Daddy spent Saturday night getting drunk and Sunday mornings sleeping off his hangovers, Mommy began attending church during the week as well as on Sundays, Daddy bought their house and they all moved in, Daddy worked more overtime to pay for the house, Mommy went to church more, Daddy drank more and more, Leona spent more and more time by herself, Mommy spent more and more time at church, Leona refused to go to church anymore and Mommy got mad, Daddy got mad at Mommy for getting mad at Leona, Mommy got mad at Daddy for drinking so much, Daddy got mad at Mommy for going to church too much, and there were no more happy times ever.

Leona ceased being the center of attention, found it increasingly difficult to get anything—much less everything—she wanted, and crying only brought harsh words and "Can't you act your age?" and "I'm much too busy to talk" and "We can't afford that" and "Daddy's not feeling well, don't bother him" and "I'm late for church" and... and Leona began to doubt that she was cute, cuddly, or worth loving…

… until the night her father caught her in the bathroom…

… and she learned a new way of getting attention, love, and everything else she wanted.

Oh, if only she could have remained a little girl *forever!*

And then, when Gordon hit her with that hammer, it was as if she'd suddenly become a child again. When she awoke in the hospital, she was waited on hand and foot every time she cried.

She was fed, washed, talked to, and cared about. She slept, ate, and dreamt. She needed for nothing.

Life was simple again.

Simple.

But not beautiful.

Not beautiful at all.

She'd spent nine years in a deep coma, constantly reliving the dreams of her childhood, totally unaware of her surroundings. The doctors had given her up for dead, said it was only a matter of time before she expired, and little was done to reconstitute her features or even to prolong her life. When Fred Foltz refused to pay for treatment, she became a ward of the state. They transferred her from a hospital intensive care ward to an institution for terminally ill indigents. She languished there for nine years before she awoke.

When she came out of her coma, she cried.

And that brought her all kinds of attention.

Doctors, nurses, physical therapists, neurosurgeons, even psychiatrists got into the act. They examined her, measured her, and studied her. They pricked her with needles, probed her with instruments, and provoked her with ten thousand questions she couldn't answer.

The hammer had damaged her corpus callosum and she was unable to coordinate the two halves of her brain. Her left hand didn't know what her right hand was doing. Though she recognized questions and wanted to answer, that part of her brain which coordinates thought and speech—the executive control center of the forebrain—had also been irreparably damaged and Leona Roberts didn't know how to say what she meant. She had to learn, all over again, how to vocalize her thoughts.

Recovery was gradual. She suffered a horrible relapse the first time she saw her face reflected in a mirror and she had to be sedated for days on end. She was transferred to a state mental hospital, where doctors misdiagnosed her condition and declared her hopelessly schizophrenic.

She spent two years in the mental hospital, locked up and restrained for her own safety. On numerous occasions she had tried to tear the flesh from her face with her fingernails, ripping and pulling as though trying to remove a Halloween mask that was glued to her skin. "It's not my face!" she wanted to scream. But the words came out of her mouth as, "How do you do? I'm pleased to meet you."

They tried to help her with drug therapy, but there was no appreciable improvement in her condition. Finally, they settled for sedation in order to keep her from hutting herself.

She slept. And as she slept, she dreamt the dream of her childhood again and again. It was a happy dream and Leona was a happy person.

And then the state experienced a significant budget crunch and the money that supported mental institutions was severely reduced, slashed fifty percent or more in an unprecedented attempt to forestall a tax increase. The facility that housed Leona Roberts was ordered to release all nonviolent inmates, those that posed no threat to society, by the end of the fiscal year.

There was nothing in Leona's medical history that held a hint of her potential to do violence to others, only to herself. And since she hadn't tried to claw her face in fifteen months, she was reclassified from "hopelessly schizophrenic" to "mentally deficient" and released to the care of a social service on the north side of Chicago.

She stayed in a halfway house for two weeks, adjusting to the real world in a way that pleased her social worker and made her seem eccentric but harmless. Leona's bed sores had completely healed, her misshapen head was covered with makeup and a wig, and she walked and sometimes even talked like a normal human being. Her responses to questions were slow and thoughtful, similar to the way a stroke victim might talk. But nothing in Leona's demeanor revealed the inner struggle between the two halves of her battered brain.

"She seems more like a child than a forty-four-year-old woman," the social worker wrote in her report to the state. "She has a hard time adjusting to reality, prefers to live in the fantasy world of daydreams, and spends hours staring off into space as though she were seeing something the rest of us are incapable of seeing. But that is to be expected, considering the nature of her trauma. Overall, she is making excellent progress. Because of her limited attention span and difficulties in concentration and communication, Leona Roberts is unemployable and will remain a welfare recipient for the foreseeable future, possibly for the remainder of her natural life. The terrible scars and misshapen features of her face will always be a handicap to her complete reintegration into society, but I feel she is strong enough to live on her own with only minimal supervision. I have found a small room for her in an uptown tenement that she can afford with her welfare stipend. I will see her twice a month for follow-up evaluations."

The next day Leona Roberts disappeared. But because there are thousands of women like Leona Roberts walking the uptown streets of Chicago, no one paid any attention to another middle-aged, slightly odd, rather unattractive figure hurrying to an El stop. Nor did anyone, as preoccupied with their own affairs as are most Chicagoans, notice which train she boarded. No one noticed, and no one cared.

Nor did Irene Koster, wealthy wife of the owner of K & R Industries, notice when her telephone rang. She had a housekeeper who took care of little details like answering the door or telephone during the day.

Nor did the housekeeper pay much attention to the caller who said, "Hello. How are you?" and when the housekeeper responded that she was fine, the woman caller said again, "Hello. How are you?" as if she were a recording. The housekeeper merely hung up on her.

That night, shortly before midnight, Leona Roberts hid in the bushes that surrounded the large yard to the rear of the Kosters' suburban ranch-style house. The neighborhood hadn't changed significantly in the eleven years since she and Gordon had owned a two-story Tudor three blocks down the street.

She waited patiently, her mind slipping occasionally back to comforting dreams of the way things were. When all the lights in the house, including the lights in the master bedroom, were out and the house was completely dark, she made her move.

She entered the side door of the two-car garage that was attached to the house. John, whether lazy or forgetful, had never bothered to lock that door in the past. Old habits were hard to change and the garage side door was still left unlocked.

Leona walked to the tool bench that ran the length of the far wall. Various hand tools were mounted on pegboard over the back of the bench: pliers, screwdrivers, wrenches, hacksaws. In the darkened garage, she had to identify each by touch, running her fingertips delicately over each tool until she came to the hammers.

She passed by the ball-peens, the mallets. They weren't what she was looking for.

Then her hand touched the hard steel of twin claws and she smiled in the darkness, yanking the head of the hammer free from the pegboard and hefting the hammer in her hand.

Still smiling, she walked to the door that connected the garage to the kitchen. She was fully prepared to smash the door to pieces with the hammer if the door were locked, but when she turned the knob, the door swung open to admit her as though she were a member of the family. In a matter of minutes, she was in the Koster bedroom, standing over the bed, the hammer in her upraised hand.

Ka-thunk!

Irene was first. Her skull cracked as the claws connected with her scalp. Her body jumped and twitched, but she didn't cry out. The impact snapped her neck and she died instantaneously.

But the noise and movement made John sit up in bed. He wasn't fully awake yet, his breath heady with the aroma of alcohol, and he couldn't see much at all in the darkened bedroom. His hand felt the bed, made contact with his wife's body, and he tried to wake her with gentle nudges to her midsection.

"Irene?" he whispered when she didn't respond.

And then the hammer hit his head with a force that sent his toupee flying clear across the room. Blood gushed from the wound in his temple and he screamed in pain.

The second blow hit him in the mouth. His teeth broke into tiny fragments and blood flooded his throat, stopping the scream so abruptly that none of the neighbors knew the night had been invaded by violence. The scream died in his throat before John Koster could die in his bed.

The third blow took off the skin of his nose before the deadly claws buried themselves in his left eye. Hard steel penetrated the brain behind his eye socket and John Koster's misery ended as quickly as it had begun.

He never felt the blows that followed.

When Leona had finished her handiwork, she searched the house for things she could use. She packed a suitcase with several of Irene's best dresses, handfuls of undergarments, and bottles of perfume and makeup. She found Irene's purse, discovered a hundred and sixty-three dollars and eighty-two cents in her wallet, and lo-and-behold a set of car keys to the Cadillac parked in the garage.

She found John's billfold in the back pocket of a pair of trousers draped over a chair. There were six one-hundred dollar bills, two fifties, and five or six smaller bills in the billfold.

You owe me this, one half of her mind told the mutilated bodies on the bed.

"I'm fine, how are you?" was what came out of her mouth. "I'm pleased to meet you," she added, unable to control the sequence of words the other half of her mind found appropriate. "What do you think about the weather?"

Fifteen minutes later she swung the gold-colored Caddy onto a westbound entrance ramp of the Northwest Tollway.

Three hours after that she parked the car in front of the Fred Foltz residence in Riverdale, Illinois.

Shortly after dawn on that Saturday morning, Leona Foltz—she no longer thought of herself as Leona Roberts—saw the man she barely recognized after all these years as her father open the sliding glass patio door and step outside for an invigorating breath of early morning air, and one half of her heart filled with love while the other half overflowed with hate.

It had taken Leona Foltz twenty-five years to return to this physical home of her childhood dreams.

But before she could make her happy dream real, before everything could be beautiful and happy again, there was still something very important she must do.

That old man, his wife, and their granddaughter—and anyone else they came in contact with and might contaminate with their filthy lies—had to die.

The same way that John and Irene, who had contaminated Gordon with their lies, had died.

Then and only then, would she finally be free to be the child she once was—innocent, beautiful, cared-for, loved.

And no one would remain alive to say that Leona Foltz had grown up to be less than perfect. And the happy dream could be real forever.

CHAPTER THIRTEEN

"I still can't believe it," said a stunned Claire Kelly. "I never imagined that a student at West, someone we knew, could turn into a cold-blooded killer. I mean, who would have thought that Joyce Roberts was capable of doing such a thing?"

"Oh, come on, Claire," Ellie Flanders grunted, obviously tired of Claire's whining. "We all knew she was crazy, didn't we? I mean, has she ever acted normal? Has she ever done any of the things normal people do? Christ, Claire, don't be such a retard! You're almost as retarded as Joyce."

"We knew Joyce was different," Linda Michaels admitted. Linda scooped a handful of peanuts from a plastic bowl and popped the peanuts one by one into her mouth. "But none of us knew she was really *crazy*. Not until now anyway."

The three girls were gathered at the Flanders' poolside patio. Ellie's parents had gone to their usual Monday night church bingo game and wouldn't be home until midnight. The girls had the house and pool all to themselves, and Ellie had already raided her parents' liquor cabinet. All three girls were rapidly getting drunk on expensive brand-name brandy.

"We're lucky *we* weren't killed, too," Claire whined. She tossed back the last of her snifter and refilled the glass. "Just think, if we hadn't left when we did, we'd be dead just like Sharon and Tony and Johnny."

"If we hadn't left when we did, maybe Tony, Johnny, and Sharon would still be alive," Linda Michaels said. "Ever think of that? We could have stopped her. All of us together could have stopped Joyce from killing anyone at all."

"Don't blame us!" snapped Ellie. "We're not responsible for what a crazy person did!"

"Aren't we?" Linda asked. Her voice sounded dreamy after four joints and two large snifters of brandy.

"Maybe if we hadn't laughed," Claire suggested. "If we hadn't gone along with your crazy stunt to get even with Tony, maybe it wouldn't have happened."

"Oh, Christ!" Ellie got up from her deck chair and paced back and forth in front of the pool. "I refuse to feel guilty about something I didn't do. Joyce was crazy. Period. End of sentence. There was nothing that you or I or anyone could have done or not done that would have kept her from killing Tony or John or Sharon. Didn't you hear the district attorney say Joyce was severely traumatized as a child? Didn't he blame Joyce's father for her psychosis? Why do you insist that we should feel guilty about this?" Ellie stripped off her T-shirt and shorts. Underneath, she wore a high-fashion string bikini that highlighted her big breasts and trim hips. "I'm going in for a swim. Anyone else want to cool off?"

"I didn't bring a swimsuit," Claire said.

"Who cares?" Ellie untied the knot at her hip. "No one's going to see us. It's too dark. Besides, Dad put up that redwood fence all around the back yard and the neighbors can't see a thing. I go skinny-dipping all the time. That's why I don't have any tan lines."

Claire took off her T-shirt. Beneath her jeans she wore see-through nylon panties. "I'm going to keep these on," she said, snapping the elastic waistband of her panties.

"Suit yourself," Ellie punned. She bunched her string bikini into a ball and tossed it onto a deck chair. Then she walked to the deep end of the pool, moonlight gleaming on her naked skin, and dove into the cool water without saying another word.

"Aren't you coming?" Claire asked Linda.

"I'm going to smoke another joint," Linda said. "Go ahead. I'll jump in later."

"Promise?"

Linda laughed. "Look," she said, "if it'll make you feel any better, I'll take off my clothes now." She slid out of her T-shirt and shorts. Braless, her breasts looked no larger than any one of the myriad pimples that dotted Linda's shoulders and back. Linda slipped her fingers under the elastic of her panties and pulled them down and off. She tossed them to Claire. "I'll even do you one better and get completely naked. Just leave me alone to do another joint and finish my drink."

Claire stared at the thick patch of pubic hair between Linda's legs.

"I've got a hormone imbalance," Linda admitted quickly. "A lot of teenagers develop differently than the norm. I have tiny tits and a thick thatch. By the time I'm twenty, I'll have breasts as big as yours."

"Mine aren't big," Claire lied. She ran her hands under the curve of her breasts. "Ellie's are bigger."

"Maybe," Linda said.

"I don't have much hair," Claire said. She slid her pants down her thighs. "You've got twice as much as me."

"It'll grow," Linda said. She drained her glass of brandy. "Believe me, it'll grow. Consider yourself lucky to be blonde. You don't have to shave your legs as often as the rest of us do."

"I shave my legs."

"Every day?"

"No."

"Then be grateful. I have to shave every day."

"Can't you use Nair?"

"Depilatories don't work. Not on me, anyway."

"Not at all?"

"Not at all."

Linda and Claire looked at each other with envy. Linda's body lacked what Claire's offered. Claire's lacked what Linda's offered. Put them together and they'd be almost perfect.

"Go swim," Linda said at last. She refilled her glass from the nearly empty liter bottle of Grand Marnier. "I'll be in as soon as I finish another joint."

Claire slipped both feet through her panties and threw the thin nylon aside. Naked, she felt vulnerable and frightened. "Promise?" she asked.

"I promise," Linda said, sipping her drink. "I want to get good and high—or good and drunk—before I hit the water."

"Okay," Claire said. She walked to the edge of the pool and stared into the dark depths, trying in vain to decipher if there was a pattern to the decorative Italian tiles at the bottom. She decided to dive to the bottom and take a closer look. "Ready or not," she challenged Ellie, "here I come."

"Come on in," Ellie coughed, spitting water from her mouth. "The water's fine."

Linda Michaels took a sip of her brandy. As Claire leapt from the deck and disappeared beneath the dark surface, Linda breathed a sigh of relief.

Her fingers sought the moist slit between her legs and rubbed it raw.

With everything that had happened in the last twenty-four hours, she needed to find release. Before she could come, however, a hammer hit her head and separated her mind from her body. Linda was already dead when the release came.

Claire caught Ellie's ankle. She felt the need to hold on, to keep contact with another human being. Ellie was the leader, had always been the leader since the three of them had entered high school. Before that, Linda had been the leader.

All through grade school and junior high, Linda was the strongest of the three. Not only was Linda's father a vice president at First City Bank, but Linda was smarter than Ellie and Claire put together. Linda's IQ in seventh grade was 152, well into the genius range. Ellie came second with an IQ of 135. Claire was last with a Stanford-Binet score of 110, barely above average.

But Claire was beautiful, as well-developed at twelve as Ellie was at eighteen. Claire attracted the boys while Linda and Ellie took advantage of the leftovers.

Claire was a blonde beauty whose body brought boys close enough for Linda and Ellie to ensnare. Linda had lost her virginity at fourteen. Ellie had lost hers at fifteen.

Claire was still a virgin at seventeen.

Maybe she wasn't as smart as Linda or even Ellie, but Claire was smart enough to graduate from high school in the top third of her class. She'd earned a scholarship at Normal and wanted to be an elementary education teacher when she eventually graduated from college. She fit into society better than either of her friends, and they tolerated her stupidity because she possessed many of the survival skills they both lacked. Linda, Ellie, and Claire had been a trio for as long as she could remember. And though Ellie and Linda both vied for control, Claire was content to play second or third fiddle. She knew her limitations and could live with them.

Now she needed to be close to the leader. She was certainly insecure, needing desperately to feel protected from the same fate that had befallen her friend Sharon. No one was safe. Only Ellie possessed the power to protect her from harm. Maybe, by holding on to Ellie's body, Claire could come out of this whole nasty affair alive. Maybe. It was all she had to hang on to.

Ellie surfaced with Claire clinging to her ankle. She spit and sputtered and prepared to dive again. But before she could head underwater, something hit her on the head.

Stunned, she floundered for the edge of the pool. Her fingernails scraped terrazzo tiles, tried to grip the slimy, wet surface to pull herself up. If she could get a fingerhold, perhaps she could pull herself from the pool before she drowned. Ellie feared death by drowning more than any other way of dying. She'd much rather be burned at the stake than drowned in water.

A second blow broke her fingers, shattering the bone from knuckles to nails.

A third blow cut into her brain. Something sharp fractured her skull and filled her head with excruciating pain. She struggled to stay afloat and couldn't.

Claire Kelly was dragging her down.

She kicked Claire in the face. Claire's hand released Ellie's ankle.

Ellie tried to swim, found that her limbs refused to obey a simple request for motion, and felt her body sink slowly to the bottom of the pool. Air bubbles escaped her mouth as she tried to scream.

Claire Kelly struggled to the surface of the pool even as Ellie sank to the bottom. Her lungs threatened to burst. She'd been underwater more than two minutes and she desperately needed a breath of air.

Her hair had barely broken the surface of the water when a heavy weight seemed to descend on her head.

Claire never knew what hit her.

When Carl called shortly after midnight, Marsha wasn't a bit surprised to learn that the three new victims were also close acquaintances of the first three victims.

Though mass murderers don't always know their victims well, selection is seldom completely random or coincidental. Victims have a psychological or symbolic significance to the killer or killers, and sooner or later a definite pattern emerges that neither victims nor killers are consciously aware of. In this case, their association with Joyce Roberts seemed to be the common denominator. Though Joyce was still unconscious and was now in protective custody in a hospital bed and couldn't be the killer, she was obviously the key to solving this intriguing puzzle. Since Joyce knew all eight victims, it was reasonable to assume that Joyce might also know the killer.

And it was reasonable to assume that the victims—some if not all—might be mere victims of opportunity, substitutes for the real intended victim. The killer was driven to commit these atrocities as a form of retribution. If the killer couldn't strike directly at the intended victim, then the killer would strike symbolically at the victim's friends and relatives. Eventually, the killer would reach his or her intended victim and the spree would end, the violence would stop. One final murder and then the killer would commit suicide. That was the usual pattern in most spree killings.

And no one would ever know the real reasons for the killing spree that had claimed so many lives. The killings would end. And law enforcement officials would simply label the case closed.

Was Joyce the ultimate intended victim? If she was, being in protective custody would prevent the killer from reaching her. And that meant the killer would kill again and again until Joyce was available to end it all.

Meanwhile, anyone who had anything at all to do with Joyce Roberts was in jeopardy. Friends, family, acquaintances were all potential targets. Even Carl Erickson, who had interviewed Joyce yesterday afternoon, could become a victim. Marsha was stunned. The realization that Carl could be a victim suddenly hit home. It *was* possible. Carl had had recent contact with the Roberts girl and that made him a prime target. She wanted to warn him, to tell him to be careful. She was suddenly aware how much she cared for Carl and it frightened her. She didn't want to lose him.

"I'll be by to pick you up in fifteen minutes," Carl told Marsha on her cell phone. "The DA and Dr. Johnson gave this one to us. They don't want to admit there's any connection to Foltz or Roberts. Drew's already committed to crucifying Joyce for the deaths of her grandparents. But with her in custody, he can't see the forest for the trees."

Carl eased the unmarked squad car into the flow of expressway traffic. He hadn't slept in nearly forty hours and his reflexes were slow and sluggish. He drove as carefully as possible, keeping a cautious eye open for late-night drunks weaving home from the bars. His own exhaustion manifested itself in the same kind of delayed response to the world around him he had exhibited during his drinking days. He felt as if he were drunk himself, a danger to everyone on the highway. He didn't dare exceed the speed limit.

The past two days seemed no more real to Carl than a dream, a nightmare. Perhaps he would awaken in the morning to discover everything returned to normal: no one murdered, no homicidal maniac running around with a claw hammer, no mountain of paperwork awaiting his attention. Maybe he should simply turn around and go home. Wouldn't it be wonderful to just go home and go to sleep?

He found himself falling asleep at the wheel as the right front tire left the pavement and bounced on the gravel shoulder. A moment later and he'd have hit a drainage ditch at forty-five miles an hour, fast enough to overturn the car and injure or kill the driver. He pulled back onto the highway just in time, barely missing a dark-colored Toyota that was right on his tail.

Carl honked his horn and the Toyota sped by in the left lane. Carl noticed that the tailgater had neglected to turn on his headlights and that explained why Carl hadn't seen him sooner. Flashing his brights on and off, Carl tried to attract the driver's attention. But the Toyota sped on and disappeared in the distant dark still without turning on lights.

"Damn fool," Carl muttered, referring to himself as much as the Toyota driver. His close call had been pure stupidity.

What if he'd hit the ditch? What if the squad car flipped over and he'd been killed? What if he'd also accidentally hit that Toyota and killed the Toyota's driver as well as himself?

He imagined himself on an autopsy table, the beautiful Dr.

Marsha Wade standing over his body. Were there tears in her eyes as she touched the scalpel to his torso?

"Don't cry," he wanted to tell her. But if he were dead, he wouldn't be able to say a word.

Though he'd known her for only a day and a half, he felt closer to Marsha Wade than any other living being. Only his mother had ever meant as much. And his mother was dead.

Carl was confused about his feelings. After his mother's death, Carl had immersed himself in his work to forget he had feelings. He'd overcome his emotions, dealt dispassionately with day-to-day encounters, and kept his personal life as uncomplicated as possible.

Then he met Marsha Wade and she'd rekindled a fire he had deliberately extinguished long ago. She had made his personal life complicated again.

Besides being beautiful and sexy, Marsha Wade was someone very special. She was not only the most beautiful woman Carl had ever seen, she was also one of the smartest. She was a medical doctor, a physician, and he was merely a dumb cop. There was a six-year age difference in their ages, and there was also an eight or nine-year education gap. Carl had another year of part-time undergraduate work before he'd earn his BA in criminology. Marsha already had her doctorate in medicine and she possessed impressive postgraduate credentials from prestigious research institutions.

If Dennis Gustafson hadn't been watching, Carl would have tried to kiss Marsha Wade last night. His lips had been close enough to hers, and she hadn't backed away. Carl was sure she wanted him to kiss her. But Carl had been acutely aware that Dennis was there, and Carl, not Marsha, was the one to quickly back away. Marsha was a medical doctor, and Carl was only a cop. He was a fool to think she could be interested in anything other than a professional relationship.

Resuming a professional attitude, Carl had tried to maintain a discreet distance between himself and the doctor the rest of the night. He hesitated to get anywhere close to her. He didn't want to make a damn fool out of himself. What if he had misread the signs. Maybe she was only playing him so he'd let her be part of the investigation. He knew he was too tired to think straight. But he couldn't stop thinking about Marsha Wade.

He was on his way to her apartment. She was waiting for him to pick her up. He felt like a teenager going out on his first date.

Preoccupied with his thoughts of Marsha Wade, Carl Erickson didn't notice the same dark Toyota that had passed him without lights now parked on the shoulder of the expressway.

Nor did he notice when the import pulled into his lane two car lengths behind him. The Toyota picked up speed. Before long it was right on his tail.

Dressed in jeans and a T-shirt, Marsha Wade waited impatiently for Carl to arrive. He was already five minutes late and she was worried.

Marsha was worried that the killer had already targeted Carl as a victim. The killer was crazy, psychotic, driven by the need to destroy. If the killer believed Carl stood in the way of the killer's reaching the real victim, Carl could easily become the killer's next victim.

And even if Carl was armed, he didn't stand a chance against a determined psychotic. When her doorbell rang, Marsha rushed to the window. She saw Carl's car parked outside.

"Thank God!" she breathed in relief and went to open the door.

Leona watched with interest as a young woman opened the apartment door and invited the detective inside. Leona debated breaking into the apartment and killing them both, smashing them to smithereens with one of the two hammers she had on the front seat beside her. It wouldn't be easy getting into the apartment and she wouldn't be able to take them by surprise as she had all the others. Besides, the detective was probably armed. She decided to wait for a better opportunity.

She started the Toyota and pulled away from the curb. Two blocks past the apartment she turned on the headlights and headed for the expressway.

She'd stolen the Toyota from Fred Foltz. The keys to the car were on her father's household key ring along with the keys to the old Jeep that Fred owned. The Toyota was one of several cars Fred had parked in his work garage behind the Foltz house. Leona was sure the car belonged to a family friend who had left it for Fred to fix in his spare time, probably needing only something minor like a tune-up or new brake shoes. The Toyota was far less conspicuous than John Koster's stolen Cadillac. She'd wisely abandoned the Cadillac Sunday evening after killing Fred and Grace. The Toyota got much better gas mileage than the Caddy.

She'd seen Fred driving the Toyota Saturday night. She'd followed him to the high school, where he waited in the parking lot for Joyce and her date to leave the prom. She'd followed Fred following Joyce and her boyfriend to the apartment on Second Street. Unfortunately, she'd fallen asleep—slipped into her happy-time dream—while waiting for the right opportunity to kill her father, and when she awoke, the Toyota was gone. She'd walked upstairs to the apartment hoping to find Joyce still there, but Joyce was gone too.

She'd killed the three kids because, as friends of Joyce, they were tainted by association. She'd killed the three girls tonight because they, too, were tainted by association.

And she'd kill the detective and his girlfriend for the same reason. Then she'd go after Joyce and put an end to the killings once and for all by bashing her daughter's brains with the hammer.

It was all Gordon's fault that this had to go on so long. If that fool Gordon hadn't flubbed the killings twelve years ago—if Leona and Joyce had been killed instead of merely maimed—then none of this would be necessary. It would have been over and done with then and there. Finished. Kaput. Ended.

Shortly after recovering from her nine-year coma, she'd been told that she and Joyce were the only survivors of Gordon's debacle. Gordon himself had blown his brains out with a shotgun, unable to find any better way to accomplish the job. She'd tried to imagine Gordon with both barrels stuck in his mouth as he strained to reach the twin triggers and finally succeeded. Too bad he couldn't have used a hammer on himself as he did the rest of the family. Too bad he wasn't still alive so Leona could have her revenge. She'd love to give him a taste of his own medicine.

But no, it was better this way. With everyone else gone, Leona was free to recreate her past through the happy dream. There was no one left to remind her that the dream had to end. Only Joyce remained to remind her that childhood eventually ended for everyone. Only

Joyce and everyone she contaminated through association.

It was almost over, this nightmare that kept her from the happy dream. Soon Joyce would be dead and Leona could finally forget about reality and dream the happy dream forever.

But first she had to kill the rest of Joyce's friends. Gary Brandt was next.

CHAPTER FOURTEEN

"Dennis can take care of the details at the Flanders place," Carl suggested, sipping coffee in Marsha's kitchen to wake up. "Why don't you stay home and catch up on your sleep tonight so you'll be bright-eyed and bushy-tailed to tackle the bodies tomorrow at autopsy?"

"You look like you need sleep worse than I do," Marsha said. "Are you sure you can drive?"

"I'll be okay," he said.

Marsha grabbed her purse and slung it over her shoulder. "I'm going, too," she said. "I want to make sure you *do* come back."

"I will," he said.

"I want to make sure you come back alive," she said.

"Worried about me?" he asked.

"Yes," she admitted. "You might be next on the killer's list."

"What makes you say that?"

"It looks to me like this killer is systematically eliminating everyone who had contact with Joyce Roberts immediately before the killings at the Foltz house. You talked to Joyce in that house the day Mr. and Mrs. Foltz were killed. You could be the next target."

"You really think so?" he asked.

"Yes," she said. "I really think so."

Gary Brandt was easy to kill. He was the last of the kids she'd seen leaving the Virusso apartment, the last of the kids the detective had contaminated with questions, the last of Joyce's friends.

She'd followed the detective most of Sunday afternoon, followed him from the apartment to the hospital to Virusso's split-level ranch. She'd stayed on his tail as he questioned Brandt, Flanders, and finally, Fred and Joyce.

Now she'd gone back to Brandt's house, slipped through an open bedroom window, and murdered the boy in bed while his parents slept in the next room.

Leona knew from her own experience that the first blow should always be aimed at the neck. If the first blow didn't rip out the vocal cords, rupture the trachea, sever the carotid artery, or render the person unconscious, the victim would surely scream. She remembered her own screams the night Gordon had hit her in the *face*. The hammer had torn her flesh and shattered her skull, but her screams continued until she lapsed into the coma. Had he hit her in the neck with the claws (as doctors told her more than once when she came out of her coma), she would have died almost instantly and never been able to make a sound. This was the type of detail her shattered mind paid close attention to.

Her mind also remembered how important it was to hide. Though she'd kept watch at the scene after each murder, she tried to stay a safe distance away to avoid being suspect. She didn't dare be questioned by the police. Any policeman who came near her would know she wasn't right in the head. She wouldn't allow herself to be stopped before Joyce was dead, even if she had to kill the entire city police force in order to finish her work.

One policeman she intended to kill anyway was that detective who'd talked to Joyce. Joyce had contaminated him through association. He had to die before Leona could hide in the happy dream.

This afternoon, while watching early-evening news on the color TV in the motel room she had rented with money stolen from John Koster, Leona saw the face of yet another man who definitely had to die. His name was Randall Drew. He was the district attorney. And he claimed to know everything about Joyce Roberts and her family history.

Drew told a TV reporter that he intended to question Joyce tomorrow morning as soon as the doctors said she was out of shock. Once he had all the facts, including Joyce's side of the story, he'd hold another news conference and release the details to the public. That was something Leona couldn't let happen. Randall Drew had to die. And he had to die tonight. Before he talked to Joyce. Before he went on TV and told the world.

If the whole world knew that Leona Roberts had grown up and had a teen-aged daughter, then they could conceivably keep her from going back to the happy days before everything changed.

Changed from good to bad.

Therefore, Randall Drew had to die. He had to die tonight. Leona Roberts caressed the bloodstained handle of the hammer on the seat beside her. She started the Toyota and drove across town. Ten minutes later she'd parked a block from Randall Drew's residence.

In less than an hour she was back in the car. And Randall Drew and his wife were dead.

On Tuesday it rained. Buckets full of water splashed the pavement and tied up traffic. It was impossible to see two feet in front of his nose, much less any car without headlights and taillights turned on. Carl wisely decided to pull off the expressway and park along the shoulder until the storm showed signs of letting up, which didn't look like any time soon.

Despite intermittent booms of thunder, Marsha Wade was sound asleep in the passenger seat of the unmarked squad car. She had been lulled to sleep by the hypnotic staccato of raindrops bouncing off the roof. Carl found it difficult to keep his own eyes open. Driving in bumper-to-bumper traffic in such conditions was hazardous at best. When Carl was half asleep behind the wheel, it was tantamount to committing suicide.

By the time Randall and Amy Drew's bodies had been examined and bagged, it was nearly noon. When Carl suggested they go home and get some sleep, Marsha had protested.

"We've got to go to the hospital," she insisted. "Sleep can wait."

"Look," he said. "You're tired and I'm tired and we are doing no one any favors by killing ourselves with lack of sleep. Right now even the killer's home in bed, resting up for tonight. We've both got to get some rest before we collapse from sheer exhaustion."

"Just drop me at the hospital and you can go home."

"Isn't there someone else who can do the autopsies?"

"I'm not going to the hospital to do autopsies," she said. "I'm going there to talk to Joyce Roberts."

"Can't it wait?"

"No, Carl, it can't. Don't you see? We have to talk to Joyce before the killer finds out that the charges have been dropped and Joyce is no longer in protective custody. Joyce is the real victim of these assaults. All the others were either substitutes for Joyce or people the killer had to get out of the way in order to reach the intended victim. Joyce is in imminent danger. The killer intends to come after her next, and you and I need to talk to her first because somehow Joyce knows the killer and might be able to give us a clue to his or her identity. I've got to talk to Joyce before the killer reaches her, because once Joyce is dead, I'm sure the killer is going to come after you. Unless the killer goes after you first. The pieces of this puzzle are all starting to fit together and I don't like the way the big picture looks."

"All right," he said. "We'll go to the hospital. But I want you to stretch out and try to get some sleep. Even fifteen or twenty minutes will help."

"I won't be able to sleep a wink," she protested. But he had insisted she try. And before they'd gone three blocks, she was out like a light.

Carl knew Marsha was right about Joyce Roberts. Though Joyce couldn't be the killer since several murders with the same MO had taken place while she was still in protective custody, Joyce had known each of the victims either directly or indirectly. That fact established a link between Joyce and the killer that was more than mere coincidence. Joyce was the key piece in this picture puzzle, the key link in the chain of murders, the one person alive who had all the answers.

Now, after going over again in his mind all the details of his initial interview with Joyce Roberts, Carl was certain the answer lay locked in those mysterious gaps in Joyce's memory. If she could be helped to remember everything that happened to her at the Virusso house and afterward, perhaps she could provide a clue to the killer's identity.

But how?

How does one go about helping someone to remember things the mind has blocked out? What would trigger the unconscious to recall images the conscious mind didn't want to deal with?

While Carl pondered these questions and waited for the rain to stop, he was completely unaware that another car had pulled off the road less than a hundred yards behind his unmarked squad car.

In the rain, even if he had seen the other car's headlights, he wouldn't have been able to tell that it was a late-model Toyota or that the driver was a woman.

Doctor Gephardt Joshi hated hospitals. During his internship he'd had to man the emergency room at an inner-city medical center that was overcrowded and understaffed. For seventy-two hours at a stretch Gephardt treated winos, drug addicts, gunshot victims, stabbing victims, and pregnant teenagers who'd tried unsuccessfully to abort their babies with a coat hanger. His experience had turned him off to conventional medicine and led to his decision to do a residency in psychiatry.

Joshi believed that doctors who treated only the body and not the mind were doomed to treat the same patients over and over again for the same injuries. Few if any diseases or traumas were naturally caused; rather, they were the result of a sick or injured mind that infected the body by sabotaging the body's immune system or drove the body to have "accidents." Those so-called "accidents" were nothing more than a form of punishment that guilty minds felt a body deserved, a form of retribution for real and imagined transgressions against God.

To Joshi, "God" was nothing more than another word for "ego."

Conventional physicians were so wrapped up in their own guilt that they refused to recognize the importance of the mind in causing and curing illness. They looked for tumors. They looked for bacteria or viruses. They wanted to cut or inoculate or prescribe. They treated the symptoms. Other doctors weren't concerned with permanent cures. But Joshi was.

And that was why he was here at Bryson Memorial on a rainy Tuesday afternoon when he could have been back in his office puffing on an old briar pipe and catching up on some of the recent developments published in professional journals. He knew smoking was bad for him. But he had an oral compulsion that only puffing on the pipe—or eating— could satisfy. At his current weight, puffing on the pipe was probably healthier than eating.

Joyce Roberts had been Joshi's patient for more than a decade. When he'd read in the newspapers that she'd been accused of murdering her grandparents, Joshi knew such a thing was impossible. Joyce wasn't a murderer. Though she may have hated Fred Foltz, she never could have killed him. Joyce didn't have it in her psyche to harm even a fly, much less another human being.

Joyce had suffered too much physical pain herself to ever think of inflicting pain on someone else. "Accidentally," perhaps, but never intentionally. No. She was not guilty of premeditated murder.

As the fat man waddled past two nurses in the hospital hallway, he heard them giggle. They were probably comparing him either to a penguin or to a caricature of Alfred Hitchcock or even to the late Orson Welles. Well, so be it. Joshi didn't mind those comparisons in the least.

In fact, he deliberately fostered the penguin image by wearing a black three-piece suit with a black bow tie and a white dress shirt. Standing only five feet four with a forty-eight-inch waist that wobbled when he walked and a big beak of a nose stuck to his face like a carrot, Joshi couldn't avoid looking like a penguin if he tried. It was something he'd learned to live with. And now he rather enjoyed being referred to as a "weird old bird." It was an identity that differentiated him from his run-of-the-mill colleagues who usually wore white coats and looked like refugees from aspirin commercials. Joshi took pride in being a bit odd. No one who ever met the man was easily able to forget him.

Nor could Joshi easily forget about Joyce Roberts. After eleven years of gently probing her psyche, Joshi felt he was on the verge of a breakthrough. Joyce had responded well to therapy in recent months and she was barely a step away from being cured. She was a pet project that would prove his theories correct once and for all.

And then this horrible thing had to happen. He tried to imagine the damage such a trauma could cause. It was bad enough that both her grandparents had been killed while she was in the same house, but being accused of their murders might have been too much for the girl's tortured mind to handle. He had to reach her before she suffered a relapse. If only he could talk to her, make her see that the deaths of her grandparents weren't her fault, then maybe he could still save her.

Dr. Joshi turned right at the end of the hall. He waited patiently for the elevator while all around him he heard the hated sounds of the hospital.

Sounds of sick people getting sicker.

He hoped he'd reach Joyce in time to save her from herself.

Leona listened to local news on the Toyota's AM/FM radio.

"Following the deaths of District Attorney Drew and his wife early this morning, the district attorney's office dropped charges against Joyce Roberts, the prime suspect in the slew of hammer homicides that have plagued this city since Sunday. Assistant State's Attorney Leslie Nash told this reporter in an exclusive interview that the Roberts girl, in protective custody at Bryson Memorial Hospital since the deaths of her grandparents Monday evening, couldn't possibly be the killer. Police are now following up on new leads and an arrest of the real killer is expected to be imminent.

"Meanwhile, city residents are cautioned to stay indoors and lock their doors and windows..." Leona clicked off the radio.

Though she'd lost the detective's car in the rain, she knew how to find him again when she was ready. Sooner or later he'd show up at his girlfriend's apartment. When he did, Leona would kill them both.

As soon as the rain let up, however, she planned to head for the hospital. Now that Joyce was no longer in protective custody, killing her would be easy. Even if Joyce had recovered from shock, she'd still be sedated, groggy, and vulnerable.

Better still, no one would expect an attack to come in a busy hospital during broad daylight. All the previous killings had occurred at night, under the cover of darkness. Leona was sure she could get into Joyce's room, finish her work, and get out before anyone suspected. Leona had spent lots of time in hospitals. She knew her way around without calling attention to herself.

Joyce and the detective were all that stood in Leona's way. Once they were gone, she'd be free. Free to go where she wanted, do what she wanted. Free to dream the happy dream forever.

Just thinking about the happy dream made her smile.

Carl couldn't wait any longer. He was about to fall asleep. It was so tempting just to doze off.

But he knew if he did, he wouldn't wake up for hours. Rain or no rain, he had to get to the hospital.

Marsha was still asleep in the passenger seat, and he decided to let her sleep. With any luck, they'd be at the hospital within half an hour. Then, after talking to Joyce, they could both go to their respective homes and sleep the rest of the day.

Slowly, carefully, he pulled back onto the expressway. Traffic was moving slowly, but at least it was moving.

The first time Gephardt Joshi saw Joyce Roberts, Joyce was only six: a tiny, frail body clinging desperately to what little life was left in her bones. She had been in a hospital then, too: a different hospital—the research pavilion at the university's teaching hospital, where some of the best medical minds in the country held senior faculty appointments—but a hospital, nonetheless. Joyce was hooked up to fewer tubes and wires now than she'd been then, but Joshi felt a sudden sense of déjà vu that sent icy shivers running up and down his spine.

He'd been called in by an eminent neurosurgeon, a colleague from the time when Joshi had himself been a faculty member at the famous Chicago medical facility.

"She'll be living in Riverdale when we've finished with physical reconstruction," the neurosurgeon had said. "You're the only competent shrink I know out there in the sticks, and I thought you might be interested in her case. She'll need years of follow-up psychological help. Even so, I'm not sure she'll ever overcome the effects of such severe systemic trauma. Our only alternative is to institutionalize her. Do you think you can do anything for her?"

Joshi couldn't turn down such a challenge. The girl was perfect to prove his theories, theories that had ostracized him from the medical community and driven him to open a practice in Riverdale rather than remain on the faculty at the university. The staid board of directors didn't want Joshi contaminating residents with radical ideas that hadn't been verified with documented case histories. So Gephardt Joshi had left the land of ivory towers behind and ventured forth into the wilderness alone to test his theories.

And Joyce Roberts was an ideal project to prove his theories. She'd suffered mental and physical trauma so severe that she'd have to be taken apart and put back together piece by piece. Her mind was his to do with as he pleased.

So he took the case and set about repairing the damage her father had done. It hadn't been easy. But he knew he could cure her with time; and he flatly refused to give up until she was a whole human being who would and could function on her own.

Fred Foltz had been a thorn in Joshi's side right from the beginning. Though the doctor had waived his usual fee in order to take Joyce as a patient, Foltz was still worried that Joshi somehow planned to pick his pockets. When he finally accepted that Joshi didn't plan to bill a penny for psychiatric services, the old man then became certain the doctor had ulterior motives for seeing the girl. Foltz had even accused Joshi of taking sexual liberties with the minor female, an accusation so ludicrous that Joshi had simply laughed it off. But when Fred Foltz tried to refuse treatment for the girl, Joshi had a heart-to-heart talk with Grace Foltz and Grace made Fred back off. Reluctantly, Foltz had let the treatments continue.

Unfortunately, Joyce's visits were limited to two ninety-minute sessions once each month, barely enough time to overcome the poisonous environment of the Foltz household. Grace was a Bible-thumping, guilt-laden woman who infected Joyce with all kinds of harmful ideas. Fred was a tyrant who punished Joyce as though he wanted to be punished himself, and Grace stood meekly by and allowed her husband to beat the girl on a regular basis. Was it any wonder that Joyce's ego was so deflated?

But Joshi had kept on relentlessly, session after session. He'd taught the girl to think for herself, to see that guilt and punishment were man-made and not divinely decreed, that most of her pain and suffering had been caused by sick minds—her father's, her grandfather's, and her own. God hadn't singled her out because she'd been bad and deserved to be punished. These things had happened to her, more often than not, simply because she allowed herself to be a victim.

She let others do things to her because her ego wasn't yet strong enough to differentiate its own identity from those that surrounded her. She saw herself only as an extension of others—a tiny link in a great chain, a small piece in a giant puzzle—rather than as a unique individual who could affect the world as much as the world affected her.

He'd tried various methods to build up her ego so it would be the equal of others. With a strong ego she'd be capable of doing anything—including healing herself completely.

Tony Virusso had been a godsend. Coming at just the right time, Tony's flattery had an effect on Joyce that an old man like Joshi could never hope to achieve. Sexual attraction reinforced everything the young man said; Joyce believed Tony's flattery because she wanted to believe it. And she wanted to believe it because she wanted *him*.

Joshi had learned of Tony's unfortunate death from the same newspaper article that told of the deaths of Fred and Grace Foltz. District Attorney Drew claimed that Joyce was responsible for the deaths of not only her grandparents, but her classmates as well. The DA had placed Joyce in protective custody at the hospital while she was in shock, but she would be arrested as soon as she was well enough to be arraigned.

When Joshi stopped at the nurse's station on the fourth floor to check on Joyce's current situation, he learned that the charges against Joyce had been dropped. District Attorney Drew, the DA's wife, and four more of Joyce's classmates had been killed while Joyce was in custody at the hospital. The sheriff's deputies that had been assigned to guard the girl were withdrawn less than an hour ago.

Joshi had no trouble getting in to see Joyce Roberts. He asked one of the nurses to lead him to Joyce's room, hand him the patient's chart, and leave him alone with his patient. The nurse did exactly what she was told.

As he squeezed his bulk into a chair next to the girl's bed, he began to assess the damages. Joyce had been heavily sedated for almost thirty hours. Her vital signs had returned to near-normal parameters, and it was safe to assume that Joyce had recovered from shock. Her body would survive. But what about her mind?

"I'm here, *Liebschen*," the doctor whispered. "I'm here to help you. Everything will be just fine now. You have nothing to worry about. Everything will be just fine."

Joshi settled back in the chair to wait. There was nothing else to do until the sedatives wore off and Joyce regained consciousness.

Despite his enormous intellect and years of superior education and training, Doctor Gephardt Joshi sometimes had to wait like everyone else for time and chance to give him his turn at success or failure.

He didn't like waiting. It made him feel insecure, out of control.

It all came back to her, flooding her with memories like waves washing over and inundating the shoreline at a time of high tide. The footsteps on the stairs, the sound of a hammer striking flesh and bone, the door crashing open and a man rushing into the room with something metallic held in his hand, men in white coats sticking her with needles and strapping her to a stretcher, the pain... the pain... the pain...

She knew she was in a hospital room, in a hospital bed, because she could smell the smells of a hospital: disinfectant, isopropyl alcohol, antiseptic, and a variety of familiar odors she recognized but whose names she didn't know. She could hear the sounds of doctors and nurses in the hallway busily making their rounds. A doctor was paged over the intercom and, when he obviously didn't answer, was paged again. She felt the IV taped to her arm tug at her skin as she tried to sit up. Her vision was blurred and she couldn't focus on anything yet without aggravating the headache that gripped her brain like a vise.

She knew it was raining outside from the constant patter of raindrops against a windowpane. The noise of the rain did nothing to alleviate her headache. The pain was almost unbearable.

She discovered the missing memory of everything that had happened to her in Steve Virusso's apartment; somehow the severe shock she'd just suffered had restored her memory. Some things about Saturday night still seemed fuzzy around the edges, but she attributed that to the large quantity of alcohol she'd unwittingly consumed while downing three or four glasses of potent kamikazes she thought tasted like lemonade.

She remembered walking home from the apartment still in a daze; she remembered trying to hide from a dark-colored Toyota that hadn't been following her at all but was merely trying to discern house numbers in the dark; she remembered walking the rest of the way home, pausing more than once to rub at the painful blisters forming on her bare feet; she remembered reaching the house after sunrise and seeing Fred Foltz sipping coffee at the kitchen table; she remembered reaching her bedroom and taking off her torn gown and throwing it in a wastebasket, and then she remembered nothing more because she was sound asleep until Grace woke her late in the afternoon on Sunday.

She also remembered a detective who had asked her question after question that she hadn't been able to answer because part of her memory was still missing then; she remembered Grandpa Fred following her up the stairs and slapping her face with a force that rattled her teeth and knocked her down; she remembered Grandma Grace's intervention and Fred's retaliation that sent the old lady flying against the wall; she remembered her grandfather picking Grace up in his arms and carrying her upstairs to the master bedroom; and then she remembered Fred coming back and dragging her by the heels to her own bedroom, where he locked her in.

And she remembered all the other times that she had woken up in a hospital bed with a headache just like the headache she had now; she remembered the pain … the pain… the horrible pain…

"Wake up."

Carl had been trying for ten minutes to get Marsha to open her eyes. She was still sound asleep in the passenger seat.

The car was hotter than hell with the windows rolled up and the outside humidity at one hundred percent. Carl struggled out of his suit coat and rolled up his shirtsleeves. He had to stay active to keep from falling asleep himself.

Finally, he opened the door and scooped up a handful of rainwater from a puddle in the parking lot. He held his fists over Marsha's face and let the water drip slowly through his fingers.

"*Mffff/jjjttxt!*" She spat out water that had entered her half-open mouth.

"Wake up, Marsha. We're at the hospital."

Marsha sat up and wiped the water from her forehead. She wasn't fully awake yet. He scooped up another fistful of water and threw it right at her.

She described her discomfort with a string of epithets he didn't think a nice girl like her knew.

"Come on," he said. "Step out into the rain and feel how refreshing—how really invigorating—rain can be."

"Where are we?" she asked.

"At the hospital. All we have to do is brave the rain between here and the front entrance. Feel up to it?"

"I'm still pretty woozy. How long was I asleep?"

"An hour. Maybe two. Grab hold of my hand and we'll run across the parking lot together. I think the rain's letting up a little. Maybe we won't get completely soaked if we run."

Marsha took his hand and tried to match his stride as they headed for the hospital's main entrance. She hadn't awakened completely and twice she stumbled and fell. But Carl's grip kept her from tumbling face-first into puddles of standing water, and she was back on her feet and running with no damage done.

By the time they entered the main lobby and reception area, Marsha was completely awake.

"Your coat," she suddenly noticed. "You left your coat in the car. Why'd you take it off?"

"It's too hot and muggy for a coat."

"Don't you keep your gun in one of the coat's pockets?"

"Yes."

"Are you wearing a gun now?"

"No. I'm not a cowboy. I only carry one gun at a time."

"Go back and get it."

"In all that rain?"

"Please, Carl. I'd feel safer if you were armed."

"Marsha, look. I don't need a gun in the hospital. There are hundreds of people here—patients, staff, visitors, even uniformed security guards. Nothing's going to happen here that'll require me to have a gun. Do you know of any place that's safer than a hospital?"

"No," she had to admit.

"Okay. Now that we both feel safe, let's find Joyce and get this over with. I'm not sure how much longer I'll be able to stay awake and I don't want to pass out here in the hospital. They're liable to keep me here."

The heavy downpour stopped.

As soon as the steady *tap-tap-tap* on the roof of the car began to abate, Leona Roberts returned to reality. She had relived the happy-dream again and again until the dream changed, turned into the nightmare that Leona's tortured mind simply couldn't face. She woke up screaming.

Her body was covered with perspiration. Beads of sweat dripped from her nose. Her dress was completely soaked.

She rolled down her window and let in a cool breeze that carried with it tiny drops of rain. She was already soaked so she didn't mind. The breeze felt good.

She started the Toyota and switched on her headlights. Though it was still midday, heavy clouds obscured the sun.

It looked almost as dark as midnight on a night with a full moon. She knew it was time.

Soon, she thought. Soon Joyce will be dead. Then, tonight, I'll take care of that detective and his girlfriend. And then there'll be an end to the killings and I'll be free to dream forever.

It took her only ten minutes to reach the hospital after she got back on the expressway.

Chapter Fifteen

"I'm here, *Liebschen*. I'm here to help you. Everything will be just fine now."

Joyce knew that voice. She recognized the slight German accent that sometimes sounded fake and sometimes sounded real. She opened her eyes and saw Doctor Joshi sitting next to her bed.

"What are you doing here, Doctor?" she asked, her own voice weak and barely audible. "I thought you hated hospitals."

"I do. I do," he answered. "But you are here, *Liebschen*, so I had to overcome my hatred of hospitals to be here when you need me most."

"Do you realize that you answered my question with a statement? You didn't answer my question with another question, doctor. Are you sure you're feeling all right?"

Joshi laughed. Joyce's vision cleared in time to catch the penguin with a genuine smile on his otherwise stern face.

"The question, my dear, is how are *you* feeling?"

"I have a headache," she admitted. "And I get dizzy when I try to sit up."

"Where is this headache located?"

"In my head. Where else would I have a headache?"

"Where in your head? Forehead? Temples? Back of the head? Exactly where?"

"Oh." She tried to pinpoint the source of pain. "Temples, I think. Both sides of my head hurt."

"Shooting pains? Constant pain?"

"Throbbing. Pounding. It doesn't stop."

"I think we can clear that up with three Tylenol tablets. Other than the headache, how do you feel?"

"Sick to my stomach."

"Nauseous?"

"Queasy."

"That's most likely a side effect of the sedatives. A good, solid meal will work wonders for your stomach. Anything else?"

"Yes." She didn't know how to tell him so she just blurted it out: "I can remember everything, Doctor."

"Everything? You remember everything?"

"The gaps are gone and I remember everything that's happened to me."

"What your father did?"

"Yes."

"You're sure you're remembering the actual event and not merely what someone told you must have happened?"

"Yes. I can remember running from my father and trying to hide from him in a tiny crawl space behind the furnace. I remember my mother coming home and I thought sure she'd save me. But she didn't. She couldn't. I even remember seeing the hammer as it hit me for the first time."

"This is a good sign, *Liebschen*. *You* know who you are. You have your identity back." Joshi sounded excited. "Now that you know your past, you can shape your future. Isn't it wonderful?"

Joshi's excitement was contagious. "I know now that I wasn't responsible for what happened to Robin. My walking into Robin's bedroom when I did, didn't cause her death."

"Of course not."

"And even if I thought Trevor got what he deserved, I wasn't responsible for his death either."

"Of course not, *Liebschen*."

"And I didn't kill my mother."

"No, you didn't."

"Nor Tony."

"How could you have thought such a thing?"

"Tony was killed because he insisted on going out with me. If he hadn't taken me to the prom and then to his brother's apartment, he'd probably be alive today."

"Or he might have been killed in an auto accident or crossing the street. Or a meteorite might have fallen from the sky and hit him squarely on the head. Any of these things are possible, *Liebschen*.

But you did not deliberately kill Trevor or Tony yourself, did you? Even if you may have wished them dead, you are not responsible for either death, is that not right? You are not guilty and you should not feel guilty. You don't feel guilty, do you?"

"No. Not anymore."

"Good." Joshi smiled. He was back in control again and things were going well. The girl would be completely cured in no time at all now. Joshi was on a roll and he wasn't about to stop.

"And you don't feel responsible for the deaths of your grandparents, do you?" he asked.

"My grandparents?" Joyce felt a terrible pain shoot through her skull as she suddenly remembered the horrible sound of a hammer hitting fragile flesh and bone in the room right next door to her own bedroom. "Fred and Grace are dead?

"You didn't know?"

Joyce felt the constructs of her newfound world completely collapse. She'd wanted Fred dead, wanted to be free of Fred and Grace and that horrible house so filled with suspicion and hate. Had she wanted it so badly that she killed her grandparents and then conveniently forgot? Had her mind played tricks on her? Had she only imagined she heard the hammer in the next room when really the hammer was in her hand when it made that horrible noise of hitting soft flesh and hard bone? Even if she hadn't done it herself, she had wished them dead. Had fate intervened to fulfill her wish? And didn't that make her just as guilty as the killer?

Tears rolled down her cheeks. She was guilty. Guilty!

She deserved to be punished.

Pain pounded her head like a drummer banging a bass drum during a Fourth of July parade.

WHAM! WHAM! WHAM!

Joshi was out of his chair and yelling for a nurse. Joyce heard him prescribe an intravenous sedative *stat*. The nurse entered the room and added something to the plastic tube taped tightly to Joyce's forearm.

WHAM! WHAM! WHAM!

Each beat of the drum was a blow to her head. WHAM! Pain. WHAM! More pain. WHAM! Excruciating pain. WHAM! Unbearable pain. WHAM!

Finally the sound subsided, the pain eased, the world went away.

As soon as she stepped from the elevator, Marsha knew something was very wrong.

A white-clad nurse carrying a vial of Pentothal was running toward a room at the end of the hall.

A booming male voice shouted for her to hurry as the nurse rushed through the door.

"I think Joyce went back into shock," Marsha told Carl. "It looks like they're going to knock her out with Pentothal until she stabilizes."

"If they put her under, how long will it be before we can ask her questions?"

"They won't let her come out until her vital signs are stable. If I were her physician, I wouldn't let you question her for twenty-four hours just to be on the safe side."

As they reached the room, the nurse had just finished adding Pentothal to the IV. A fat man in a dark suit, obviously a doctor, was timing Joyce's pulse rate.

"Who're you?" challenged the nurse.

"I'm Dr. Wade," Marsha said softly. "I'm on staff here at Memorial. This is Detective Erickson. What happened to Joyce?"

"I thought she knew her grandparents had been killed," the fat man answered. "She had a relapse when I casually mentioned that they'd been murdered. She was doing so well that I didn't think before I spoke."

"And you, sir?" Carl asked. "Who are you?"

"Dr. Joshi. I'm Joyce's psychiatrist."

"Are you working with the DA's offices, Doctor?"

"I'm Joyce's personal psychiatrist," Joshi answered. "I'm in private practice."

"We need to ask Joyce some important questions, Doctor," Marsha said. "It's imperative we talk to her as soon as possible. How long will she be under?"

"I don't believe in anesthetizing a patient any longer than is absolutely necessary, Dr. Wade. An unconscious mind seldom cures itself; the unconscious doesn't recognize pain and therefore it's useful only as an escape mechanism. But there is no real growth, no development of the personality, unless a balance can be achieved between the unconscious, the subconscious, and the conscious parts of the human mind. I want Joyce conscious as soon as she's stable, but I won't chance another relapse."

"Of course," Marsha said. "But when will she be conscious again?"

"When can you talk to her? Not until I've had a chance to ascertain her ability to withstand the shock to her psyche that questions will inevitably impose. Her mind is extremely fragile, Doctor. The natural tendency of the human mind to avoid pain sends Joyce into a state of shock where she tries to escape—to hide—from reality. A single word can trigger associations with other words or events in her past which hurt her—caused her immense pain—and then her subconscious mind takes over and blocks out everything else. Unfortunately, she also suffers from a deflated ego and an overabundance of guilt. Sometimes her subconscious won't let her forget the pain as a form of punishment for her perceived guilt. And since her ego isn't strong enough to stand up to the subconscious and fight, she becomes a victim in flight from her own self-imposed pain."

"I didn't ask for a diagnosis, Doctor. I need to know what kind of time frame we're talking about. When can we reasonably expect the girl to respond to questions?"

"Tomorrow. Sometime tomorrow she should be strong enough to answer your questions."

"That'll be too late," Carl said. "We need to talk to Joyce before tonight."

"Impossible."

"Nothing's impossible, Doctor," Marsha Wade insisted. "We *must* talk to Joyce as soon as she's stable. We want you to be in the room when we question her, and we want you to monitor her condition while we're asking our questions. But we are certain Joyce is the killer's next intended victim, and the killer won't wait until tomorrow. If we don't talk to Joyce today, she might not be alive to talk with tomorrow."

Joshi blanched.

"Can you help us, Doctor?" Carl asked. "It really is a matter of life or death."

Joshi shook his head. "I've just administered Thiopental Sodium intravenously. I chose Pentothal over Propofol because Pentothal is a rapidly-acting anesthetic that also reduces intracranial swelling. But the half-life of Pentothal in infusion is twelve hours. We'll have to wait until the effect wears off. And I can't stop the flow of Pentothal until Joyce shows substantially stabilized vital signs."

"You don't have to stop the flow, Doctor," Marsha suggested. "Just reduce it. Thiopental Sodium should redistribute to the rest of the body within ten to twenty minutes." She raised the girl's eyelids with the tip of her index fingers. "She's completely under. You can safely reduce the IV flow at this time and she should gradually emerge from the anesthetic without complications. We'll be able to question her before she's completely conscious and she'll answer automatically, unaware of the ramifications of her answers."

"You mean to use the Pentothal like truth serum?"

"Yes, Doctor."

"Don't you feel that would be unethical?"

"Not under the circumstances, Doctor," Marsha insisted. "We'd only ask what we need to know to save her own life, and nothing she says would or could be held against her in a court of law. We already know Joyce isn't the killer, Doctor. But we think she knows who the real killer is, and maybe—if we're lucky—she'll reveal the killer's true identity. Don't you think it's worth the chance?"

Joshi considered it a moment. Then he turned to the nurse and asked her to leave. "Under no circumstances are you or anyone else to enter this room until I give permission. Is that clear, nurse?"

"Yes, Doctor," she said.

"You may hear screams when the girl comes out of sedation," he added. "Please disregard them. I'll let you know if the patient needs anything."

"Yes, Doctor," the nurse said. She left the room and closed the door behind her.

Dr. Joshi turned the knob that regulated the intravenous flow of Pentothal to his patient, thus reducing the amount of anesthetic being added to a standard solution of life-sustaining glucose. He checked the patient's pulse, made a mental note of her improved skin color, and monitored her respiration.

"She'll be coming out in a matter of minutes," Joshi said. "Maybe ten, maybe fifteen." He looked fondly at her face. "She's a strong girl, you know. She's been through hell and still stayed human. Anyone else would have gone completely mad."

"You care a lot about her, don't you?" Marsha remarked.

"I care about all my patients, Doctor," Joshi said. "Each is a unique human being and well worth my caring and concern"

"How long has Joyce been one of your patients?" she asked.

"Eleven years," Joshi answered"

"Then you've watched her grow up, haven't you?"

"Yes, of course."

"And you've tried to protect her?"

"Of course." Joshi smiled at the unconscious girl. "I'd never let her be harmed again. I'll always protect her."

"I thought so," Marsha mumbled more to herself than aloud. "You've became too attached to your patient for your own good, Doctor. And definitely too attached for your patient's good. You're acting like she's your daughter rather than just another patient. You're not her mother, Doctor. You're her physician. You've lost your objectivity, Doctor, and you may have lost your ability to act in the patient's best interest."

"You'll be just fine, *Liebschen*," Joshi whispered to the girl. "You'll be just fine. I'm here to take care of you."

Leona tried to think of a way to hide the hammer.

She'd have to walk past dozens of people in the lobby, dozens more in various hallways, and nurses and doctors on the floor where Joyce's room would be located. Leona had spent plenty of time in hospitals herself. She knew no one would try to stop her if she kept the hammer well hidden. But where could she hide it?

It wouldn't fit inside her purse.

Nor would it fit under her dress without being overly conspicuous. No matter how hard she tried, she couldn't think of a way that would work.

Just then a brand-new Subaru SUV parked next to the Toyota. Leona watched a man leave the Subaru carrying a big bouquet of long-stemmed cut flowers wrapped up in pretty paper. He also held onto a helium-filled balloon tied to a red ribbon. Written on the balloon was the message to "Get Well." As she watched him walk toward the hospital entrance, Leona knew what she had to do.

She drove to a nearby florist shop and bought a similar bouquet. Before she returned to the hospital parking lot, she slid the hammer into the center of the bouquet. Nestled amid long stems and hidden by wrapping paper, the hammer was now invisible.

Leona left the Toyota in the lot and walked slowly toward the main entrance, carrying her flowers in her right hand. The rain had recently changed to light drizzle, and she was barely wet when she entered the main pavilion.

She hadn't bothered to buy a get-well balloon.

"She's in REM," Marsha said. "Joyce should be conscious enough for questions in another minute or two."

"What's REM?" Carl asked.

"The rapid eye movement stage of sleep," Joshi contributed. "REM is the stage of sleep where dreams frequently occur. It's the intermediary step between the total unconsciousness of delta, or deep sleep, and the alpha rhythm stage of semi-consciousness. During the alpha rhythm phase a person is neither fully awake nor completely asleep."

"When Joyce reaches alpha, we can ask our questions," Marsha added. "She'll be awake enough to hear our questions and verbally respond, but she won't be able to think about what she's saying. Her responses will be automatic."

"You'll communicate directly with her subconscious," Joshi said. "Her conscious mind will still be too numb to interfere and she'll have to answer truthfully, without elaborate artificial constructs or fabrications getting in the way. Please make your questions simple interrogatories that she can answer without difficulty. She'll be able to identify people, places, and events; but she won't be able to think about their meaning. If you ask her to think, she may become confused, disoriented."

"I'll start the questions," Marsha offered. "She should be about ready. Doctor Joshi will regulate the flow of Pentothal to keep the patient just below the threshold of consciousness during our interrogations."

Marsha leaned over the bed and spoke softly into Joyce's ear. Carl could barely hear Marsha's questions.

"Joyce, can you hear me?"

The girl's eyes remained closed.

"Joyce," the pathologist repeated, raising her voice slightly. "Can you hear me?"

A frown appeared on the girl's forehead. Her eyeballs moved back and forth beneath her closed lids. Her lips barely moved as she whispered, "Yes."

"Can you remember what happened the night of your senior prom?"

"Yes," the girl said again.

"Will you tell us everything that happened between the time you left the prom and the time you returned home?"

"Yes."

"Tell us now. Don't leave anything out."

The girl told them everything she saw or heard in greater detail than Carl had thought humanly possible. She told of walking up the back stairs to the kitchen of Steve's apartment, describing the color of the walls, the intensity of the light, even the number of steps up the stairs. She described the other people in the apartment: what they wore, where they sat, and their personal relationships. She identified the sweet smell of marijuana in the air and the awful odor of beer and alcohol that seemed so repugnant to her sensitivities but was somehow also exciting. She told of Tony leaving for the bathroom and Ellie introducing her to a lemonade-like drink that Gary Brandt made in a blender. She told of passing joints, additional trips to the kitchen to refill her glass with kamikazes, Tony returning from the bathroom to hit Ellie in the stomach, Ellie rolling unladylike on the floor, Tony picking Joyce up in his arms and carrying her into the bedroom, the glare of the overhead light that reminded her of the bright lights in a hospital operating room, Tony undressing her and then himself, what she felt as he played with her body and primed her for the plunge into womanhood, the door bursting open and Ellie and her friends laughing and staring before coitus could be consummated, the fight between Tony and John Grabowski.

When Joyce mentioned being stalked by a dark-colored Toyota after fleeing Virusso's apartment, Carl knew it was the same car that he had seen yesterday without headlights, the same car that had stalked him on the expressway very early this morning. Joyce's description of the car and its lack of headlights matched his own experience to a T. He made a mental note to contact DMV for a printout of all late-model, dark blue or possibly green, Toyotas.

Joyce ended her tale after she threw her torn gown into a wastebasket in a corner of her room. "I crawled into bed and fell asleep," she said. "That's all I remember."

"Joyce," Carl said. "Do you remember a detective talking to you on Sunday?"

"Yes," she said

"Will you tell us everything that happened in your house after the detective left?"

"Yes," she answered again.

"Tell us now. Don't leave anything out."

"I knew Grandpa was mad at me," Joyce began. "I wanted to get away from him before he hit me. I started up the stairs to hide in my bedroom but he came after me."

Carl listened as the girl told of the blow to her head that nearly knocked her out. Joyce said she watched, horrified, as Fred sent Grace reeling against the wall. Grace's glasses flew from her face and shattered to shards. Her dentures broke and pierced her lips. She slumped to the floor and didn't move. Joyce thought she might be dead.

Fred must have thought so, too. He stared at the old woman's body for the longest time before trying to move her. He bent his knees and lifted her limp body from the stairs. Then he carried her slowly up the twelve remaining steps to their bedroom.

Minutes later, he came back for Joyce. He grabbed her ankles and pulled her unresisting body up the seven steps to the second-floor landing. Then he dragged her down the hall to her room and dropped her unceremoniously to the floor next to the bed. She heard him leave and lock the door behind him.

Nightfall descended, and the light coming through the open drapes turned golden, then gray, then black. Joyce heard her grandfather's slow tread on the stairs as he limped down to the living room and then another flight to the basement. She heard him moving around, mumbling to himself. Then she heard glass shatter and the sound of pounding on the floor as though he were building something in the basement. Once or twice the hammer sounded like it missed its mark and hit the floor. She recognized the sound of hardened steel hitting cement.

And then there were footsteps on the stairs again, but they weren't her grandfather's footsteps.

"It's Mommie," she said. "Mommie's home! Mommie will save me. Daddy can't kill me when Mommie's home. Everything will be fine now Mommie's here. Mommie will protect me."

"Her mother's dead, isn't she?" Marsha asked Dr. Joshi. "Didn't the father kill everyone in the family except Joyce?"

"Actually, no," Joshi said. "The mother survived. She was hospitalized in a nursing home. She was in a coma for nine years, and when she miraculously recovered from the coma, she was diagnosed as hopelessly insane and placed in an institution. Because Fred Foltz wanted everyone to believe that Leona Roberts had died in the hospital, he told Joyce her mother was killed by blows from a claw hammer. He threatened to remove Joyce from my care—to find another psychiatrist—if I even hinted to Joyce that Fred had lied and Joyce's mother hadn't died. Believe me, I wanted to tell Joyce that her mother was still alive, but I didn't dare until the girl turned eighteen." He looked at Joyce with tears in his eyes. "We were so close to a cure, *Liebschen*, and I couldn't risk losing you. Could I?"

"Doctor, don't you see what you've done?" Marsha nearly screamed at him. "You've allowed your feelings for your patient to cloud your professional judgment. You're her doctor, not her mother. You need to act like her doctor."

"Doctor," Carl asked anxiously, "where is Leona Roberts now?"

Before the doctor could answer, the door to the room burst open. A middle-aged woman stood in the doorway. Her face was horribly misshapen and scarred. Her lips were spread wide in a ghastly grin that displayed gaps where some of her teeth were missing as she said, "How do you do? I'm pleased to meet you."

Then she rushed into the room and hit Carl in the face with a bouquet of flowers that she held in her hand like a hammer.

CHAPTER SIXTEEN

Chunk!

Carl felt jolting pain as the fistful of flowers smashed into his face. There was something hard hidden in the center of the bouquet and it cracked his left cheekbone and splintered two teeth.

But the sprig of flowers had partially cushioned the blow and kept his face intact. If the hammer had hit directly, the whole left side of his face would have been pulverized.

He knew he had to react quickly or a second blow would put him out of commission permanently. Despite his extreme exhaustion and the debilitating dizziness caused by what likely was a mild concussion, he grabbed the woman's arm and tried to wrench the flowers from her hand before she could swing again at his head.

She was stronger than she looked. Though her body was frail and emaciated, the woman exhibited the veritable strength of ten tigers. *Madness does that to a person,* Carl thought, fighting vainly to subdue her. *Madness turns ordinary men and women into animals and I must become an animal or go mad myself if I want to stop her. This looks like one I'm not going to win.*

They grappled across the room, knocking the IV stand and Dr. Joshi to the floor.

Marsha reacted instantly. She pulled the IV needle from Joyce's arm and threw it aside. Then she jumped into the fray to help Carl.

"Stay back," Carl warned too late to stop her from interfering. Marsha grabbed at the flowers and they pulled free of the wrapper. She held a handful of flowers while the madwoman still held the hammer.

The second blow, uncushioned, hit Carl in the forehead. The sound of his cranium cracking reverberated in his brain like a thunderclap, and it was the last thing he heard as his knees turned to rubber and he lost his tenuous hold on the woman's arm that was all that kept him from falling, and he fell to the floor in a pool of his own blood.

Marsha's worst fears were realized as she saw Carl go down. Blood gushed from his forehead and sprayed the killer's face as Carl released his grip and fell to the floor.

Now the killer was free to come after Marsha or go after Joyce. Which would it be?

Marsha's heart skipped a beat as the killer looked her way.

And then the woman took the first step in Marsha's direction and Marsha knew she was next. Why hadn't she insisted that Carl go back to the car for his gun? She'd had a premonition that the killer would come after Carl when he least expected it, when he was unarmed and least able to defend himself.

But who would have expected the killer to attack openly and in broad daylight?

Marsha shoved aside all recriminations. It was too late to change anything now. The killer was coming for her with the hammer, and there was nothing to do but fight or die. Or maybe fight and die anyway.

Though eleven-and-a-half years had passed since last she'd heard that voice, Joyce recognized it instantly. In her alpha state, Joyce was completely aware of sounds and sensations, but she was unable to respond unless directed to do so. With her subconscious in the fore, in fact, she was total unthinking awareness without will. And she had no control at all over any of her motor functions.

When Dr. Wade and Detective Erickson had asked her questions, her half-conscious self had reacted as though it had just received instructions from her conscious self. Though her own consciousness had been inactivated by chemical receptors in her brain which were effectively blocked from bonding by the Pentothal in her bloodstream, her subconscious-self recognized carefully worded suggestions as though they were commands from her own consciousness. In the alpha state, the subconscious mind is highly susceptible to such suggestions. Hypnosis and meditation work on basically the same principle as Pentothal, inducing a trancelike alpha state that responds well to specific suggestions. No sooner had Joyce recognized her mother's voice than she heard the dreaded sound.

Chunk!

This time she knew it had come from right here in this very room. It hadn't come from next door. It hadn't come from her memory. The sound had come from right here, right next to the bed where her body lay immobilized.

And then she heard other noises that she couldn't identify, scraping noises.

When she felt a tug on her arm, she knew something was pulling at her IV needle. Then the tape pulled off and the needle slipped free of her skin.

Within seconds her conscious mind was struggling back from oblivion. It tried to take control again, but Joyce's subconscious mind fought her conscious mind for possession.

Then she heard the second horrible ka-chunk! and her subconscious yielded possession of her brain to her consciousness as though it knew its own survival depended on the conscious control of her body. Joyce opened her eyes. And then she screamed.

Marsha Wade had spent her entire life believing that violence was wrong. She'd never been able to conceive of a situation when violence was justified.

Yet, she knew that violence was real. It was a worldwide phenomenon that had spread like a plague to infect more and more people every year.

She'd seen its effects in the case histories of thousands of autopsy victims: gunshot victims; knife-wound victims; rape victims; and the battered and beaten, bruised bodies of defenseless, victimized children.

Violence was something Marsha Wade didn't understand. Her fascination with forensic medicine had grown into a need—an obsession—to learn the nature of violence in all its forms. She was sure that once she understood the causes of the various forms of violent activity, she could look for a cure.

Now, confronted with raw violence in the form of a crazed killer, she knew no cure was possible. Violence had to be met with more violence. If Marsha Wade expected to come out of this alive, she, had to kill the killer.

Or find some way to outsmart her.

But time had run out. The time-bomb was about to explode.

Leona Roberts advanced one step at a time, holding the hammer above her head, claws pointed at Marsha's face. Three more steps and she'd be within striking distance.

Marsha could see cunning in the woman's eyes, cunning and hatred and something else, too: the determined set of her badly damaged facial features betrayed an obsession with death that could only mean one thing.

Leona Roberts wanted to die.

When the time-bomb exploded, Leona expected to go up in smoke with the rest of her victims. Leona saw herself as a victim. There was no hope, Marsha knew at once, no way to talk her out of killing them all. Yes, the killer wanted to die. But she felt she wouldn't earn the right to die until everyone else in the room had preceded her.

She had already eliminated Carl, hadn't she? If he wasn't dead, he'd soon expire from loss of blood. Then, once Leona had taken care of Marsha and Joshi, she'd go after Joyce.

And then she'd turn the deadly claws on herself.

"It won't work," Marsha said aloud. "You can't kill yourself with a hammer. You can't get enough leverage to do more than knock yourself out. You won't be able to finish the job when you're unconscious."

But the woman was beyond reason and Marsha's words didn't register in her mind.

As she stepped forward and swung the hammer, Leona said, "I'm fine. How are you?"

Joyce had seen the hammer in her mother's hands, poised to strike. The deadly claws, coated with blood, looked like the fangs of a venomous snake about to bite.

Joyce screamed.

Leona, momentarily distracted by the scream, turned her head. Joyce saw at a glance that her mother wasn't her mother anymore. Leona's face was a mask of hideous scars. Unlike Joyce who had undergone extensive facial reconstruction, Leona had a face that looked inhuman.

As Joyce watched in horror, Leona turned away to complete the task at hand. The monster that had once-upon-a-time been Joyce's Mommie took another step forward and swung the hammer.

In a blur of motion, Dr. Joshi's black-clad bulk hurled itself between the two women, knocking the younger one out of the way before the claws could connect.

K-thunk!

The full force of the hammer hit Joshi on the back like a ton of bricks. Twin claws ripped through the cloth of his suit coat and embedded in his right shoulder. He bellowed in pain as he fell to the floor with the hammer still buried in his flesh.

Leona, surprised to have the hammer torn from her hand, reached down to retrieve it.

But the other woman was quicker. She threw herself to the floor next to the fat man, and her fingers reached out to grasp the wooden handle of the hammer. With the practiced skill of a surgeon excising a tumor, the younger woman removed the hammer from Joshi's back.

She was on her feet in an instant. The hammer was in her hand.

And like a butcher chopping a piece of meat with a cleaver, she wielded the weapon right at the face of the monster....

Leona saw the hammer coming.

Though she wanted to duck out of the way, her duploid mind wasn't able to translate the thought into action before the hammer hit.

Ka-thunk!

The claws cut through her skin and fractured her forehead. Blood spurted every which way. There was a momentary sensation of excruciating pain, and then the pain passed.

But Leona was still standing on her own two feet. The hammer dangled idly from the hole in her forehead. The stupid bitch had let go of the hammer.

With a great deal of effort, Leona willed her arm to move upward. Her fingers opened and grasped for the handle.

And clamped shut around the familiar feel of raw wood. She pulled the hammer free. Chunks of bone and pieces of skin clung stubbornly to the metal claws. Blood gushed from the open wound and nearly blinded her.

Then she turned away from the horrified woman and looked down at the terrified child lying on the bed.

She smiled.

It was almost over. Everything was ending just the way she wanted.

The bitch could wait. She'd done Leona a great favor by using the hammer on Leona. If Leona had the strength, she would repay the favor and hammer the woman to death.

But first, like a good mother, she had to take care of Joyce.

Marsha had heard of such things happening. There were documented histories of men who returned from war with shrapnel buried in their brains, men who functioned normally despite a trauma that should have killed them instantly. She recalled one case of a man who had a piece of straw pierce his brain during a tornado, and the man walked ten miles afterward without even noticing the ends of the straw sticking out both sides of his head.

There were other cases, too, where victims were able to survive traumatic head injuries. But Marsha didn't have time to think of them now.

Marsha knew the woman wouldn't last another three minutes with her head bleeding like a sieve. In fact, the woman should have lost consciousness by now. But obviously, she hadn't.

And, in less than three minutes, Joyce would be dead and the killer could come at Marsha with a thirst for vengeance.

Marsha looked around the room for something—anything—to use as a weapon.

Why, oh why, hadn't she insisted Carl bring his gun?

Though Joyce had her eyes tightly closed as the hammer connected with her mother's head, she couldn't shut out the dreaded sound.

When she opened her eyes, she was surprised to see her mother still standing. The hammer, dangling from Leona's forehead, looked ludicrously like Tony's half-limp penis.

Then, while Joyce watched incredulously, Leona's hand reached for the hammer and pulled it free.

And, as if she knew Joyce was watching, Leona turned to the

bed and smiled.

It was a horrible smile, full of hate and loathing. On an already disfigured face, it looked more like a death grin than a smile.

Joyce cringed in fear as she saw her mother raise the hammer.

And when Leona took the first step toward the bed, Joyce lost complete control of her bladder.

I'm acting like a child again, Joyce realized, embarrassed by her lack of control. I'm almost eighteen and I still act like a child frightened of the dark.

Looking up into a face that seemed ten times more terrible than the face of the boogeyman she'd imagined as a child, Joyce knew she had to come to grips with her worst fears.

Or die.

That isn't the boogeyman, she told herself. That's my mother. And that's the way I would probably look, too, if I hadn't had all that painful surgery.

Joyce remembered the way her mother used to look: beautiful, self-assured, always well dressed and professionally coiffured. The pitiful hag who came toward her now looked nothing like the woman Joyce had once known.

Perhaps Grandpa Fred had been right in claiming that Leona Roberts had died eleven long years ago. Maybe she'd been dead and buried and this apparition standing before Joyce now was little more than a ghost or a ghoul come back from the grave to haunt the living.

Joyce suddenly realized that she didn't want her mother back. Not the way Leona was now, certainly. But not even the way she was then.

Leona Roberts had never acted like a mother should, not even when Joyce was a child and needed a mother.

And Joyce didn't want to be a child again. Tomorrow she'd turn eighteen, legal age. At eighteen she'd be emancipated, free of childhood and parents and dreadful nightmares of the boogeyman that haunted the dark.

Joyce decided to grow up one day ahead of schedule.

Marsha saw the woman raise the hammer over the girl's head. But even as Marsha moved quickly toward the bed, she knew she wouldn't be able to stop the hammer from falling.

It was the girl herself who saved the day.

As though refusing to ever again be a victim, the girl lashed out with a foot and caught her mother squarely in the midsection. The kick came so unexpectedly that Leona was caught completely off guard. The hammer fell from her hand and bounced on the floor next to the bed.

But before Leona could retrieve the hammer, a hand snaked out from under the bed and snatched it away.

"No!" the demented woman shrieked. And then the steam seemed to simply go out of her sails as loss of blood took its inevitable toll.

Was this the end of the nightmare? Marsha wondered. Or was this merely the calm before the storm? Marsha reached for the fallen woman and felt for a pulse. What little was left was irregular and failing.

Then Marsha turned around and peered under the bed. She saw Carl Erickson's pain-filled, half-conscious face looking up at her from where he lay in a pool of his own blood.

In his right hand he held the deadly claw hammer, clinging desperately to the handle as though his very life depended on it.

There is no remembrance of former things; neither shall there be any remembrance of things that are to come with those that shall come after.

Ecclesiastes 1:11

EPILOGUE

Joyce came across a fragment from Euripides during her first week in college: "Those whom the gods wish to destroy, they first make mad."

Another fragment from Euripides went: "The sins of the fathers are visited upon the children by vengeful gods."

Of course, in the original Greek, the word for "God" that Euripides had used had probably meant more "The Fates" rather than the singular male form of deity preferred by Christians. In fact, the ancient Greeks most often viewed "The Fates" as women, though today one tends to think of God as male and Fate as neuter. Modern man simply can't conceive of women affecting and sometimes controlling man's destiny. Joyce thought it a shame that men seemed so blind to the simple truth that they couldn't see the forest for the trees. Anything a man could do, a woman could certainly do, too.

Carl Erickson had to learn that fact the hard way. After weeks in the hospital, Detective Erickson was released to Dr. Wade's personal care. Marsha brought Carl home to her apartment, took a leave of absence from work, and nursed him back to health. She fed him and bathed him, tended to his wounds and changed his bandages. She even donated six pints of her own blood—one pint a week—to replace the blood he'd lost during surgery.

Joyce wouldn't be surprised if Marsha and Carl someday decided to get married.

Gephardt Joshi required sixteen stitches to close the gaping wound in his shoulder. Marsha Wade's expert excision of the claws had kept damage to a minimum, and Joshi's total blood loss turned out to be less than a pint. Other than a dislocated shoulder and a large, painful knot on the top of his skull, Dr. Joshi said he felt like himself again within twenty-four hours. The knot on his head resulted from hitting his head against the wall and inadvertently knocking himself unconscious. A man with his momentum should never run blindly across the room, Doctor Wade liked to chide her colleague. But this one time, she admitted, she was grateful he had.

Joyce, on the other hand, had recovered better than anyone might have imagined. She came out the true victor of the incredible battle that took place in that isolated hospital room one rainy Tuesday almost four months ago. All of her emotional scars finally healed and she became a whole woman with a stronger identity than most women her age were expected to have.

And during the next two years, the last of her physical scars were scheduled to be corrected through cosmetic surgery. Marsha had made arrangements for the reconstructive surgery to be accomplished at the university hospital where Joyce attended classes as a pre-med student. Most of the work could be done on an outpatient basis and wouldn't interfere with her studies.

Joyce had inherited her grandparents' estate. There was enough money in Fred's bank accounts to pay for Joyce's undergraduate education. Proceeds from the sale of the Foltz house would provide for her medical studies.

Marsha herself claimed to have come out of the battle with a new understanding of human nature. Though she was no closer to a cure for all violent behavior, she said, she now knew that some forms of violence called for violence in return. She felt Carl was right in hating violence so much that he was even willing to become violent himself—within legal limits—in order to put an end to killing and carnage. Marsha's respect for Carl and his principles seemed to grow and grow every day they were together. Joyce told them she was happy for them.

Joyce looked forward to Thanksgiving vacation. Marsha and Carl had invited her to Thanksgiving dinner, and Dr. Joshi would be there, too. Joyce thought of them as her family, now that Fred and Grace were dead.

Doctor Joshi had published a case study of Joyce Roberts and her miraculous recovery that brought him accolades from many in the psychiatric community.

The police had managed to fit together all the missing pieces of the puzzle, and Joyce was horrified to learn that Leona—released from the mental hospital without being cured—had gone on a rampage and killed more than a dozen people. The hospital claimed they'd notified Fred of his daughter's release, but Fred refused to sign for their certified letter. Fred had long ago disowned his daughter, and nothing would make him acknowledge she still existed. Had he known Leona had been released, or had he taken Leona home immediately after Leona's release from the hospital and helped her to heal, he might have prevented his own death.

And the deaths of so many others, too.

Or maybe it had already been predetermined by "Fate"—or a vengeful "God"—and nothing Fred Foltz did or didn't do made one iota of difference. Joyce didn't believe that, of course. No more than she believed in blind chance playing a part in human destiny.

What she did believe in, at long last, was herself.

AFTERWORD BY THE AUTHOR

Claw Hammer was first published in 1989 by Pinnacle Books. The story itself has haunted me most of my life. I'm extremely grateful to Crossroad Press for the opportunity to finally revise this tale and tell it the way I wanted to tell the story in the first place.

I lived in Chicago and worked at the American Society of Clinical Pathologists' Chicago headquarters, directly across West Harrison Street from the Cook County Medical Examiner's office, when I wrote Claw Hammer. My ASCP job was to sell continuing education classes to pathologists, and I got to sit in on many of those classes because I was the person who registered pathologists for various courses, set up microscopes in classrooms at conference centers, ran the overheads and slide projectors, hawked new books published by the Society or the College of American Pathologists, and hosted cocktail parties for the docs at national medical conferences. One of those ASCP classes featured the latest techniques of tool mark analysis available to forensic pathologists interested in identifying the instrument of death. I was fascinated to learn about the variety of ways people, more often than not, used common household implements to kill beloved family members and friends. That fascination manifested in Claw Hammer and many of my other novels.

That class also reminded me of several terrible tragedies that had happened to grade-school classmates of mine in my own hometown of Rockford, Illinois. I recalled awakening one dawn, when I was only about eight or nine, to the sound of sirens. I learned that a neighbor had allegedly gone crazy during the night and killed his entire family—all but one daughter who survived—with a claw hammer. The milkman, the same milkman who had just delivered milk to my house, discovered six broken bodies when he entered the neighbor's house to put milk in the refrigerator as he normally did twice a week. In those Father Knows Best and Leave It to Beaver days of the early 1950s, people were very trusting and nobody ever locked their back doors. All that changed, of course, after an entire family was murdered in our close-knit suburban neighborhood. It never dawned on us that locking the doors would do no good if the killer lived inside the house and had keys to the locks.

Not long after that first tragedy, the mother of another female grade-school friend was electrocuted in her bathtub. Supposedly, a radio fell off a shelf and added 110 volts to an afternoon bubble bath that fried the lady's brains and turned her into a boiled lobster. Police arrested the lady's husband and charged him with her murder. My young friend had to leave school to go live with her grandparents. I never saw her again.

One of my favorite uncles, Eric Ekebom, was a Rockford police detective sergeant and I remember asking to see his gun when I was too young to know any better. He told me he hadn't had to use his gun even once in more than twenty years on the police force. He did carry a gun, he explained, but he said he really didn't need one because "Good detectives use their brains and not guns to catch criminals." I'll always remember that.

When Pinnacle Books bought two of my novels and wanted them delivered right away, I wrote a rough draft of Claw Hammer, more an outline than a novel, and sent it off with the expectation I would have time to revise and polish the manuscript later. I had one day between the time I received the page proofs and the deadline for getting the completed novel back to New York in time to make the publishing window. I overnighted the proofs back. I have never missed a deadline. In the old days when I was learning the newspaper business, we published what we had in order to make a deadline. "Go with what ya got," the city editor called out as the daily deadline approached. Some stories were incomplete or inaccurate, but we knew we always had the next day's edition to round out the details or publish a correction. I'm glad Claw Hammer endured to see a next edition.

Computers make the writing and publishing businesses much easier. Revisions don't require retyping the entire manuscript. Editors e-mail page proofs, and writers e-mail corrections back.

I actually had time to make revisions and correct page proofs. I accept full responsibility for any errors you find in this edition. I hope you found the story a good read.

ABOUT THE AUTHOR

Paul Dale Anderson loves to read and write horror, dark fantasy, thrillers, and science fiction. He's an active member of SFWA, HWA, and ITW, and was previously represented by Barbara Puechner of the Peekner Literary Agency. When Barbara died with his breakthrough novel still half-finished, he switched to writing non-fiction. Paul went back to college and earned an MS Ed. and most of a doctorate in Educational Psychology and earned an MA in Library and Information Studies from the University of Wisconsin. He taught creative writing for Writers Digest School (both Novel and Short Story) and for the University of Illinois at Chicago.

He returned to fiction writing with a vengeance in 2012, completing his breakthrough novel and seventeen other novels, and began writing fresh fiction that crossed genres.

Two of his published novels, Claw Hammer and Daddy's Home sold very well, and several of his anthologized short stories have reappeared from major publishers. One of those short stories adapted to graphic novel format was recently re-released in hardcover and paper in J. N. Williamson's Illustrated Masques.

He is also a Certified Hypnotist and National Guild of Hypnotists Certified Instructor.

Curious about other Crossroad Press books?
Stop by our site:
http://store.crossroadpress.com
We offer quality writing
in digital, audio, and print formats.

Enter the code FIRSTBOOK
to get 20% off your first order from our store!
Stop by today!

Made in the USA
Lexington, KY
12 July 2018